D1454593

SILVER ROSE

Hertfordshire, December 1470

My dearest Tom,

It seems an age since you went to fight for noble Edward of York. Do you remember the Outlaw's Oak, where you gave me the silver rose? I wear it still close to my heart . . .
A dreadful thing has happened. My stepfather has betrothed me to an old Lancastrian knight. I would rather die than marry him! So I am going to run away, and find you wherever you may be . . .

God have you safe in his keeping, my dearest love, until we meet again.

Alys

Books by Jill Eckersley
in the Spectrum Imprint:

BREAKING AWAY

Point R♥mance

SILVER ROSE

Jill Eckersley

Complete and Unabridged

spectrum
LARGE PRINT

First published in Great Britain in 1998 by
Scholastic Children's Books
London

First Large Print Edition
published 2000
by arrangement with
Scholastic Children's Books
London

British Library CIP Data

Eckersley, Jill
  Silver rose.—Large print ed.—
  (Point romance)—Spectrum imprint
  1. Great Britain—History—Wars of the Roses,
  1455 – 1485 —Fiction
  2. Love stories
  3. Young adult fiction
  I. Title
  823.9'14 [J]

  ISBN 0–7089–9525–X

Published by
F. A. Thorpe (Publishing)
Anstey, Leicestershire

Set by Words & Graphics Ltd.
Anstey, Leicestershire
Printed and bound in Great Britain by
T. J. International Ltd., Padstow, Cornwall

This book is printed on acid-free paper

1

September 1470

'Alys! Alys!'

Alys Sherwood gave a guilty start, pulled her linen shift on over her still-damp body, and hid behind the biggest of the gnarled old apple trees in her stepfather's orchard. On this sultry September day, the tree was heavy with fruit, and provided enough cover for Alys to scramble hastily into her gown and begin to braid her long dark-brown hair.

'Alys? 'Tis I! Wherever are you, sister?'

The calling voice was nearer now and Alys breathed a sigh of relief as her sister Cecily, scarlet in the face from running, appeared round the orchard wall. When she saw Alys and took in her wet hair and bare feet, her eyes widened.

'You haven't been swimming in the river again? Oh, Alys! You know what Dame Eleanor said . . . '

Alys shrugged and tossed her head.

'Let her say what she likes. I care not!

1

On a hot day like this, nothing will serve but to swim in cool water. And Dame Eleanor need not worry, I didn't go near the millpond where the men are. I went right upstream, beneath the willow trees. No one saw me, there was no one to see except a few sheep! Besides,' and Alys grinned at her sister, 'Dame Eleanor will never know! Even my hair will soon dry in the sunshine, so unless you tell her . . . '

'You know I would never do that,' said Cecily loyally.

Alys slipped her arm around her sister.

'And what brings you running across the orchard on such a day, as if hounds were after you?'

Cecily sighed.

'I wanted to warn you, sister. Our father has just returned, and seems to be in a thunderous temper. Giles and Robin have already had a beating, and have been sent to the gatehouse tower with a promise of nothing but dry bread and ale for their dinner. 'Tis a shame. Cook is making mutton pasties, I can smell them,' continued Cecily, who liked her food.

Alys's face darkened.

'Sir Hugh's been grouchy as a bear for days now. Lord knows what ails the man!'

she complained. 'You shouldn't call him father, Cecily. He is but our mother's husband, and an evil toad at that. Our father, our *true* father . . . '

' . . . was a brave knight who died fighting for his liege lord, the Duke of York,' Cecily finished. 'I know that, sister, and I know you always call him Sir Hugh. But you remember our father and I . . . I was only four years old when he rode away, and sometimes I forget.'

'I will never forget,' said Alys briefly. 'Nor can I forget that Sir Hugh is not a gentleman, whatever his birth and lineage. Look at the way he treats our lady mother! The Manor is hers by right, yet she is naught but his servant, there to share his bed and pander to his whims, to run his household and bear his children, poor Mother!'

'But, Alys,' said Cecily helplessly, 'what else can she do? Every woman needs a husband to protect her, and 'tis natural to bear babies when you are wed. Besides, you love Giles and Robin and Joanna and Katherine, don't you?'

'Of course I do,' said Alys, thinking of the half-brothers and sisters who shared her home, and also, fleetingly, of the tiny, waxen forms of the twins her mother had borne the previous winter, who had sickened and died of a fever before they had been weaned. Her mother had not complained. Lady Philippa never complained. She had just grown ever more thin and pale and spent more time on her knees counting her rosary-beads and praying — for more babies? For a kinder, less brutal husband? Alys didn't know. She, herself, was often tempted to pray for Sir Hugh to be summoned away, perhaps to France, where his former mistress, the ex-Queen Margaret of Anjou, plotted and schemed to place her witless husband Henry the Sixth back on England's throne.

And let him stay away a good, long time. All would be well, and we would live happily at the Manor if he was gone, Alys thought rebelliously.

Suddenly another thought occurred to her.

'So what did Robin and Giles do to deserve their thrashing?' she asked.

Cecily giggled.

'Oh, Alys, it was comical, truly it was! You know their tutor, Brother Matthew?'

Alys did. The young monk came from a

4

local monastery, five mornings a week, to teach her young half-brothers reading, reckoning, and some Latin. He had a wispy blond tonsure and fine, fair skin like a girl's, and he blushed whenever she or Cecily walked by. He was quite the wrong person to be in charge of two mischievous small boys, who were far more interested in knightly games and their ponies than they were in book-learning.

She nodded.

'Well, Rob, or it may have been Giles, found a grass snake, and took it into the hall, and hid it among Brother Matthew's books. When he saw it, he leapt into the air, and then out of the hall! I would never have thought he could move so fast! And he bumped into Margery the washer-woman, and sent her linen flying, and she sat down in a puddle of spilled ale and soaked her gown, and she scolded, and Dame Eleanor came running in and scolded, and Giles and Robin laughed until they nearly split their sides, and then Fa . . . I mean Sir Hugh . . . came striding in to find out what all the noise was about . . . '

'And he beat them. As usual,' said Alys scornfully.

Her sister nodded.

'They were brave, and didn't cry, though Rob came near it. I'll wager it will be a day or two before they can sit down easily though,' Cecily said.

'Poor brats. It was only mischief, not worth a thrashing,' said Alys. ''Twould be punishment enough to make them miss their dinners. Perhaps I could take them a mutton pasty each up to the gatehouse tower, after Mother and Sir Hugh have retired this evening.'

Cecily paled.

'Oh, take care, Alys,' she begged, 'or you will be beaten too!'

Alys knew this was true. She had felt the hardness of Sir Hugh's hand, and even his leather belt, when she had given him a pert answer, or not treated him with enough respect. Sir Hugh Drayton liked his women to be meek as lambs, and as silent, with downcast eyes and ladylike demeanour. He ignored Cecily, who was terrified of him and kept out of his way as much as possible. Alys, who loathed him more than she feared his unpredictable temper, found it hard to stay respectfully silent when he bullied her gentle mother, frightened her half-brothers and sisters, and ill-treated the servants.

She rolled over on to her stomach on the parched grass of the orchard and looked up at Cecily.

'It surely can't be just Giles and Rob's antics that have angered Sir Hugh,' she said thoughtfully. 'Perhaps he has had bad news. Perhaps wool prices have fallen, or there is trouble in London again.'

Even here, twenty miles away in the Hertfordshire countryside, there was sometimes news of the power struggle between the young King Edward the Fourth, the exiled Queen Margaret, and the powerful Earl of Warwick and his family. As her father had died fighting for the Duke of York, Alys was a passionate supporter of the King, his son. And not only for that reason!

'They say that Edward the King is the handsomest man in England, Cecily,' she said out loud. 'Tall, golden-haired, truly kingly. A brave knight and a noble warrior, far better to reign over us than witless Harry of Lancaster. He is nothing but a milksop, half-daft, who lets his wife do his fighting for him! Oh, Cecily, don't you long to go to London, to see the court, like our cousins of Aylesbury?'

7

'Perhaps we will, one day,' Cecily said hopefully. ' 'Tis not so far, only two days' riding. They say London is a fair city, the finest in Christendom. It would be wonderful to see the King himself, and his queen. Our cousin Mary says she is beautiful, the Lady Elizabeth Woodville . . . '

'Beautiful enough to make King Edward anger the Earl of Warwick by marrying her, instead of some foreign princess,' agreed Alys, yawning. ' 'Tis like a tale from some old romance, the handsome prince who goes out hunting in the forest, meets a fair young widow, and marries her in secret! When I am wed, I'll make my husband take me to court; yes, and you too, Cecily, and we'll find a handsome knight for you among the King's courtiers!'

Cecily blushed.

'It will be years before that happens, sister, and you not even betrothed,' she protested. Then, as she saw the look on Alys's face, her eyes widened.

'You're not . . . Alys! Sister! Has . . . has Tom spoken to our fa . . . to Sir Hugh? Or rather, has our uncle the Earl spoken on Tom's behalf?'

Now it was Alys's turn to blush.

'Tom?' she said airily. 'Who said anything about any 'Tom'? I know no Tom I could wed — I was only day-dreaming, Cecily. After all, I'm sixteen now, and a marriageable woman. I know it must happen one day . . . '

'Don't tease, Alys,' said Cecily. 'You know I mean Tom Taverner, who else would I mean? The last time we visited our cousins of Aylesbury, he never took his eyes off you the whole time.'

'I'm sure I never noticed,' said Alys, her nose in the air. 'Why, Tom Taverner is no more to me than . . . a brother. 'Twas he, after all, who taught me to swim, and to ride, when we played together as children. If he looked at me when we visited our cousins, it would be . . . because I had a pimple on my nose, or he misliked my green gown, or thought I had grown taller since he saw me last . . . '

Her voice trailed off into silence and it was Cecily's turn to laugh.

'Well, if you can't see what's happening, sister, I'm sorry for your poor wits,' she said. 'You will be fortunate if Tom Taverner takes you for his wife. He's young, and strong, and good-looking in

9

his way with those broad shoulders and that smile, and he's of good family too. His father owned great lands in Yorkshire, I believe. And he's in the household of our uncle of Aylesbury, so if he asks Sir Hugh for you, he cannot object, for 'tis an excellent match . . . '

'You think so? You really think Sir Hugh would agree?' Alys gasped, clutching her sister's hands.

'Why should he not? Tom will be knighted one day, and he's of good family, as I said . . . '

'Oh, Cecily,' Alys cried, 'I care not for his family! I'd wed Tom Taverner if he were a . . . a pig-keeper!'

Cecily burst out laughing.

'I thought you said he meant no more to you than a brother?' she said slyly, and Alys dimpled.

'I hardly dared to hope,' she admitted. 'But are you really sure he kept looking at me, when last we visited our cousins?'

'Of course he did. Even Mary remarked on it.'

'We shall see him next week, when our cousins come over for the harvest-home feast,' said Alys thoughtfully. 'What can I wear, Cecily? Not my green gown again, for sure. You can have that, 'tis too tight across the bosom for me. Our lady mother had a beautiful length of apricot silk sent up from London. She'll never wear it. Sir Hugh likes to see his wife in dowdy greys and violets. Perhaps I could persuade her . . . '

'Tom Taverner will not notice what you wear. What do men know of gowns and jewellery?' said Cecily the practical. 'You have but to gaze at him with big eyes, and look away when your eyes meet, and blush a little, and sigh, and he'll be trapped like a rabbit in a snare. That's if he isn't already.'

Alys looked at her sister in admiration and astonishment.

'You're remembering the tales of high romance Dame Eleanor used to tell us when we were children,' she laughed. ' 'Tis hard to imagine greeting Tom Taverner with a blush and a coy look, when he was pushing me into cow-pats and dropping spiders down the back of my gowns not long ago!'

'But things are different now. You're not children any more,' Cecily reminded her. 'And Tom didn't look at you like a lad looks at a sister and playmate, but as a grown man looks at his lady and his love.'

Alys's heart thumped and a shiver ran down her spine at her sister's words. Could her most precious, most secret dream, that until now she had shared with no one, not even Cecily, possibly come true? Tom, she thought longingly. Tom Taverner . . . Sir Thomas, no doubt, one day, when he has proved himself to the Earl of Aylesbury, and through the Earl to the King and the house of York. Sir Thomas and Lady Alys Taverner . . .

She could not remember when Tom had begun to be more than a childhood playmate, just one of the tangle of children and dogs who romped and squealed around the Castle and the manor grounds. Tom's family came from the North, from faraway Yorkshire, Alys knew, but he had been placed in her uncle the Earl of Aylesbury's household at the age of eight, first as a page, then as a squire, to learn the warlike skills and courtly manners befitting a landed knight. They had always been friends, she and Tom, playing, laughing, squabbling over trifles, sharing games, scoldings, mischief and beatings, like the others. She remembered Tom taking her into the hay-barn, where one of the swarms of Castle cats had given birth to a litter of wriggling kittens.

'Take one. Take one for your own. It won't be missed,' he had assured her, picking up one of the tiny, squirming, black-and-white creatures. It had mewed as she held it and tried to suckle from the bodice of her gown, much to Tom's amusement.

'It needs its mother,' Alys had said, setting the kitten down. 'But 'tis a kind offer, Tom. Next time, when it is a little older.'

She hadn't thought he would remember, but he did, and on her next visit to the Castle he had placed the half-grown cat in her arms and insisted she take it home, where it was named Tib and had proved a useful ratter, and an affectionate pet besides.

When was it that she had started to see Tom as more than just one of the Earl's squires, to look for him in the crowd, to feel disappointed if she couldn't see his tousled blond head across the crowded hall? When had they begun to exchange those long, questioning looks, looks that made her feel warm and fluttery and uncertain of herself? She couldn't remember, but that was when Tom's laughing face had begun to haunt her dreams, both day and night.

She found a button from his doublet and kept it for a keepsake, hidden under her pillow. Even Cecily didn't know that. And when she had seen him once, smiling and joking with her cousin Mary, pain as sharp as a sword-thrust had caught at her heart. Oh, she knew there was nothing between them, for kindly Mary was stout, and plain, and betrothed to the wall-eyed son of Sir William Enderby, but still Alys felt that Tom's smiles and jokes and warm looks should be for her, and her alone.

'I pray you're right, Cecily, and Sir Hugh approves the match,' she said anxiously.

'Stay on the right side of him, and he will,' answered her sister sensibly. 'I feared he might cancel the harvest-home feast, with his temper being so foul.'

'Not he!' said Alys scornfully. 'Not when the Earl and Countess and their household are bidden to join us. Sir Hugh is much too proud of his aristocratic connections, or rather our mother's aristocratic connections, to risk offending the Earl by cancelling the invitation! It sickens me to hear him sometimes. 'My kinsman the Earl' he says, and 'Brother Aylesbury' he says, and he flatters our aunt the Countess with sweeter words and prettier compliments than ever he gives our mother! How I hate the man!'

'I know,' said Cecily gravely, 'but if you're wise and clever, you'll keep it to yourself, sister. Be meek and gentle. Drop him a low curtsey when you meet. Say 'Yes, Father', 'No, Father', 'As you wish, Father' and one day, Tom Taverner could be yours!'

The church bell struck the hour and Alys suddenly realized she was hungry, and began to think with pleasure of Cook's mutton pasties. She pulled her scuffed leather shoes back on, straightened her gown, and smoothed her hair anxiously.

'How do I look?'

'Like a young lady of good family,' grinned Cecily, 'and not like a hoyden who has spent half the day lolling on her back in the orchard and swimming beneath the willow trees! Dame Eleanor will have something to say, she wanted us to help her in the still-room, or finish our embroidery.'

'I have something that will sweeten Dame Eleanor's sharp tongue,' said Alys, remembering. She showed her sister a plaited reed basket filled to the brim with big, luscious blackberries. 'There! I haven't been idling my time away, or not completely. Besides, Dame Eleanor's bark is worse than her bite, and you'd think she'd have enough to do with Joanna and Katherine, not to mention helping our poor mother.'

Dame Eleanor was the large, bustling woman who had been, first, Lady Philippa's personal maid, and then nurse to Alys, Cecily, and their young half-brothers and sisters. As Lady Philippa had grown older and frailer, Dame Eleanor had taken over more of the housekeeping. Now, she either did or supervised most of the endless tasks involved in running the manor. Dressmaking, child-care, nursing the sick, brewing, baking, ordering stores: Dame Eleanor did it all. She was up at five every morning and slept only after she had seen the children, the household servants, and her mistress to their beds. Sharp-tongued, tireless, and golden-hearted, she was determined that Lady Philippa's daughters should grow up to be fine ladies and make good matches, and she nagged and scolded them with that end in view! Much as she might grumble at Dame Eleanor's rules, sometimes earning herself a sharp slap for disobeying them, Alys loved her old nurse as much as her gentle, faded mother.

With the basket of blackberries held between them, Alys and Cecily crossed the orchard, passed the Manor fish-ponds which provided eel and carp as a change from mutton, fowl and fat bacon at the dinner-table, made their way through their mother's herb garden and into the courtyard. Horses and ponies whickered gently in the stables, hens scratched in the dust, Margery the washerwoman hobbled across to the gatehouse with a basket of linen, and bold-eyed Moll the kitchen-maid, her black curls tangled and her gown cut lower in the bosom than was seemly, exchanged languishing glances with Jake Woods, Sir Hugh's lecherous bailiff.

Inside the Manor, in the great hall, all was bustle and confusion as the servants ran this way and that setting out the trestle tables and benches for dinner under the eagle eye of Dame Eleanor. Two of Sir

Hugh's hunting hounds squabbled over a bone in the middle of the hall, and a stray chicken pecked hopefully among the trodden-down rushes, food scraps, and other rubbish on the floor. From the kitchen at the far end came the sound of clattering pots and the savoury smell of mutton pasties. Alys and Cecily both sniffed appreciatively.

'So there you are, the pair of you,' said Dame Eleanor. 'Not before time, Miss Alys, either! I looked for you earlier, and where were you . . . ?'

'Picking blackberries, good dame,' said Alys demurely, before her old nurse could begin to scold. 'Look, I have a whole basketful — the juiciest berries you ever saw!'

Dame Eleanor's stern expression softened.

'Well, well,' she said, looking over the berries with an expert eye, 'there'll be some to stew, and some to preserve for the winter, there. Thank you, Alys. And now, out of my way, both of you! Your lady mother awaits you in her solar, and I must find that good-for-nothing trollop of a kitchenmaid . . . '

'She'll not find Moll,' giggled Cecily, as

the two girls made their way up the spiral stone staircase to their mother's solar. 'By now, she'll be tumbling in the hay-loft with Jake Woods, if I know anything of Moll!'

Alys knocked on the heavy wooden door and her mother's gentle voice said, 'Enter!'

The girls went in and made their curtseys. The room seemed dark, cool and quiet after the thundery heat of the day and the bustle of the great hall. It was simply furnished, with a big carved chair in which Lady Philippa sat sewing, a spinning-wheel, several chests for clothes and two or three plain wooden stools.

'God's greetings to you, Mother. Dame Eleanor said you wished to see us,' said Alys respectfully. Lady Philippa smiled and her careworn face lightened.

'Ah, yes, my daughters,' she said. 'I was just thinking, 'tis time you both had new gowns for the visit of our kinsfolk next week. I've had some silks and other stuffs sent up from London, so you may choose what you would like.'

Cecily kissed her mother's cheek.

'That's kind of you, Mother,' she said. 'But it's Alys who needs a new gown for the feast, because . . . '

Her voice trailed away as Alys shot her a warning look. She had no wish to confide her hopes to her mother. Not yet. If Tom was truly interested, well, that would be different, and perhaps she could enlist her mother for an ally.

'Because?' said Lady Philippa questioningly.

'Because my old green gown is so tight, I've given it to Cecily,' Alys said hastily, peering at her reflection in the looking-glass on the wall. Her hair was glossy and shining after her swim, and she wasn't *too* sunburned. Was that a spot on her nose? She wished her mother kept some of the little pots of rose-petal and marigold creams that her cousins of Aylesbury used on their complexions. But the Lady Philippa had no use for such things.

When her mother unrolled several lengths of cloth from one of the storage chests, Alys made a dive for the apricot silk and held it against her face.

'This one, if it pleases you, Mother,' she said.

'Ah, yes. It suits you, suits your colouring. I had a gown in just that shade when I was about your age,' smiled Lady Philippa. Alys looked at her mother's greying dark hair and the fine lines beneath her shadowed eyes. It was hard to imagine that she had once been sixteen years old, with hopes and dreams and all her life before her.

There was a clattering noise on the staircase, the heavy door swung open, and Sir Hugh Drayton strode into the room, bringing with him an overwhelming stench of ale, horses, and stale sweat. Lady Philippa rose to her feet.

'Greetings, my lord and husband,' she said uncertainly, 'what brings you here?'

'I come to tell you we have a guest for dinner,' grunted Sir Hugh. 'He has ridden far, and must be honoured, and welcomed to my house.'

'Of course, husband,' murmured Lady Philippa.

Alys longed to ask who the stranger was, but remembering what Cecily had said, she kept her eyes cast down and did not speak.

'You too, girls,' Sir Hugh ordered. 'I trust you will mind your manners!'

'Yes, Father,' Cecily whispered, nudging Alys, who managed to force out 'Yes, Father' too.

'Yes. Well. See to it,' Sir Hugh went on,

turning on his heel and almost falling over the hound who had followed him up the stairs. He kicked out at the dog irritably, and it yelped.

'Who can he be, this mystery traveller?' Alys wondered out loud, when her stepfather had stamped off downstairs again.

'Best not to ask,' said her mother gently. 'We live in troubled times, Alys. All we need know is that this stranger is Sir Hugh's guest, and as such we owe him honour.'

Alys had plenty of time to study her stepfather's guest from her place near the foot of the family dinner table. Sir Hugh had muttered an introduction — the man was a Robert Bevill, Saville, or something of the kind — and both men had made it clear that the women of Sir Hugh's household counted for nothing. The stranger's greasy jerkin was travel-stained and he, too, smelled strongly of the stables as he gave the sketchiest of bows to Lady Philippa, Alys and Cecily. No courtier, then, Alys decided, or not by the look of him. He seemed to be a messenger of some kind, given to muttering with Sir Hugh in quiet corners, glancing round suspiciously all the while. He looks shifty, Alys decided, I could swear he and Sir Hugh are plotting something. But what can it be?

After dinner, during which she had managed to wrap two mutton pasties up in a napkin to take to her young half-brothers, Alys managed to put the unpleasant stranger out of her mind. He'll be gone tomorrow, she consoled herself, and then it's only a few days more till the harvest-home, and I shall see Tom!

Her heart skipped a beat at the thought.

'What's this I hear about a new gown for you?' said Dame Eleanor, bustling up to Alys and Cecily as they sat over a game of chequers as dusk fell. 'And a *silk* gown, no less, and who's to make it? You? 'Twill fall apart on first wearing if I leave it to you!'

Alys blushed. Unlike her mother and Cecily, she didn't care for needlework and had little skill. Cecily looked up.

'We'll work on it together, Dame Eleanor,' she said. 'Mother, Alys and myself, and young Bella, Margery's daughter, has some skill with her needle. Don't worry, it will be ready in time. Come, Mother has retired to her solar already. If

23

we go up now, we can make a start tonight!'

As her sister headed for the spiral staircase, Alys murmured an excuse, and sped out of the hall and across the courtyard to the crumbling old gatehouse tower where Robin and Giles were confined. The key was in the lock, so she let herself in and said, 'Ssh! I've brought you food — Cook's mutton pasties, and some apples from the orchard!'

The two lads turned dirty, tear-stained faces towards her with exclamations of delight. Alys hugged them awkwardly.

'I heard about your prank — for shame, both of you,' she said. ' 'Tis wrong to tease poor Brother Matthew, but you have paid for it with a thrashing, and I would not see you starved as well.'

'Thanks, Alys,' muttered Giles, through a mouthful of pasty.

Alys locked the door behind her and ran down the shabby stone staircase as quickly as she could. The hall was deserted now, as dusk had fallen, and she started with surprise as she heard the jingle of coins and low, muttered whispers.

'In Christ's name, who's that?' came an angry voice, and her stepfather and his

24

visitor came out of the shadows. Alys felt a chill of fear.

' 'Tis . . . 'tis only me, Alys. A message for . . . Dame Eleanor,' she said hastily.

The two men glanced at one another. The stranger seemed to be hiding something behind his back.

'Away with you, girl. 'Tis surely time you were abed,' blustered Sir Hugh.

Alys needed no more telling. Whatever are they about? she asked herself as she sped across the hall. Why is Sir Hugh giving money to this shabby stranger, and in so secretive a manner? Is he leaving now, at night? And where is he bound?

She shivered suddenly. It's not my concern, she thought. Best put it from my mind, as Mother suggested, and think of music, and dancing, and apricot-silk dresses, and a smile from Tom Taverner. Or maybe, even, a kiss . . .

2

September 1470

Alys woke early on the morning of the harvest-home feast. Shivering a little, whether from excitement or the chill morning air she could not tell, she crept out of the bed she shared with Cecily and over to the window. She gave a sigh of relief when she saw the sky — blue, cloudless, promising a glorious day. Already she could hear the faint sounds of movement from the Manor kitchens as the servants prepared for a day of feasting and merrymaking. Alys pulled her chamber-robe tighter around her. When would the Earl and Countess of Aylesbury and their household arrive? They should have started out before dawn, for she knew her stepfather was planning a deer-hunt and he would want to leave before the sun was too high in the sky.

Shall I go hunting too? Alys thought. For sure, Tom will, and the other young men and squires. Although many

well-born ladies enjoyed hunting, hawking, hare-coursing and other such sports,
her aunt the Countess had often said it
turned her stomach. Cousin Mary was a
poor horsewoman, and her own mother
far too delicate to relish a gallop across the
woods and fields in pursuit of hare, deer
or wild boar. Would Tom think her wild
and unladylike if she hunted with the men,
rather than staying behind to gossip with
the ladies?

There would be other sports to watch if
she stayed behind. Some of the villagers
had spent the previous day setting up
archery targets. There would be tilting at
the quintain, which her young half-
brothers enjoyed. A beech trunk, greased
with mutton fat, had been laid across the
stream with a prize for anyone who could
cross without falling in. There would be
dancing later, and music, and Margery
the washerwoman turned fortune-teller,
promising handsome husbands to the
giggling village girls, and games of
hot-cockles and hoodman-blind . . .

Alys whirled round, pulled the coverlets
off Cecily's sleeping body, and began
tickling her sister unmercifully and crying,
'Wake up, get up, sleepy-head, 'tis a fine

27

morning for our harvest feast!'

Cecily groaned and tried to pull the pillow over her head, but Alys was too quick for her and whisked it away. Cecily sat up, blinking and rubbing the sleep from her eyes.

'Have our cousins of Aylesbury arrived?' she demanded, yawning.

'No, not yet, and it's as well for you they haven't,' Alys replied, scrambling into her shift and then into her gown. 'What would Sir Hugh say, or Dame Eleanor, if they arrived and we were not there to greet them? Come, sister, let's go down and break our fast together, and then out into the courtyard to wait for them!'

By now wide awake, Cecily climbed out of bed and dressed as swiftly as her sister. The Manor was beginning to come to life. Doors banged, cocks crowed, sheep bleated plaintively in the distance, and from the nursery came the sound of childish chatter as Dame Eleanor prepared the two little girls for the day ahead.

Alys and Cecily hardly had time to gulp down mugs of ale and slices of bread and fat bacon before they heard the jingling of spurs and harnesses which meant that riders, a large party of riders, were approaching. Sir Hugh hastily drained his ale, belched loudly, fastened his doublet, and ran his hands through his thinning, greasy hair.

'My brother of Aylesbury approaches,' he announced with satisfaction. 'Wife, come! We must greet him together, 'tis only fitting.'

Lady Philippa rose from her seat and laid her thin hand formally in Sir Hugh's big, grimy paw. Followed, at a respectful distance, by Alys and Cecily, Robin and Giles, and with Joanna and Katherine clinging to their nurses' hands, they went out of the hall and across the courtyard. Old Toby, the gatehouse keeper, was sweating as he unbolted the big studded wooden gates. A tall young man on a prancing bay horse rode through them.

'Their Graces, the Earl and Countess of Aylesbury,' he announced.

Suddenly, the courtyard seemed crowded with people, dogs and horses. Alys stood back for a moment, her eyes searching the crowd for a familiar blond head. Surely he would come. He had to come! Where was he? Could he be ill? Had he been sent away on some message or errand, perhaps even home to his family in the North?

For a moment, Alys felt sick with disappointment. What should I do, she thought despairingly, after all Cecily's teasing, all my hopes, if Tom isn't here?

And then she saw him, at the back of the crowd, dismounting from a stocky piebald pony, tossing the reins to a stable-boy, and ruffling young Robin's hair. He was smiling, and looking round. Could he be looking for her, Alys? Her heart began to thump, slowly and painfully. I'm here, I'm over here, Tom Taverner, she thought, willing him to turn those sea-blue eyes her way. When he did, she gasped, and felt as though she might swoon. He had seen her! Her and Cecily. Oh, dear God, he was coming over! What should she say? What should she do?

He smiled, brushed a lock of untidy blond hair from his forehead, and swept her a courtly bow.

'Lady Alys, Lady Cecily. God's greetings to you both,' he said formally.

Oh, Lord, here he is, before me, and I'm scarlet as a poppy and tongue-tied as a booby! What *will* he think of me? thought Alys desperately.

'G-good day to you, sire,' she managed to stammer.

Cecily bobbed a curtsey, glanced from Tom's questioning face to her sister's blushing one, and said innocently, 'Oh, there are my aunt the Countess and cousin Mary! I must bid them welcome!' Then she disappeared.

There was a silence. Alys looked at her feet, at the stable door, at her sister's retreating back, anywhere except at Tom. I can't believe this, she thought. This is Tom Taverner, my old playmate, and I'm struck as dumb as Daft Will in the village, who can neither hear nor speak!

'You . . . you are welcome to our harvest feast, Tom,' she said faintly. At last she managed to look up at him, and he was smiling. Suddenly, she stopped feeling shy. Everything was going to be all right, she was sure of it.

'Am I truly welcome, Alys?' Tom said softly. He was standing close to her, so close that she could see the soft blond hairs on his upper lip, the mole high on his left cheekbone. The stray lock of hair had fallen into his eyes again. I could brush it

31

back, Alys thought daringly, I could touch him . . .

'I'm glad to see you, Tom Taverner,' she told him. 'It has been too long since last we met. 'Tis good to see you, and to have a fine day for our harvest-home.'

Tom glanced up at the sky.

'Indeed,' he said, grinning. 'We have not always had such good fortune, have we? I remember one year when you and I were caught in a rainstorm with some of the others. We'd tried to build a raft and sail it down the millrace, and Matt the miller's son almost drowned, do you remember?'

Alys laughed and nodded, feeling easier with him than she had done for weeks. In spite of the new, disturbing feelings that made her blush and feel weak at his nearness, he was still Tom, still her friend and playfellow.

'Sir Hugh, my stepfather, plans a hunt,' she told him as they strolled over to join the others. 'Will you ride with them?'

'I can but try!' said Tom ruefully, nodding towards the piebald pony. 'Two of the Earl's best hunters have gone lame, and old Patch there is no horse for hunting! He'll surely be left behind when the others go in for the kill. But I care not, 'tis the ride that I like, and sunny weather, and good company. Will you ride with me, Alys?'

Cecily was right, Alys thought joyfully. He must like me!

'I will if I may,' she said, suddenly doubtful. What would Dame Eleanor say if she rode off with the hunt like a man — or, worse, lingered behind the others with Tom Taverner? But 'tis a feast-day, she thought, I can do as I will!

'My mare Joliet grows plump and lazy, a gallop would do her good,' she added.

They were still smiling foolishly at one another when Cecily came up with Cousin Mary and her betrothed, as plain as she was and with eyes for no one else.

'God's greetings, Alys,' said good-natured Mary, giving her cousin a hearty kiss. 'Has Cecily told you our news? Our fathers have agreed at last, and William and I are to be wed at Christmas-tide. I say 'tis too long to wait, we've been promised a year already, but there was so much to-do over dowries and settlements and the Hall where we are to live, out in Essex I hear, not that I've seen it, but William says 'tis a fine fair little manor, and the land is good for cattle if not sheep, and of course his father is an old man now, and sickly, and William is to inherit Enderby Hall one day, so all may be well and for the best . . . '

'Peace, Mary!' said her husband-to-be, a solemn young man who was as silent as Mary was talkative. 'You chatter like a magpie! Let Lady Alys speak!'

'I was only going to say I wish you well, cousin,' Alys laughed. 'But we shall miss you. Your new home must be several days' ride away . . . '

'Oh, no matter, we'll visit one another, of course we will,' said Mary calmly. ' 'Tis more than time I was settled with my own household, and babies, God willing. I'm eighteen years old, cousin! My mother the Countess had borne three children by the time she was my age.'

'We look forward to your wedding feast, Lady Mary,' said Tom politely. 'Christmas-tide, did you say? May we all be there to wish you Godspeed!'

'Aye, well, as to that,' said William Enderby, glancing over his shoulder and lowering his voice, 'I hope we shall all be together at Christmas-tide, but', he shook his head, 'if it were my choice, I would marry my Mary tomorrow, and take her to Essex straight away.'

For no real reason, Alys thought of the stranger who had come to the Manor the previous week, and disappeared as suddenly and mysteriously as he arrived. She felt a chill of fear.

'Why, William?' she asked, frowning. 'Is anything wrong? What have you heard?'

'Don't worry, Alys,' Tom broke in. 'It's just that there were some rumours of a landing by the exiled Earl of Warwick and his followers. Just rumours, I'm sure. The Earl my master believes that Warwick has been plotting with Queen Margaret to put Lancaster back on the throne and unseat our sovereign lord, King Edward.'

'If it's true, there could be trouble,' said William Enderby gloomily. ' 'Tis all very well for knights, and those who love to fight and long for deeds of valour, but I'm a plain man, myself. All I want is a comfortable home, a good wife, and sons to follow me on my own lands. War holds no promise for men like me!'

Alys looked pityingly at Mary. What must it be like to be betrothed to someone as plain, as stolid, as unheroic as William Enderby? But Mary was discussing court

35

fashions with Cecily, and not listening. I'm sure *Tom* would go and fight, if war came, Alys thought, lifting her chin proudly. Just like the heroes in the old romances Dame Eleanor used to tell us. Just like my brave father . . .

' 'Tis too fine and fair a day to worry about plots and rumours,' she cried gaily. 'Come, Tom, to the stables! I want to saddle Joliet, and then we'll follow the hunt!'

Sir Hugh, the Earl, and some of the other young squires were keen huntsmen and were soon off across the fields, pursued by a pack of yapping, squabbling hounds. As Tom had suspected, his mount, old Patch, seemed to have little interest in the chase, and Alys found that even her sweet-natured lazy mare Joliet could outrun him.

'Lord, for some decent horse-flesh,' groaned Tom, as the sound of the hunting-horns faded in the distance while Patch ambled along at his own pace. 'I swear, Alys, that when I win my knight's spurs, I'll buy myself a fine Arab stallion, the best I can afford! 'Tis more than time this old nag was put out to grass. The children can have him.'

But he leaned over to pat the old pony's neck affectionately while Alys, who loved animals, looked on approvingly.

'I mislike seeing a noble beast torn apart by hounds anyway,' she said. 'I know 'tis a natural thing, and we need venison and other meats to see us through the winter, but ... I don't watch the pig-killing, either.'

'Nor I,' said Tom cheerfully. 'I find more sport in knightly combat. I've brought my longbow, and plan to test my skills on the archery targets this afternoon. I've practised jousting with the other lads by the hour, and the Earl has told me I'm as skilled as any in swordplay. Lord, I wish ... ' He broke off.

'Tell me. What do you wish?' said Alys. This was a Tom she hadn't met before, neither a merry playfellow nor a disturbing stranger, but a mature young man, grown thoughtful for his scant seventeen years.

'I wish there was some way I could prove myself worthy of knighthood,' Tom went on, after a pause. 'Hunting, hawking, archery, even swordplay at the Castle, they are only games, Alys. Children's games. And I'm no longer a child. I'm a man! Perhaps it sounds foolish to you, but I long to test myself in true knightly combat. I owe loyalty to my lord the Earl, and through him to our sovereign lord King Edward, and I want to prove myself worthy of their trust. Like the knights of old, like Roland, or Charlemagne, or even King Arthur himself. And here I am, instead, playing boys' games, as if I was but seven years old, not seventeen!'

Alys drew rein and turned to face him.

'I understand, Tom,' she said gently. 'My own father was a true and brave knight who died fighting for the House of York at Wakefield, when I was but a child. I, too, long to be judged worthy, worthy of his memory.'

'I saw the King once, you know,' Tom said. 'I went to London with the Earl and Countess and the Lady Mary and others of the household.'

'Tell me, tell me,' said Alys eagerly. 'I should love to go to London and see the King's court. My cousin Mary says that King Edward is a handsome man.'

'So he is, and a true king,' said Tom reverently. 'And yet, 'tis also true he has the common touch. The people love him. He strode through the crowd like . . . like a god among men, so tall and golden and laughing, yet he'd stop to greet an old friend, to shake the hand of a poor man or to pinch the cheek of a pretty young wench. No wonder men long to do him knight's service!'

'Who was he with?' breathed Alys, spellbound.

'His brother of Gloucester, him they call Dickon.'

'And is he tall and kingly, too?'

Tom laughed.

'No, my lord of Gloucester looks like a changeling at that glittering court. He's slight and dark and looks uncomfortable, as though he'd sooner be on horseback on his Northern moors, or else fighting. They say he's a fierce fighter.'

'And the Queen? Did you see the Queen? Mary says she's beautiful!'

Tom hesitated.

'Yes,' he said shortly, 'Queen Elizabeth is fair, but I thought her a cold and haughty woman, Alys. King Edward jests, and laughs, and speaks to all and sundry. The Queen is silent, and looks . . . as though there was a bad smell under her nose! Mind you,' he continued, laughing, 'there may have been! London is a fair city, Alys, but it stinks, believe me! And the noise! Church bells, pedlars and chapmen and street traders bawling their wares, horses neighing, a flock of geese cackling, a group of drunken sailors roaring out a tune, 'twas like St Albans on market day, but fifty times as loud! I wonder the men and women of London don't all go deaf. Were it not for seeing our lord the King, I would have been happy to leave.'

'Oh, Tom,' sighed Alys enviously, 'you are so fortunate. I long to go to London! If only I was a man . . . '

She looked up, caught his eye, and found she couldn't look away. A strange feeling swept over her and her breath caught in her throat.

'I . . . I'm very glad you're not a man, Alys,' Tom said. 'And, I swear, there was no lady at King Edward's court so fair as you; no, not even the Queen herself!'

Alys felt a fiery blush spreading from her neck to her cheeks.

'Th-thank you, Tom,' she stammered. Tom looked as though he wanted to say something else, but instead he dug his heels into his pony's sturdy sides.

'Come up, come up, Patch,' he muttered roughly. 'I think I hear the hunting-horns approaching.'

Sure enough, some of the other riders came into view a few moments later, followed by the hounds, licking their chops and looking pleased with themselves. The Earl and Sir Hugh soon followed, Alys's stepfather with a fine deer slung over his saddle pommel.

'Good sport today, young Tom!' said the Earl pleasantly as he rode by.

Alys didn't get another chance to be alone with Tom. When he went in for the archery contest she and Cecily, Cousin Mary and William Enderby, and some of the other young squires stood and watched. When Tom was placed second, after Philip de Blayne, the Earl's finest archer, Alys glowed with pride. Some of the village lads staged a mock sword-fight, and when tempers began to fray Matt the miller's son, a beetle-browed youth with the build of an ox, sent them all down to the mill-stream to try their luck on the greasy pole. By the time four or five of them, including Matt, had had a thorough soaking, Alys's sides were aching with laughter.

The warmth and merriment of the day seemed to have affected everyone. Even

Sir Hugh had lost his usual ill-tempered scowl, and managed to smile when each of the villagers brought him their harvest gifts — a freshly-baked loaf, a dozen eggs, a bag of apples and pears. Lady Philippa chatted quietly to her sister the Countess, the Earl discussed horses and hunting with anyone who would listen, and the children ran around, getting under everyone's feet and sneaking titbits from the kitchen when Cook wasn't looking. Even Dame Eleanor, her face bright scarlet from sampling the harvest ale, forgot to scold when she discovered a huge, jagged tear in Alys's hunting gown.

'I'll mend it tomorrow, I promise,' smiled Alys, giving her old nurse a hearty kiss.

And I hope tomorrow never comes, she added silently to herself, for there has never been a day like today, and there never will be. Tom Taverner says I'm fair, fairer than the Queen herself!

It was a thought to be cherished, to be held close in her heart and pondered on later, when she lay abed beside the sleeping Cecily. We rode together, she thought, and he told me what was in his heart, his dreams of knightly combat. He must like me. He must . . .

The cool of the evening brought more laughter and merry-making as the great feast that had been prepared was finally served. Roast mutton and venison turned on a spit, savoury broths, brawns and pies, stewed fowl, pike and carp from the Manor fish-ponds, were followed by sugared cakes, great dishes of fruit from the orchard and — in honour of the Earl and Countess — a great 'subtlety' made of marchpane in the shape of their own castle, with tiny banners in the Earl's colours fluttering from its sugar roof! There were oohs and aahs of pleasure as the two pastry-cooks brought it in and set it down on the high table, in front of the guests of honour.

' 'Tis almost too fair to eat!' laughed the Countess, and Sir Hugh's mottled cheeks crimsoned with pride. He had been drinking since early morning, and was somewhat the worse for strong ale. He staggered to his feet with difficulty and raised his mug high.

'A toash . . . a toast!' he roared. 'To our resh . . . respected kinsfolk of Aylesbury. My brother, my shish . . . my sister. May they live long and prosper!'

43

He stifled a belch, none too successfully, and Alys looked away, embarrassed. He's a pig, she thought, a snorting, sniffling, sweaty swine! God send me a kinder husband, I pray, than He sent my lady mother! How can she bear to share his bed?

She raised her own mug dutifully and caught Tom Taverner's eye across the crowded hall. He smiled and winked at her, and Alys felt better immediately.

After the meal, there was music, and dancing. Blind Gwilym, the Earl's Welsh harpist, played and sang sad old ballads from his native land, and even though no one understood the words, the plaintive melodies were enough to catch at the heart. Alys saw Cecily wipe away a sentimental tear, and even her own eyes felt damp. But tears soon turned to laughter as a troupe of tumblers burst into the hall, cracking jokes, leaping on one another's shoulders, turning cartwheels and somersaults, all accompanied by flute, pipe and tabor.

Then, when the dancing began, Alys felt her heart begin to beat fast again. Would Tom choose her for his partner? Or would he dance with one of the other girls, with

Cecily, or Mary, or no one at all?

The minstrels struck up a gay carole, and the Earl rose to his feet.

'Come, my lady,' he said to the Countess, 'let us lead the dance!'

They were soon followed by Mary, who loved dancing, dragging a very sheepish-looking William Enderby with her; Cecily, blushing and protesting when one of the Earl's young squires held out his hand to her, and then by a crowd of servants and village folk. Stout Dame Eleanor was pulled into the weaving, moving circle of dancers by Matt the miller, Moll the kitchenmaid tossed her curls in time to the music, and even small Joanna, with Katherine and a gaggle of the village children, jigged merrily about with the rest.

Alys went on sitting at the table, her cheeks burning. Where was Tom? He seemed to have disappeared in the crowd. Everyone will notice, she thought, mortified. Everyone is dancing, even the old and the stout and the plain and those with two left feet like poor William Enderby. Everyone but me . . .

She whirled round as she felt a tap on her shoulder.

'Lady Alys,' said Tom formally, 'will you be my partner?'

Her smile gave him his answer and he took her hand and led her on to the floor. His hand felt strong and warm, the palm a little calloused from swordplay and hard riding. If we could stay like this for ever, Alys thought dreamily as they circled the floor, her hand in Tom's, the music playing, the candlelight reflected in his eyes . . .

The minstrels changed their tune to a country dance and Alys was swept up the line to other partners — Matt the miller, Cecily's young squire, even the Earl himself. When the dance brought her back to Tom again she felt hot and breathless, but still as if she could dance for ever. I'll remember this day, this night, all my life, she thought. Yes, even when I'm a crooked old dame with no teeth and bones too creaky for dancing, I shall remember the night I danced with Tom Taverner, and he told me I was fairer than the Queen herself.

The candles burned lower. Sleepy children were borne off to their beds, ale-flushed villagers crept back to their cottages, and Sir Hugh sat slumped in a pool of wine at the high table, snoring loudly. Lady Philippa said farewell to the Earl and Countess alone, except for Alys and Cecily.

'Take care of yourself, sister,' said the Countess briskly, with a disapproving look at the drunken Sir Hugh. 'We shall meet again soon, God willing.'

'Aye, and if not before, then for the wedding of young Mary and William Enderby,' said Lady Philippa. 'He was well chosen, my sister. He's a fine young man and will make Mary a good husband.'

Mary blushed and looked at her feet. The horses were brought round from the stables. Some of the young squires mounted at once, carrying lighted torches, as the road to the Castle led through woodland, and there could be outlaws abroad. There were kissings and huggings and promises to meet again.

'Psst!'

Alys looked round. Tom Taverner, not yet mounted, stood in a shadowed corner of the courtyard, beckoning to her. Glancing round to make sure no one was watching, Alys slipped over to him. With his blond hair haloed against the light of the torches, he looked more handsome than ever.

'Alys, I . . . ' he began.

With those sea-blue eyes gazing into hers, Alys felt as though she could not have spoken if her life depended on it.

'I . . . I,' Tom stammered. 'Alys, I would ride with you again. That is, if . . . if it would please you.'

Alys could only nod.

'Then . . . meet me by the Outlaws' Oak in Dedham Forest, at twelve of the clock, three days from now,' he said urgently. 'Can you do that? Will you be missed?'

'No,' she said slowly. 'I spend much time alone, either picking fruit, swimming in the mill-stream, or exercising my mare Joliet. I could come, Tom, and yes, it would please me to ride with you again. It would please me very much!'

They smiled at each other. Then, very gently, Tom took both her trembling hands in his.

'Oh, Alys,' he breathed. She looked up into his eyes, feeling as though she were drowning in their depths, as his soft lips met hers in the gentlest, the sweetest of kisses.

'Farewell, dear Alys,' he murmured, his

touch as light as thistledown on her hair. 'Until we meet again, God have you in His keeping.'

He turned abruptly and strode away to where his pony was waiting, already saddled and ready to leave.

'Farewell, Tom,' Alys breathed.

Then she stood gazing after him, her thoughts in turmoil. Slowly, wonderingly, she raised her fingers to her lips, the lips that Tom had kissed, so warmly, so sweetly.

I love you, Tom Taverner, she thought, and there was no surprise in the thought, but only a tender, glowing joy.

3

'Faster, Joliet! Can't you go a little faster?'

Breathlessly, Alys urged the little mare on, digging her heels into the horse's plump chestnut sides as they sped along the woodland path towards the ancient tree known as the Outlaws' Oak. Glancing up through the sun-dappled leaves, Alys saw that the sun was already high in the sky. It must be past twelve, she thought frantically. He won't be there! He'll have gone, he'll think I'm not coming, that I was just flirting with him! Oh, a curse on Dame Eleanor and her wretched mending! Why must she keep me back to finish that seam, today of all days? I could have finished it this afternoon instead — yes, and done my mother's share and Cecily's too, and gladly — if I could only spend this hour with Tom Taverner!

There! At last, the great shape of the Outlaws' Oak stood before her. Panting, Alys slowed Joliet to a trot, and looked about her. Was he there, or had he given up and ridden back to the Castle? She gnawed her thumbnail anxiously.

'Tom?' she called. 'Are you there, Tom?'

There was a rustling noise further along the path and Tom emerged, smiling, from a willow copse. He was mounted on a fine bay hunter, not old Patch. When he saw Alys he leapt from the saddle and ran across to her, his hand outstretched.

'Alys! Oh, Alys, I thought . . . '

'You thought I wasn't coming,' she finished for him. 'I'm so sorry, Tom. I know I'm late. Dame Eleanor kept me, fussing and fussing about some stupid mending, until I thought I should go mad!'

She slid from Joliet's saddle into Tom's waiting arms. He greeted her with a warm, loving kiss, which lingered until they finally broke apart, breathless and laughing. Alys's heart thumped. He's even more handsome than I remember, she thought adoringly, and he likes me, at least . . .

She blushed as she remembered how eagerly she had returned his kiss, though there hadn't been any mention of love between them. Perhaps I have been too bold, too forward, she thought

51

uncertainly . . . or he could just be flirting with me? Then she looked up into his sea-blue eyes, and as his arms tightened around her, all her doubts melted away.

'Oh, Tom,' she sighed happily, ' 'tis good to see you!'

'And you,' he said. 'I wondered if perhaps you would not come at all!'

'But I said I would!' she retorted, in mock indignation.

'Aye, but what girls, young ladies, say, is not always what they mean,' Tom replied soberly. 'They tease, they flirt, they make promises and break them again, till a man doesn't know whether he's on his head or his heels!'

Alice drew back and gazed at him, wide-eyed.

'And where did *you* learn so much about young ladies and their habits?' she asked. 'Indeed, I might not have come, if I'd known I was coming to meet a practised flirt! You could have broken hearts all over the county, for all I know!'

'No, I have not,' said Tom, flushing. ' 'Tis just what the other lads say, the squires and young knights at the Castle. When you didn't come, I thought that perhaps you were just playing a game, making a fool of me because you knew how I felt about you!'

There was silence for a moment.

'But, Tom . . . ' Alys breathed, 'I didn't know . . . how could I know?'

He looked at her, very straight and true. There was no sound in the clearing but the rustle of leaves and the chink of the horses' bridles as they cropped the grass. Alys felt as though she could hardly breathe.

'Why, I love you, Alys,' Tom said simply. 'And when I'm knighted, I want you to be my lady, my wife. What do you say?'

'Oh, Tom,' Alys gasped, 'I . . . I know not *what* to say! Of course, of course I love you, too, but . . . this is all so sudden . . . '

'Nonsense!' said Tom, suddenly practical. 'We have known one another for years. My lady the Countess is your aunt, we're of an age to be betrothed . . . '

'Betrothed . . . ' Alys echoed.

It was all happening, just as it had done so often in her dreams. She felt so happy that she wanted to cry, or laugh, or turn somersaults across the clearing, like the tumblers at the harvest-home feast. Tom loves me, she thought. Tom loves me, and I love him, and he will ask his master the

Earl, and the Earl will ask Sir Hugh for me . . .

'Cecily says Sir Hugh will be sure to approve the match,' she said out loud.

'Oho! So you and your sister had it all planned, did you? And there I was, thinking it was all my idea,' Tom teased.

Alys blushed.

'I thought I'd better make sure of you, before someone else did,' he went on.

'Someone else?'

'Yes, I thought perhaps Philip de Blayne, you know the Frenchman, the Earl's top archer? He's looking for a wife, and he's a comely man, or so they tell me.'

Alys snorted.

'Philip de Blayne? You thought I would look twice at Philip de Blayne, with his mincing airs and his monkey-face? And he's old, Tom, he must be past thirty! I pity the girl who marries him, for she'll be fighting him for the looking-glass each morning! If he is the kind of man they breed in France, I'll stick with Englishmen, thank you!'

Tom grinned.

'I'm glad to hear you say it! But Philip isn't the only one who has looked your way. What about Alan of Bedford, or Will

Enderby's brother Ralph?'

Alys made a face.

'Ralph Enderby's a mere child, scarcely out of petticoats . . . ' she objected.

'I do beg your pardon, Grandmother,' said Tom, with a mocking bow. 'I seem to remember young Master Enderby celebrating his sixteenth this past summer, just a few months after your feast-day, my lady!'

'All the same, he's but a boy,' Alys giggled. 'And as for Alan of Bedford, his idea of courtship is to talk for hours on end about his father's lands and cattle and sheep and orchards. I swear, he must have described every fleece, every barrel of ale, every side of beef, every turnip! 'Tis not any woman's idea of a romantic wooing, Tom. I was so bored I could have screamed!'

'My style of wooing pleases you more, does it?' said Tom, smiling down at her.

'You know it does.'

'Oh, Alys, Alys . . . '

She felt his warm hands in her hair, loosening her braids, running the long, shining strands through his fingers, and moved closer into his arms, wondering how it was possible to feel so happy. We'll be wed, perhaps, next year, she thought, and Tom can take me to London before we go up to his estate in Yorkshire. My new home! What will it be like, I wonder?

'Tom,' she said out loud, 'what is your home like? What is Yorkshire like? Is it very different from Hertfordshire?'

Tom laughed.

'In truth,' he said, 'I can hardly remember Broughton Hall! Don't forget, Alys, I was only eight years old when I came to the Castle as a page, and I've only been back once, five years ago when my father died, God rest his soul. My mother runs the estate now, and will until I'm eighteen and a knight.'

'Your mother?'

Alys tried, and failed, to imagine her own mother doing such a thing. Dame Eleanor, perhaps, or the Countess . . .

'Yes, my mother. She's a formidable woman, I remember that much,' said Tom proudly. ' 'Twas really my mother who brought my sister and me up. My father was an old man and ailing, even then. As for Yorkshire, Alys, well, some parts are fair and wooded and very much like this, but there are also wild moors with no trees at all, just heather and bracken as far as

56

the eye can see, and no towns or even villages, just shepherds' huts and the tracks used by travellers and pilgrims going to the great Abbey at Whitby, on the coast. We stayed one night in York when my father died. That's a fine fair city too, as fair as London. Or so all Yorkshiremen think, though Londoners disagree!'

'I long to see it,' said Alys happily. 'We never go anywhere, Cecily and me. Once or twice to St Albans on market day, with my aunt the Countess and Mary, but that's all.'

'I remember. I was there with you when those piglets escaped into the market-place. Lord, what a to-do there was!' Tom chuckled.

'Oh yes, when one of them knocked that fat priest right over, Cecily and I thought we should die laughing.'

Tom stroked her cheek gently and his hand tightened on hers.

'I shall be the kindest husband,' he said, 'and I promise that you shall go to York as often as you please, when we're living at Broughton Hall. And your sister shall visit us, and your cousin Mary, and my sister. We shall be merry!'

'Your sister?'

'Elizabeth,' Tom nodded. 'She is older than I, and has two little children. Her husband died of a fever last year though, so she is back at Broughton Hall with the children, or she was, when last I heard, six months ago.'

Alys leaned against Tom with a happy sigh. She was already imagining her new home, much like the Manor, only without the baleful influence of her stepfather. No one shall bully *my* servants, or beat *my* children, she thought angrily. Tom and I will rule Broughton Hall by kindness, and not by fear! Our crops will flourish, our sheep and cattle will thrive, our servants will love us, our children will be plump and healthy, there'll be music and dancing and the sun will always shine!

'When shall we tell them?' she said dreamily, her head on Tom's shoulder.

'Leave it to me,' he replied. 'The Earl is away this week, and I can do nothing until he returns. But then . . . '

Alys shivered.

'I hope Sir Hugh will not make difficulties over my dowry,' she said.

Tom squeezed her hand.

'You know I'd take you without a dowry,' he said tenderly. ' 'Tis you I want,

Alys, not your father's money.'

'Nevertheless, I will bring it,' she said. 'Sir Hugh would be only too pleased to get his filthy hands on it, but 'tis mine, mine and Cecily's! It's kept in a chest in Mother's solar, and she and Dame Eleanor both have keys. Anyway, I'll wager Sir Hugh will be only too pleased to see the back of me. He has no use for daughters! And he will be able to boast to all and sundry about his kinsman, Sir Thomas Taverner of Broughton Hall in Yorkshire!'

'Let him,' said Tom. 'What do we care? Once you are truly mine, my love, you need never see that drunken old sot ever again!'

'Never would be too soon for me!' Alys laughed. Even thinking about her step-father couldn't take the edge off her happiness. I'm betrothed, she thought. I'm promised to the man I love and soon nothing shall part us!

Suddenly, she noticed how the shadows had lengthened, and scrambled to her feet.

' 'Tis time I was leaving,' she said. 'Dame Eleanor thinks I am with Cecily, and Cecily will be getting worried.'

'I'm needed at the castle, too,' said Tom,

helping her to mount Joliet. 'Shall we meet here again, Alys? On Sunday, after Mass? 'Tis easy enough for me to get away then.'

Alys nodded and bent down so that Tom could kiss her again.

'Sunday it shall be. God keep you till then, my dearest love,' she said softly.

'And you, my Alys.'

She raised her hand in farewell, gave a gentle tug to Joliet's reins, and trotted away down the path towards the Manor.

When she arrived home, there seemed to be more hustle and bustle than usual, and when she led Joliet into the stables Jack, the stable-boy, was feeding and watering two strange horses, both sweat-stained, as if they had been ridden long and hard. As he was busy, she attended to Joliet herself.

'What's happened, Jack? Are there visitors? I didn't know Sir Hugh was expecting anyone?' she asked, puzzled.

Jack's cheeky face broke into a grin. He adored Lady Alys, who had saved him from more than one beating by pleading for him with her stepfather.

'I know not,' he said, wiping his nose with the back of his hand. 'No one tells me, do they? It's just 'Take care of the

60

horses, Jack!' 'More hay, Jack!' 'Water for Sir Hugh's stallion, Jack!' '

'You can't fool me,' Alys laughed. 'You always know what's going on! Come on, don't tease, who are the strangers?'

Jack glanced over his shoulder and lowered his voice.

' 'Tis that Saville, that was here before,' he muttered, 'and another gentleman, a Frenchie or some such, jabbering away in his heathen tongue. I don't know for sure, but they're saying that Warwick, you know the great earl, has landed in the West Country and is marching east, with the King's brother, the traitor Duke of Clarence. Mind,' as Alys's eyes widened in shock, 'it could be no more than a rumour, so don't worry, my lady. They'll not bother the likes of us!'

Frowning, Alys crossed the courtyard and went into the great hall. She was thinking about what Tom and Will Enderby had said at the harvest-home feast — that if Warwick invaded and tried to put mad Henry of Lancaster back on the throne, it could mean war. Fear gripped her suddenly, as if a black cloud had crept up and blotted out the sun. All the plans she and Tom had made seemed no more than dreams, fairytales, for if war came Tom would be there, fighting for the King and the House of York, just like Alys's father. Alys's father, who had died fighting . . .

'Cecily!' Alys called, trying to control her rising panic. 'Cecily? Dame Eleanor? Where are you?'

'I'm here, child. Where else would I be?' said Dame Eleanor, bustling out of the still-room, looking so sane, and normal, and exactly as she had always done that Alys was reassured. Perhaps Jack was mistaken. He was only the stable-boy, after all. Even if the Earl of Warwick and the Duke of Clarence had landed, it need not mean war. The people loved handsome King Edward. No one wanted Daft Henry back again.

'I see we have visitors,' she said carefully, hoping that Dame Eleanor wouldn't notice her flushed cheeks and shining eyes. 'Who are they, do you know?'

Dame Eleanor shrugged.

'Two more for supper, that's all I know. 'Tis as well we have an extra barrel of salted pork,' she grumbled. 'Nay, child, I haven't seen them, they've been shut in the bailiff's room with your father since they arrived. Men's business, no doubt, nothing to concern us. What have you been doing, young lady? Your hair looks like a rat's nest, your braids are loose, and as for your gown . . . '

Alys wondered what Dame Eleanor would say if she knew she had spent half the afternoon in Tom Taverner's arms. She'll know soon enough, once we are honourably betrothed, and she'll be pleased I've made a love-match, she thought, hugging her secret safe. Meanwhile, I must find Cecily! If I don't tell someone soon, I feel as though I shall burst with excitement!

She found Cecily busy with her needle in their bedroom, altering the old green gown Alys had given her.

'I wish I was tall and slim like you, sister. 'Tis more elegant,' she began with a sigh. Then, when she saw Alys's face, she dropped her sewing and leapt to her feet.

'Alys! I have no need to ask if you met Tom, if all went well, I can see it in your face! It's as if . . . as if a candle was shining behind your eyes! What did he say? What did you say? Come, tell all!'

'Hush, Cecily,' Alys replied, squeezing her sister's hands. 'It was wonderful, much better than I had dared to hope. Cecily, Tom and I are betrothed!'

Cecily gasped.

'Betrothed! Then he has spoken to the Earl, and Sir Hugh?'

Alys laughed and shook her head.

'No, no, 'tis but between us at the moment. A secret, Cecily! No one is to know but Tom, and me, and you of course, until the Earl comes back at the end of this week. But Tom knows the Earl will agree and he thinks, as I do, that Sir Hugh will be glad to get rid of me, especially to Sir Thomas Taverner of Broughton Hall! Oh, Cecily, just think, by next summer, I could be wed, and living in Yorkshire!'

Cecily hesitated for a moment and then hugged Alys hard.

'I'm pleased for you, truly. T-Tom Taverner will make you a good husband,' she faltered.

Alys's smile faded and she slipped her arms round her.

'What is it, sister?' she asked gently.

Cecily gave a sob and hid her face in Alys's shoulder.

'I . . . I'm happy for you, Alys, really I am . . . but I shall miss you so much,' she wept. 'I knew it must happen one day, 'tis

64

only natural that we both should wed, and be parted, but I shall be so lonely . . . '

'No, you won't, or not for long,' said Alys firmly. 'Tom says you can visit us as often as you like, and I promise, Cecily, as soon as Tom and I are wed and settled, we will look around for some nice gentleman in Yorkshire to be your husband!'

Cecily gulped, and sniffed, and stopped crying. Then Alys remembered the strange horses in the stables, and the rumour Jack had told her.

'Did you know that that Robert Saville is back? And with another man, some foreigner?' she demanded. 'What can it mean, Cecily? I don't trust that man, nor our stepfather, either!'

Cecily bit her lip.

'Moll the kitchenmaid told me there were soldiers in the village too. Ten or a dozen of them, she said.'

'Soldiers? What do they want?'

'Just passing through, the sergeant-at-arms told Moll.'

'But where are they bound? Is it true, then, that the Earl of Warwick has landed and is marching on London?' Alys persisted.

Cecily shrugged and looked frightened.

'I . . . I don't know. Moll wouldn't think to ask them, would she? 'Tis enough for her that there are a dozen lusty lads in the village for her to flirt with!'

Alys shook her head. The fear that she had managed to push to the back of her mind refused to go away. She couldn't forget what Tom and Will Enderby and the others had said. There might be war, fighting, killing. The idea of her brave Tom riding off to fight for his king seemed real, no longer a romantic dream. I don't want him to go, Alys thought. 'Tis all very well to dream of heroes, and knightly combat, like the tales of long ago, but Tom could be wounded, even killed!

'Cecily,' she said. 'I must find out what our stepfather is planning!'

'But how?' demanded Cecily, ever practical. 'When has he ever shared his plans with anyone, even our lady mother? He comes and goes just as he pleases, and so do his friends and cronies. If you seem to pry, 'twill only anger him, and that will mean a beating.'

Alys bit her lip.

'All the same, I must know, and get word to Tom if there's a plot against our lord King Edward,' she said stubbornly.

66

Fortune seemed to be against her. At supper she was placed too far down the table to hear what her stepfather and the strangers were saying. They didn't seem to talk much anyway, being preoccupied with shovelling baked salt pork into their mouths, washed down with mug after mug of new ale. They're louts, I hate them all, thought Alys in disgust, as she watched Robert Saville wipe his greasy fingers on his doublet. The Frenchman gazed across the hall, his eyes narrowed, now and again picking at his blackened teeth with his knife, glancing this way and that as if he expected to have to flee for his life at any moment. Alys felt more and more certain there was something going on.

After the meal, when the ladies had retired, Alys tiptoed back down the narrow staircase and squeezed herself into one of the alcoves in the kitchen passageway, hoping that she would be near enough to overhear the men's conversation. Her heart was hammering, for she knew that if she was discovered, she would be beaten, or worse. These were desperate men, plotting treason, who would have no mercy on spies or eavesdroppers.

However much she strained her ears, she could hear little but low murmurings, and the chink of coins. Now and again, a name was mentioned. Plymouth. Montagu. Northumberland. The names meant nothing to Alys, but she resolved to remember them, to tell Tom on Sunday. Eventually, cramped and stiff, she crept from her uncomfortable hiding-place and went back upstairs to her bedroom.

Cecily was already asleep, but Alys found that she tossed and turned and could not sleep. Her happiness with Tom seemed a faraway dream. She crept out of bed and sat by the window, gazing out across the woods and meadows towards the Castle, where Tom would be sleeping. God keep you safe, my love, whatever befalls us, she thought, and a tear slid from between her eyelids and made a damp patch on her bed-gown. Would this night *never* pass? And the long, weary days till Sunday, when she would see Tom again?

This time he was not smiling when he rode out from beneath the Outlaws' Oak to meet her.

'Tom . . . oh . . . Tom . . . ' Alys gasped, sliding from Joliet's back and flinging herself into his arms. 'Something's wrong, I know it is!'

He gave her a quick, preoccupied kiss, then gripped her arm so hard that it hurt.

'What have you heard, Alys? Tell me!'

'Why . . . that . . . that the Earl of Warwick has landed . . . ' she faltered. 'And there have been two strangers at the Manor, and soldiers in the village, according to Moll our kitchenmaid. One of the strangers is a Robert Saville. He came before, my stepfather gave him money, and he rode away. The other man is foreign, says little, looks shifty. I . . . I heard them talking, but all I could make out were some names . . . '

'Names?' said Tom sharply.

'Yes. Plymouth, Montagu, and Northumberland.'

Tom frowned, and was silent.

'What does it mean, Tom?' Alys begged, really frightened now. He took both her hands in his and looked into her eyes.

'My love,' he began in a hoarse voice, 'I wasn't going to tell you until I left you today, but it seems you know already . . . '

'Know?' Alys cried frantically. 'I know nothing, Tom! Tell me!'

'Hush,' he said. 'Word came to the

Castle two days ago that the Earl of Warwick, and Clarence the King's brother, have landed in Devonshire, at Plymouth we believe. There are soldiers with them, French soldiers.'

'So it's as you feared. They plan to take King Edward's throne and give it back to Henry of Lancaster and his fierce French wife,' Alys breathed.

Tom nodded.

'King Edward is in Yorkshire, Alys. There has been trouble there too, a rising of some kind. That devil Warwick had his hand in that, too, no doubt! We hear that the King, his brother Dickon of Gloucester, and their followers are marching south.'

'And Montagu? Northumberland?'

Tom shrugged.

'Great lords in the North, I believe. They may support our king, or turn their coats when they see how Warwick fares in battle against him.'

'Battle,' echoed Alys faintly.

Tom's hands tightened on hers.

'Yes, my love,' he said softly, 'it may come to that. The King has sent word to the Earl of Aylesbury, my master, to join him and fight the rebels. We set off for the

North tomorrow.'

A thousand thoughts rushed through Alys's mind. Everything seemed to be happening so terrifyingly fast. Her love for Tom, his love for her, their betrothal, their future wedding, all seemed like a dream long past. Instead, Tom would ride away to fight, perhaps to die.

'Oh, Tom, don't go! I can't bear it if you go!' she wept, clinging to him.

He held her tight against him and when she looked up, she saw that his lips were quivering too, so that he looked less like a soldier, and more like a frightened seventeen-year-old boy. But then he squared his shoulders, lifted his chin, smiled, and cupped her face in his hands.

'Don't say that, Alys,' he said gently. 'You are a soldier's daughter. You know that I would be dishonoured if I did not fight for my king against these upstart rebels. 'Tis my duty, 'tis what I have been trained for! I wanted to prove myself in knightly combat, now I shall have the chance! And we shall prevail, Alys, have no doubt of that. King Edward is the rightful king. The country prospers under his rule. He is a bonny fighter, and so is his brother Dickon. You need have no fear for me, I shall be safe under their command! Did not the Earl say I was as skilled in swordplay as any? And he has promised me a fine war-horse, the best his stables have to offer! We shall soon destroy Warwick and his poxy French followers, just like King Arthur and his knights slew the evil Sir Mordred! I shall be back with you before you know it! Come, sweetheart, don't weep. I want to remember you smiling.'

Alys looked up at him, so tall and proud and clear-eyed, and felt ashamed of her tears. I wanted a handsome knight to fight for me, didn't I, she told herself, her heart swelling with pride. Tom was right. Nothing could happen to him while he fought for his king, handsome, golden Edward of York. He would soon come safely home, and . . .

'And we shall wed, shan't we, when you come home?' she said out loud.

Tom laughed.

'Of course we will, Alys, my love. I am fighting for you, and for our love, just like the knights of old! Come, give me a token to take into battle with me!'

'But I have nothing!' Alys said. Then she removed one of the blue silk ribbons that bound her braids. 'Here, love,' she said, 'take this!'

Tom kissed the ribbon and placed it inside his shirt, next to his heart.

'And I have something for you,' he said, taking a small leather pouch out of his saddle-bag.

'For me? What is it?'

'Open it. Open it and see!'

Alys opened the pouch and took out something wrapped in a scrap of ivory silk. It was a rose pendant, a silver rose, exquisitely worked, on a fine silver chain.

'Oh, Tom,' Alys gasped, 'it's beautiful!'

Tom undid the clasp and fastened it around Alys's neck where it lay against her skin beneath her gown.

'I have no betrothal ring to give you, Alys,' he said seriously, 'but this pendant has been in my family for generations, and my mother gave it to me to keep when my father died. 'Tis a Yorkshire rose. Keep it, my dearest love, and wear it in remembrance of me. When the fighting is over, I shall come back and claim you as my bride.'

Her heart too full for words, or even tears, Alys just nodded. Tom flung his arms round her and they exchanged a last, desperate kiss. Then Tom loosened her arms from about his neck and mounted his horse.

'Fare well, my dearest lady, until we meet again,' he said formally.

'God keep you, Tom,' said Alys, her head high.

He swung his horse round and rode away without looking back. Half-blinded by tears, Alys watched him go, until his horse's hoofbeats faded away into the distance. Then, very slowly, she mounted Joliet and turned towards home. She could feel the silver rose pendant warm against her skin. Wear it for me, Tom had said. I shall, Alys thought fiercely. I shall be brave, and strong, for Tom's sake, and I shall wear the silver rose until we meet again.

4

December 1470

Alys was woken, before daybreak, by Tib the cat, who had crept into the bedroom during the night and leapt on to the bed she shared with Cecily, snuggling down between them for warmth.

'What's amiss, Tib?' said Alys sleepily. As soon as she put her arm out to stroke the little cat's fur, she felt the bitter chill of the winter's first frost and shivered, pulling the wolfskin rug tighter round her and moving closer to Cecily. She could hear faint sounds from below; the creak of the winding gear from the well in the courtyard as the maids drew water, and smell woodsmoke from the kitchen fire. It must be almost time to get up. But what is there to get up for, she thought gloomily, just another dreary winter's day, cold and grey. Her fingers were too stiff and chilblained to work on her embroidery, and Dame Eleanor would want her to help with the baking or the brewing or the salting of meat and fish for the long winter months ahead.

I wish I was a man, Alys thought rebelliously. Men do as they please in this world, with no one to answer to. They go hunting, they go to London on business, like my stepfather, they go off into battle, like Tom . . .

Oh, Tom . . .

Automatically, Alys's hand went to the silver rose pendant, tucked away beneath her linen bed-gown. If it wasn't for this, she thought, I could almost believe that Tom was a dream, like the handsome knights in the old tales! More than three months he has been gone, and I have heard nothing. Not that I expected to hear. If there have been battles, Tom would have more on his mind than sending word to me! And who would he find to send word, anyway? He's but a squire, not a great lord with a dozen messengers at his command.

She and Cecily had talked about it, over and over again, as they sat with their needlework, or played chequers, or sat by the fire in the evening while Alys strummed her lute and Cecily sang.

'No news is good news,' Cecily would

say, trying to cheer her. 'If anything
. . . well, if the news was bad, they would
hear at the Castle and the Countess would
send word to our lady mother, wouldn't
she? Don't worry, Alys. Tom will be safe
with the Earl!'

'That's what he told me,' Alys replied
with a sad smile. 'He said that I was not to
worry, that the Earl and King Edward
would protect him.'

'And so they will,' said Cecily stoutly.
'You need only be patient, Alys.'

'Patient!' Alys grumbled. 'Have I not
been patient enough? You don't know
what it's like, Cecily, to sit, and sew, and
smile meekly, and say, 'Yes, Sir Hugh' and
'No, Dame Eleanor', when your heart is
breaking from loss and you long to *do*
something, anything!'

'But there's nothing you can do,' Cecily
pointed out. 'You cannot go off fighting
with the men, with Tom and the Earl. A
battlefield is no place for a woman.'

'I would if I could,' said Alys muti-
nously. ' 'Tis shameful that I have never
even learned to lift a sword. I could strike
a blow for Tom, and for King Edward!'

'Oh, Alys!' Cecily protested, shocked.

So Alys could only wait, and hope, and

remember Tom's smile, and his sea-blue eyes, and the way he had kissed her before he rode away. He had promised to come back and claim her as his bride, and she knew he would keep his promise — as long as he wasn't wounded, or killed, or dead of some fever and lying in a ditch somewhere, miles away.

She scrambled out of bed, wanting to escape such unpleasant thoughts. Cecily was right, she thought determinedly, if there was bad news, my aunt the Countess would have let us know. All will be well, I must have faith!

Shivering, she pulled off her bed-gown and got into her shift, long hose and woollen gown, with a fur-trimmed surcoat for warmth. Her fingers were almost too stiff from cold to braid her hair. Murmuring, ' 'Tis, morning, sister — and a cold, frosty day, too!' to wake Cecily, she opened the heavy door and hurried down the draughty staircase to the hall, where at least there was a fire. Dame Eleanor greeted her with a mug of hot, spiced ale and some new-baked bread.

'So there you are, lazy slug-a-bed,' she said crossly. 'And where's that idle sister of yours? When I was your age, Alys, I was up at six of the clock every morning, summer and winter, helping to milk my father's cows. If I was late down I went without my breakfast until the work was done! You young folk have an easy time these days!'

Alys, who had heard all this before, smiled at her old nurse.

'Don't scold, Dame Eleanor,' she pleaded. ' 'Tis the first really cold morning we've had! Now that I am up and about, I can help you preserve those apples and pears and quinces, and I'm sure Cecily will help too.'

'Hmm,' sniffed Dame Eleanor. 'I'm not sure more fruit doesn't go into your bellies than into my preserving pots . . . but thank you, Alys. I could do with your help, and your sister's. Young Katherine awoke this morning with a swollen throat and a fever, and I shall have to tend her myself, Sally the nursemaid being taken sick herself yesterday . . . '

'Nothing serious, I hope?' said Alys.

'No, no, just the same swollen throat. My soothing mixture, the one with honey and herbs and blackberry syrup, is most efficacious. Sally and young Katherine will soon be better.'

'I'm glad,' said Alys, thinking to herself

79

that Dame Eleanor's medicine sounded drinkable, for once. She hadn't forgotten the disgusting potion she had been given when she'd eaten some tainted fish that had upset her!

Cecily came into the hall, rubbing her hands together and yawning.

'I hate winter,' she grumbled. 'The damp, raw days are so unpleasant. When 'tis bright and sunny and we can go out riding, or skating on the village pond, then 'tis agreeable. And, I was just thinking, it will be Christmas quite soon!'

'What sort of Christmas shall we have?' said Alys bleakly. 'There will be little cause for feasting at the Castle, with the Earl and half his followers away.'

'And what about Mary's wedding?' Cecily pointed out. 'She and Will Enderby were to be married, were they not? That cannot happen with the Earl away!'

Alys and Cecily looked at one another, the same thought in both their minds. Would Sir William Enderby still agree to marry his son to Mary, if things did not go well for the Earl her father?

'Poor Mary,' said Alys sympathetically. 'She has waited so long, too long, for her bridal day. 'Twould be a shame if it didn't happen!'

'If what didn't happen, my daughter?'

Lady Philippa came into the hall from her private prayers in the Manor's tiny chapel, and accepted a mug of ale from Dame Eleanor.

'We were speaking of our cousin Mary's wedding, mother,' said Alys respectfully. 'It was to be at Christmas, don't you remember? But with times so uncertain, and the Earl away . . . '

'I am sure my sister and her husband will do whatever's best,' Lady Philippa said. 'But . . . hark, what's that?'

There was a commotion in the courtyard, the jingle of horses' bridles, the yapping of dogs and the sound of raised male voices. Alys and Cecily exchanged glances, and Lady Philippa rose to her feet.

' 'Tis Sir Hugh,' she said, her voice betraying neither gladness nor sorrow. ' 'Tis my husband come home!'

The great doors swung open and Sir Hugh strode in, his hounds at his heels, followed by five or six other men. Alys recognized Robert Saville and the skinny Frenchman who had left the Manor in the autumn, just before Tom rode away. Lady Philippa and the two girls curtseyed deeply, and so did Dame Eleanor, coming in from the kitchen.

'Bring food. We must have food and ale,' Sir Hugh commanded, not even looking at his wife and stepdaughters. He strode to his usual place at the head of the table and sat down, indicating with a gauntleted fist that his followers should do the same. Alys, almost on her knees on the rush-strewn floor, looked up at him furiously. How dare he treat our lady mother with such disrespect, she thought. If it wasn't for her, he wouldn't be Lord of the Manor here, nor would he be able to boast of his connections at the Castle! Who does he think he is?

To her great surprise, Lady Philippa rose from her knees and approached the high table, where the men were devouring a cold roast fowl, tearing it apart with their bare hands.

'Welcome home, my husband,' she said with great dignity. Sir Hugh looked up, apparently noticing her for the first time. Alys noticed that a couple of the other men looked embarrassed.

'Oh. Greetings, lady,' said Sir Hugh

carelessly. 'Is all well at the Manor?'

Lady Philippa nodded.

'Good. Good!' Sir Hugh smiled wolfishly and took a deep draught of his ale. 'Excellent, I should say.'

'Then your business in London was successful, husband?' ventured Lady Philippa.

Sir Hugh slapped his thigh and looked round at his companions, grinning.

'Aye,' he said, 'I think I could rightly say that! My . . . er . . . my 'business' went very well indeed!'

Alys edged closer to her mother, desperate for news. If Sir Hugh had really been in London, whatever his 'business' was, he would know what had happened to the King, to the Earl of Warwick's rebellion — and, indirectly, to Tom.

Sir Hugh finished eating and sat back, patting his belly.

'Sit down, my lady,' he said. 'I bring news from London, news that affects us all!'

Alys's heart began to thump and she felt Cecily's hand steal into hers and grip it tightly.

'And you, too, girls,' said Sir Hugh. 'This will affect you, too, I suppose, in one way or another.'

'What has happened?' asked Lady Philippa calmly.

'Changes. Many changes. Indeed, I hardly know where to begin,' said Sir Hugh. 'But, to be brief, we have a new king, or, rather, our old king back again. Edward of York is fled, and Henry of Lancaster is back on the throne.'

Alys felt the colour drain from her face. Oh, God, she thought. Tom . . .

Her mother was frowning.

'But . . . but how can this be?' she said. 'We thought . . . it was said that King Henry had lost his wits and was being led by his fierce French wife, Queen Margaret! And . . . Edward of York was safe upon the throne, helped there by the great Earl of Warwick . . . '

Sir Hugh smiled smugly.

'Warwick? Nay, he has no love for Edward now!' he boasted. 'Ever since the Yorkist king became a man and began to choose his own counsellors, and his own wife! Edward's court was packed with his wife's family, the Woodvilles, and no room there for the Earl of Warwick . . . '

'So he turned traitor, and gave his support to Lancaster instead!' Alys burst out scornfully. Sir Hugh looked at her as though a piece of the furniture had spoken.

'Take care, Lady Alys,' he said, his voice silky with threats. 'Take care what you say. The Earl of Warwick is no traitor, but a loyal subject of the King's Grace, that's His Grace, King Henry the Sixth of Lancaster! As are we all!'

'All?' cried Alys, heedless of Cecily's warning hand on her arm. 'But we're not, I'm not . . . '

Sir Hugh jumped to his feet.

'I said, as are we all!' he roared. 'I owe loyalty to the King's Grace and the House of Lancaster, and so do my family, by God! I will not be defied!'

For a moment, Alys met her stepfather's eyes. I hate him, she thought, him and his plots and his schemes and his turncoat friends. My father died fighting for York, my Tom is away fighting for York, and now Sir Hugh wants me to pledge loyalty to Lancaster, to Tom's sworn enemies. I won't do it!

Lady Philippa leaned forward and murmured something to her husband. Sir Hugh snorted angrily and glanced over at Alys.

'Aye. Well. I have more to think of than ill-mannered chits of girls,' he said.

Alys felt Cecily tugging at her skirt.

'Sit down, sister,' she muttered, ' 'twill do no good to anger our stepfather!'

Alys sat down, biting her lip in frustration. She knew Cecily was right. There was nothing she could do. Besides, if she was banished to her room, or to the gatehouse tower, she wouldn't hear the rest of the news from London.

'So Henry of Lancaster is back on the throne, with Earl Warwick's help,' said Lady Philippa soothingly. 'How did it happen? And where is the King ... I mean where is Edward of York?'

'Fled. Exiled to Burgundy, or the Low Countries, I know not where,' gloated Sir Hugh. 'Ran like a whipped hound with his tail between his legs, him and his youngest brother Gloucester and a handful of misguided followers!'

'And ... my brother-in-law of Aylesbury? How did he fare? Was he not a supporter of King Edward?' said Lady Philippa carefully.

Alys held her breath, but Sir Hugh just shrugged.

'I know not,' he said. 'If our brother-in-law is wise, he will have crept back to the Castle and will lie low for a while, till King Henry and my lord of Warwick have forgotten he ever supported Edward of York! Meanwhile, there could be rewards — land, money, even titles — for those of us who have supported Lancaster all these years. They're saying the French queen will come over to England when the weather permits. Perhaps she will remember me. I served her once, long ago, and Margaret of Anjou was ever one to reward loyalty. Yes, wife, the fortunes of this family are on the rise, with our new king. As soon as the Queen arrives, I will go to London and pay my respects. You could come with me. Who knows, there could be a place at court, or a rich husband, for your daughters, places in Warwick's household as pages for Giles and Robin . . . '

Oh, no, thought Alys, tears stinging the back of her eyes. I can't bear it! London, the court, all the things I dreamed of seeing, once upon a time, and now they mean nothing, for Tom is not here!

'Alys,' Cecily murmured, under her breath, 'you don't think our stepfather really means to marry us off to rich

Lancastrians, do you? I . . . I shouldn't like that at all!'

Icy fingers of fear clutched Alys's heart.

'He can't do that,' she said flatly, knowing, deep down, that Sir Hugh could do anything he wanted. If he chose to marry her and Cecily off to his cronies, rather than a disgraced Yorkist, he could do it!

'No,' she breathed. 'No, I would rather die! He cannot drag me to the altar by force, nor make me recite wedding vows to someone I loathe. I will marry Tom Taverner, or no one!'

'And I shall become a nun, rather than marry a man I hate,' said Cecily calmly. 'I have always longed to have a husband and babies, but rather than a bad husband, I would take the veil. 'Tis not so bad a life in a convent, at least you have the fellowship of the other sisters. Better that than be wed to a man who beats you, or treats you cruelly.'

Alys leaned forward again to hear what Sir Hugh was saying.

' . . . no battles at all,' he said. 'Edward of York was marching south, expecting support from Lord Montagu, but then Montagu decided to support Warwick

88

instead, and Edward and his men escaped from Norfolk in small boats. It might have been better for us if they had been taken or killed by pirates, but, alas, the word is that they landed safely in Holland.'

Well, that's something, Alys thought. The true king seems to be alive and safe, no thanks to the traitor Montagu. But where is Tom?

It was only when he had finished gloating over Lancaster's triumph that Sir Hugh seemed to remember his duties as host and Lord of the Manor. Lady Philippa, Alys and Cecily were presented to the men he had brought with him. And a sorry, scrofulous lot they were, too, Alys thought scornfully — the greasy Robert Saville, the shifty Frenchman, a couple of pimply youths whose beards were scarce grown, and a slobbering old knight called Sir Henry Capshaw, who wheezed as he shovelled in his food and wiped his dirty hands on his even dirtier cloak before taking hers in a clammy grip.

Ugh, Alys thought, as the fat knight's piggy little eyes, almost hidden in folds of bloated flesh, bored into hers. He must weigh twenty stone at least!

'Charmin'. Charmed to meet you. I

admire a likely young wench,' he muttered lecherously, before Alys could pull her hands away. He smelt of sweat and garlic.

'Will you excuse me, Sir Henry?' Alys said, as meekly as she could. 'I . . . er . . . Dame Eleanor needs me this morning. We are preserving fruits for the winter.'

Sir Henry smiled, revealing a mouthful of blackened stumps.

'Useful as well as beautiful, my dear, heh heh!' he said.

Alys longed to turn around and slap the ugly, sweating face, but knew that her stepfather would beat her black and blue if she insulted one of his guests. I'd better just stay out of his way, out of everyone's way, she decided.

As she and Cecily sliced apples and pears, stoned quinces, and prepared honey syrup, they discussed what Sir Hugh had said.

'But what do you suppose has happened to Tom?' Alys fretted. 'Did they meet up with the King, and go into exile with him? Or did they return to the Castle?'

'The Earl could have gone to King Henry's court, to make peace with him,' Cecily suggested.

'Never!' said Alys proudly. 'Or . . . I

90

don't know, even if the Earl could do such a thing, for the sake of his family, Tom never would. He saw King Edward once, Cecily. He told me he was a true king, tall and handsome and kingly, yet with the common touch. He would never betray Edward! But . . . but . . . if only I knew where he was, if he was safe!'

Cecily squeezed her hand.

'Don't worry, sister. I'm sure we'll get word from the Castle soon,' she said.

Over the next few days Alys wished with all her heart that her stepfather had not returned. The atmosphere at the Manor seemed to have changed overnight. The servants crept around, either sullen or frightened, Lady Philippa spent more and more time in prayer, and even the children seemed to have forgotten how to laugh and play. Sir Hugh swaggered around with his friends, looking so pleased with himself that Alys longed to slap his smug face.

'Anyone would think he had put King Henry back on the throne single-handed,' she complained to Cecily. 'Yet he did nothing, as far as I can make out, but give money to the Lancastrian cause. Money from the Manor coffers, that rightfully belongs to my lady mother, to you and me and the children!'

Cecily shook her head sadly. The two girls spent most of their time helping Dame Eleanor with the household chores and in tending little Katherine, who soon got over her fever and was her rosy self again. Once, going to the stables to see her mare Joliet, Alys was surprised by Sir Henry Capshaw, who squeezed her waist and tried to plant a wet kiss on her cheek. Luckily, she managed to dodge, and rushed out of the stables, disgusted.

'I can't bear that man. He looks at me as if ... as if I was a marchpane sweetmeat he'd like to devour!' she said when she and Cecily were alone in their bedroom. 'When will he and the others leave, do you suppose? I long to see the back of them! I only wish our stepfather would go, too!'

'Dame Eleanor said that Sir Hugh has bidden them stay with us for the Christmas feast,' said Cecily glumly. She, too, had been troubled by sly pinches and lewd remarks from one of the spotty young squires.

'Oh, no! A right merry Christmas we shall have this year!' said Alys sarcastically.

But, just a week later, a messenger rode

up to the Manor, a messenger in the livery of the Earl of Aylesbury. Alys, crossing the courtyard on her way back from the bakehouse, felt her heart miss a beat. He slid from his horse and bowed politely.

'I have a letter from the Countess, for her sister, the Lady Philippa Drayton,' he said formally.

'My lady mother is in the nursery. I can take it to her,' Alys said. Then, remembering her manners, she added, 'You will take refreshment, sir? A glass of wine, perhaps, or our good ale?'

Jack, the stable-boy, led away his horse, and Alys took him into the hall and sent for food and drink before flying up the stairs to the nursery where her mother and Dame Eleanor were playing with Katherine and Joanna.

'A letter, mother. From my aunt the Countess,' Alys gasped. Her legs suddenly felt too weak to hold her up and she sank down on the children's bed. What would the Countess's letter say? Would there be news of the Earl, or Tom?

Lady Philippa broke the seal, scanned the letter and looked up, her careworn face lightening. Not bad news, then, Alys thought, weak with relief.

'We are bidden to the Castle on Christmas Eve, to celebrate the marriage of your cousin Mary and Sir William Enderby,' said Lady Philippa.

Sir William, thought Alys. Then Will's father must have died, God rest him. But . . .

'Then . . . is the Earl at home? At the Castle?' she enquired innocently. Lady Philippa continued to read her letter.

'Yes,' she said absent-mindedly, 'he is back, but he has been wounded, my sister says, though his wound is healing well. My poor brother-in-law!'

Alys's heart gave another bound. Wounded! What did that mean?

'He was in battle, then? He fought for King Edward?' she ventured.

' 'Twas hardly a battle, he and his men were set upon by Lancastrian knights, and heavily outnumbered, it seems,' her mother said. 'Ah, well-a-day, why must men always be fighting, always be killing?'

' 'Tis their nature, drat them,' said Dame Eleanor dryly.

'So the Earl and his party have returned to the Castle? They haven't fled to Holland with King Edward?' Alys persisted.

Her mother shrugged.

'So it seems. Anyway, the Earl is well enough now to attend his daughter's wedding. 'Twill be a quiet affair, I should imagine, with the Earl only just up from his sickbed, and Will Enderby mourning his old father. Poor Mary, 'tis not what she planned! Well, we must all go over to the Castle and wish them good fortune.'

'Indeed, yes,' said Alys demurely, keeping her eyes cast down to hide her joy. The Earl was back, and Thomas with him! 'Tis strange he hasn't sent word, she thought happily, as she sped down into the hall to find Cecily and give her the good news, but perhaps he was busy, or sick, or he was waiting to surprise me on Mary's wedding day!

She thought of asking the Castle messenger, but when she got downstairs she found he had already left.

'I'll wear my apricot silk again, 'tis most becoming,' she said excitedly to her sister. 'Oh, Cecily, imagine! Three months now since I saw Tom! Do you suppose he has spoken to the Earl? Perhaps the Earl will ask Sir Hugh for me while we are at the Castle! Tom *said* that when he returned he would claim me as his bride! He will be disappointed not to have been able to defend King Edward in battle, though.'

Christmas Eve dawned crisp and cold, but sunny; a perfect winter's day. How fair the world is, all trimmed with ice, like fairyland, Alys thought as she rode along, well wrapped in a fur-lined cloak. She managed to avoid the wheezing Sir Henry Capshaw by urging Joliet on when he tried to ride alongside her. Not even Sir Henry's unwelcome attentions could spoil her mood today. As well as Mary's wedding day, this could be the day of my betrothal, she thought.

When they arrived at the Castle, all was bustle and confusion. Lady Philippa, Dame Eleanor, Alys, Cecily and the two little girls were whisked away at once to the Countess's solar, where three or four maids scurried around the flustered Mary, bringing her lavender water, a circlet of dried flowers for her hair, a gold brooch, a necklace of pearls.

'Indeed, I don't know whether I am coming or going!' chattered Mary, when she saw her cousins. 'I never imagined a bridal day would be like this, so many people, so much rushing about. You are well come, Alys, Cecily, Aunt Philippa!'

Alys kissed her cousin's flushed cheek.

'And we are happy to be here, dear Mary,' she said warmly.

'You look most fair. A lovely bride, my dear,' said Lady Philippa.

It was almost true, Alys reflected. No one could ever have called Mary beautiful. She was too plump, her nose too big, her mouth too wide. But today, she glowed with love in her rose-pink gown, and her happiness made her beautiful. As Mary and Will stood in the Castle chapel and the priest blessed them and sprinkled them with holy water, Alys felt a lump in her throat. Be happy, cousins, she thought, and may you be blessed with many children!

As they left the chapel, Alys looked eagerly to left and right. She saw some of the other squires, Alan of Bedford, sporting a new ginger beard, and young Ralph Enderby, Will's brother — but where was Tom? Why had he not sought her out? Cold fear began to steal into her heart and suddenly the day didn't seem so merry. Something is wrong, Alys thought, as the chattering throng of wedding guests made their way into the great hall of the Castle for the wedding feast. Before she was shown to her place by the Earl's servants, Alys darted over to Alan of Bedford, so worried that she forgot to be discreet.

'Alan,' she panted, 'where's Tom? Tom Taverner?'

'Tom?' said Alan. 'Oh, aye, I forgot you wouldn't know, Lady Alys. Tom's not here. He's with the King . . . er . . . I mean Edward of York, in the Netherlands!'

Alys gasped and all the colour left her face.

'But . . . but . . . what happened?'

'Happened? Well, the Earl and his men were set upon by a group of Lancastrian knights. 'Twas bad luck they met, not a deliberate ambush. The Earl was wounded, and fell, but Tom and one or two of the others managed to get away and reach York and his party in Norfolk. The last we heard, they had all landed in the Low Countries where', his voice dropped, 'they say Edward is planning to raise an army and reclaim his throne.'

Alys sat down, feeling sick with disappointment. She had longed and longed for this day, dreamed of seeing Tom again, and now . . .

'Dear God,' she murmured, 'he might

be anywhere! He might be dead!'

She sat still, frozen with misery, as the Earl's minstrels played a merry tune and the wedding feast was brought in. Through a mist of tears, she saw Cousin Mary's radiant face and Will Enderby's proud one; the Earl and Countess smiling fondly at their daughter and new son-in-law. I must be brave, Alys thought, her throat aching as she tried not to cry. I mustn't spoil Mary's bridal day with tears.

She could neither eat nor drink, but she was vaguely aware of food being served, and toasts to the happy couple drunk. The Earl rose and made a gracious speech. Then, to her horror, her stepfather Sir Hugh rose to his feet. Oh, *no*, thought Alys, embarrassed, what is he going to say? Dear God, is that drunken fool going to shame us all? Lady Philippa and the Countess looked bewildered, and Cecily confused.

Sir Hugh banged his glass on the wooden table and gazed blearily out across the company.

' 'Tis a fair day, a wedding day,' he slurred. 'And my good wishes to my lovely . . . er . . . my lovely niece Mary and her husband!'

Mary smiled and blushed.

'And I have more good newsh . . . news,' Sir Hugh went on. 'There will shoon be another wedding, for I have a betrothal to announce!'

There was silence in the hall. What does he mean? Alys thought.

'Yesh!' cried Sir Hugh. 'I am pleased to announce the betrothal of my daughter, Lady Alys . . . '

'Me?' Alys gasped, as everyone turned to look at her.

'My daughter, Lady Alys,' Sir Hugh went on, 'to my trusty and well-beloved friend — Sir Henry Capshaw!'

5

December 1470

Alys sat as though she had been turned to stone, while the wedding guests clapped and cheered, and those who knew who she was pointed her out to those who didn't.

This can't be happening, Alys thought, frozen with horror, as the Earl's minstrels struck up a merry dance and Will Enderby, blushing and stumbling, led his new wife out on to the floor. I didn't really hear what I thought I heard. My stepfather can't have promised me to that lecherous old toad Sir Henry! He can't! He wouldn't!

Then she glanced along the tables at Sir Hugh's smirk of self-satisfaction, and realized that this was no nightmare, but the cold, hard truth. Instead of being betrothed to handsome Tom Taverner, she was to be given in marriage to a repulsive old man, old enough to be her grandfather! God help me, Alys thought frantically, what can I do? As she looked around the hall, her eyes fell on Sir Henry himself. He lumbered to his feet, leering, and headed in her direction.

'A dance, Lady Alys?' he wheezed, holding out a grubby, wrinkled hand. Alys snatched her hand away.

'No,' she hissed. 'I shan't dance with you! And I won't marry you, either!'

Little Joanna, and Alan of Bedford, sitting nearest her, turned round in surprise when they heard the anger and desperation in her voice. Alys was amazed at her own boldness, but Sir Henry seemed unperturbed.

' 'Tis your stepfather's wish, my dear,' he said calmly, leaning across the table to pinch her cheek. At the touch of his clammy fingers, Alys thought she might be sick. Jumping to her feet so abruptly that she overturned the bench she was sitting on, and holding up her apricot-silk skirts, she turned and fled from the hall, not caring if her stepfather saw her and was angry, not caring if the whole wedding party was watching, only knowing that she had to get away.

But where can I go? she thought, her heart hammering, as she leant against the icy stone of the Castle walls, ignoring the curious stares of the Earl's retainers and one of the stable-lads. Here in the outer courtyard, sleety snow was falling and a vicious, icy wind whipped her hair across her face and cut through her thin silk gown. Alys began to shiver, too shocked and frightened for tears.

'Lady Alys? What's amiss?'

It was Jack, the Manor stable-lad, who had come over to the Castle with them to help take care of the horses. He was carrying two heavy pails of water, which he set down when he saw Alys.

'Oh, Jack,' Alys muttered through chattering teeth, ' 'tis . . . 'tis a terrible thing! My stepfather has just announced my betrothal! To that dreadful Sir Henry Capshaw! Whatever am I going to do?'

Jack's cheerful, freckled face fell and he bit his lip.

'Sir Henry? A careless oaf who mistreats his horses! That's bad, Lady Alys. And you were sweet on young Tom Taverner, weren't you?'

'How did you know?' Alys gasped.

'I've eyes in my head, haven't I?' retorted Jack. 'Grand folk always think servants are stupid, but we see more than you know, Lady Alys, believe me.'

'I . . . I suppose you do,' said Alys listlessly.

'Come on, you can't stay out here, you'll catch your death,' said Jack. 'It's warmer in the stables with the horses, and your mare Joliet will be pleased to see you. She knows her mistress, that one!'

Numbly, Alys followed Jack into the dimly-lit stables, warmed by the breath of a dozen fine mounts, including her little mare, who whickered with pleasure when Alys stroked her soft muzzle and laid her weary face against her neck. It seemed days, weeks, since she had set off from the Manor that morning in high spirits, thinking she was going to see Tom.

I imagined that today might be my betrothal day, she thought, and it was! But not as I planned it, as I dreamed it, oh, Tom, Tom . . .

At last the tears came and she sobbed broken-heartedly against the little horse's smooth chestnut coat. She could still hear the music from the hall, the laughter, the pipings and carollings and drumming as the minstrels played, and was reminded of herself and Tom, dancing together at the harvest feast, his sea-blue eyes gazing down at her, and then that final kiss that had seemed to draw the very soul out of her body and bind it to his — for ever.

'I will not marry Sir Henry!' she whispered. 'No, no matter what my stepfather says, not if he beats me, not if he starves me, not if he drags me to the altar by my hair, he will never make me say 'I will!' I love Tom Taverner, and I belong to him. He said he would return to claim me for his bride, and he will. All I have to do is keep faith with him, and that I'll do, I swear!'

Fumbling, she pulled the silver rose pendant Tom had given her out of the bodice of her gown and kissed it.

'I swear by Almighty God and His Holy Mother, that I will keep faith with Tom Taverner, my true love, as long as we both shall live!' she said out loud.

'Fine words, Lady Alys,' said Jack, coming round the corner with a pitchfork of hay for Joliet, 'but what can you do? Your stepfather is a hard, cruel man, and unless I'm mistaken, Sir Henry Capshaw is another. They'll not take kindly to being defied!'

Alys lifted her chin proudly. The time for tears and panic-stricken flight was past, for was she not the daughter of one brave knight and the lady-love of another? Whatever her stepfather's evil plans, she would outface and outwit him, and endure all, for Tom's sweet sake.

'Alys? Sister? Are you in here?' came a breathless voice, and Cecily rushed in. 'Jack, have you seen . . . oh, there you are, Alys! Sister, you must come back, the Countess and our lady mother are looking for you.'

For a second, Alys's courage wavered, but then she said calmly, 'Indeed? Then I won't disappoint them, I will return to the hall. Tell me, Cecily, is our stepfather *very* angry?'

Cecily made a face.

'Well, he's rather drunk,' she admitted, 'but our mother has managed to convince him 'twas just shyness, and surprise at the honour done you, that made you rush out like that!'

'And Sir Henry? What did he say?'

Cecily's lip curled in disgust.

'He said it was quite natural you should be overcome with shyness!'

Alys snorted.

'Shyness! I told the disgusting old goat I'd never wed him if he was the last man alive! He must be brim-full of conceit if he could think that was shyness!'

The two girls left the stable and walked across the courtyard in silence. Just before they reached the great oak door of the hall, Cecily turned to her sister.

'Oh, Alys,' she faltered, 'what are you going to do? Be careful, won't you? If Sir Hugh has made up his mind to give you to Sir Henry . . . '

'Well, I have made my mind up, too,' declared Alys. 'I am not a warhorse, or a deer-hound, or a bolt of cloth, to be given to one man or another as a gift, a chattel! I have chosen my own husband. I will marry Tom Taverner, or no one!'

As they entered the hall, Joanna and Katherine came dancing up to them, their faces alight with excitement.

'Alys, Alys,' Joanna cried, 'you're to come up to the Countess's solar right away. We are making Cousin Mary ready for her wedding journey!'

'And she's promised me an' Joanna sweetmeats, for being good girls today,' added little Katherine solemnly.

'Has she, poppet?' Alys laughed. 'Then Cecily and I will come with you, and see how she fares.'

Relief flooded through Alys as she

hurried along the side of the hall and up the stone staircase to the Countess's private apartments. At least my stepfather and Sir Henry can't trouble me here, she thought. Mary, inclined to be tearful now that the moment of parting from her family had come, was being dressed in a thick velvet cloak lined with fur, and maids were packing linen and trinkets into small wooden chests that would be carried by a string of pack-ponies on the long journey to Mary's new home in Essex.

'Oh, Alys, I shall miss you,' Mary gulped, throwing her arms around her cousin.

'And I you,' replied Alys. 'But we shall visit one another, Mary, I promise!'

'Aye, in the spring, when the weather improves, and I shall show off my fine housekeeping,' said Mary, trying hard to smile. 'But Alys,' she lowered her voice, 'is it true that you are betrothed to Sir Henry Capshaw? Or was it just that my father's good wine had fuddled your stepfather's wits?'

'It seems not,' said Alys coolly. 'He wishes me to marry Sir Henry.'

Mary looked doubtful. Like all girls, she had been brought up to obey her father's wishes, but the Earl was a kindly soul and would never have wed her to a man she detested. It seemed that Alys was not to be so lucky . . .

'Shall you be happy with him, do you think?' Mary enquired. 'I hardly know the man, and they do say 'tis better to be an old man's darling than a young man's slave . . . '

When she saw the expression on Alys's face, her voice trailed away.

'I will not marry Sir Henry, Mary,' Alys said through gritted teeth.

Mary's eyes widened.

'Then what will you do?' she said.

Alys shook her head.

'I'll think of something, don't worry. Sir Henry revolts me, Mary, and I . . . I . . . well, I love Tom Taverner . . . '

Mary gasped and clapped her hands.

'Oh, yes, of course! Dear Tom, he'd be the perfect match for you, were he to return with the King . . . er, with Edward of York, I mean. But, Alys, it will not be easy to change your stepfather's mind.'

'I know,' said Alys. 'But enough of this, Mary, 'tis your wedding day, not mine! I hear the carriage out in the courtyard, your husband will be waiting for you.'

109

Mary hesitated.

'Cousin,' she said seriously, 'if . . . if things go badly for you, remember Will and I are on your side, yours and Tom's.'

Alys managed to smile in spite of the lump in her throat. Dear Mary, she thought, dear, fortunate Mary, wed at last to a good young man who loves her. To think that I pitied her, once, because Will is not handsome and dashing and gallant like Tom Taverner, a dull farmer and not a brave knight! Now they are wed, and will live out their lives in love and peace together, while Tom and I . . .

She bowed her head so that Mary shouldn't see the tears that sprang to her eyes.

'Farewell, Cousin Mary,' she said. 'May fortune and happiness go with you!'

Alys stood with her mother, aunt and sisters in the courtyard as the Earl's carriage and the train of packponies slowly set off across the drawbridge and turned eastwards towards Enderby Hall. Mary pulled back the velvet curtain and waved until she was out of sight, and Will, trotting alongside on a sturdy bay horse, waved his hat with a flourish. They turned the final corner, and were gone.

'We, too, must soon be leaving,' said Lady Philippa to the Countess.

'Oh, no,' her sister replied. 'Stay for the Christmas feast, all of you! 'Twill be quiet here for the Earl and myself, with the last of our daughters wed. Stay and keep us company.'

Lady Philippa smiled.

'I will ask my husband,' she said, 'but I should love to stay. Wouldn't you, Alys? Cecily?'

Cecily nodded, smiling, but Alys shivered suddenly.

'I . . . I don't feel well,' she said. 'The wind has been so cold, I feel quite feverish . . . '

Well, it's only half a lie, Alys consoled herself, as the Countess hurried her up to her private apartments, where a fire blazed in the hearth, and sent a maid scurrying to bring hot ale and a warmed rug for Alys's frozen feet. I *do* feel strange, light-headed and a bit unreal, and if I can keep to my bed for a few days with a supposed 'fever', I need not see Sir Henry before he has to leave!

So Alys spent that Christmas season huddled in blankets in the Countess's solar, sipping chicken broth and picking at delicacies her kindly aunt sent up to tempt the invalid's appetite. Dame Eleanor came to see her several times, but Alys pretended to be asleep whenever she heard her old nurse's heavy footsteps on the stairs. She had no wish to be dosed with any of Dame Eleanor's foul potions!

On the fifth day, Cecily came to see her, her face wreathed in smiles.

'They've gone!' she announced ecstatically, 'the whole boiling of 'em! Sir Henry Capshaw, Ferret-face Saville, Pimples and Big-Ears!'

Alys giggled at this rude description of her stepfather's cronies. It seemed an age since she had felt like laughing.

'Sir Hugh, also? Has he gone?' she said hopefully.

'Not he,' Cecily told her. 'He's out hunting with the Earl today, and says we shall return to the Manor tomorrow.'

Alys looked thoughtful. She knew, of course, that she would have to face her stepfather one day, and she still wasn't sure what she was going to say to him. But she couldn't hide away in bed for ever. She knew Sir Hugh was quite capable of storming up the stairs and dragging her

112

out of bed if he suspected her of shamming.

In the end, he rode over to her as soon as he saw her mount Joliet for the journey home.

'Feeling better, my daughter?' he enquired silkily, his eyes as cold and hard as granite pebbles. Alys tried to look demure.

'Yes, thank you,' she said.

'Good, good. Your betrothed, Sir Henry, was most concerned for your health, and disappointed that he didn't see you again before he left,' Sir Hugh went on. 'He and I have discussed the arrangements for your wedding, though.'

'My wedding?' echoed Alys faintly.

'Yes. Sir Henry wishes it to be soon,' said Sir Hugh, chuckling. 'He's most taken with you, my dear, as ardent as a young man half his age, I swear!'

Oh, no, Alys thought, her stomach churning. If they are planning a quick wedding, I too will have to think fast. If I refuse to marry him, what am I to do? Still, Cecily is right, it will be best to keep my stepfather sweet and pretend to agree with everything he suggests. For the time being . . .

'When will Sir Henry return?' she enquired innocently. Was it her imagination, or was there a flicker of satisfaction on Sir Hugh's face? He obviously thought she had given in, and would agree to the marriage. Think again, old toad, she thought angrily.

'Oh, two or three weeks. He had but gone to London to pay his respects to our sovereign lord, King Henry,' said Sir Hugh.

Two or three weeks, Alys thought, that's all the time I have . . .

In fact, it was scarcely two weeks later when the hall door flew open, bringing with it a flurry of snow, and Sir Henry Capshaw was announced. The family were just finishing dinner, and Alys's heart sank when she saw the fat knight, ruddy-faced from cold and wearing so many wraps and cloaks he looked bigger and flabbier than ever.

Sir Hugh rose to his feet.

'Greetings, my trusty friend,' he said. 'Is all well?'

Sir Henry nodded and looked over at Alys, who was trying to hide behind the stout figure of Dame Eleanor.

'Greetings, Lady Philippa, Lady Alys,'

he said meaningfully. Lady Philippa inclined her head gracefully, and Alys just nodded.

'Come, come, this won't do,' blustered her stepfather. 'Alys, remember your manners! What sort of welcome is that to give to your betrothed, when he has ridden from London in a snowstorm just to be with you? Give Sir Henry a kiss!'

Alys didn't move, even when Sir Henry shambled forward, pulled her, unresisting, into his arms, and clamped his wet lips on hers. He smelt of sweat and rotten teeth. Alys's stomach heaved, and, unable to prevent herself, she shoved him away so hard that he stumbled and almost fell. His self-satisfied smirk disappeared and he glared at her.

'Little wildcat!' he muttered. 'Wait till I have you alone!'

'Never!' hissed Alys. Then her stepfather intervened.

'Alys!' he roared. 'What is this? How dare you insult Sir Henry, my guest, my honoured friend, and the man you are to marry? What's the matter with you, girl?'

Alys was silent.

'I'm sure my daughter meant you no disrespect, Sir Henry,' said Lady Philippa soothingly. 'She was always a flighty creature, you know how young girls are . . . '

'Hmm,' said Sir Henry, recovering his dignity. All would have been well if Sir Hugh had not snapped, 'Flighty? The girl's a lack-wit, madam, with the manners of a gutter urchin! Sir Henry, here, is doing me a favour taking her off my hands, she has never been anything but trouble! Alys, you owe your betrothed an apology!'

Still Alys said nothing. Sir Hugh began to tap his foot impatiently.

'Alys?'

His voice was dangerously low. Suddenly, Alys spoke.

'Yes?' she said, and to Cecily's amazement, she was smiling.

'Apologize to your betrothed!'

Alys looked at Sir Henry, then at her stepfather.

'I have no betrothed,' she said in a clear little voice. 'I will not marry Sir Henry, for I love another!'

Both men gaped at her, and Cecily began to cry.

'What's this?' blustered Sir Hugh. 'Do you dare to defy me, girl?'

'I won't marry Sir Henry,' repeated Alys.

With a roar of fury, Sir Hugh leapt to Alys's side and grabbed her shoulder so hard that she almost screamed with pain. He was white to the lips with anger and there were flecks of foam at the corners of his mouth.

'Husband . . . ' Lady Philippa protested feebly, but he shoved her aside.

'How dare you!' he repeated. 'Wretched girl, how *dare* you? 'Tis not your place to tell me whom you will or won't marry! I stand in place of a father to you, and if I choose to give you to Sir Henry in marriage, you will do as I say!'

'I won't!' said Alys.

Then she gave a cry of pain as Sir Hugh's heavy fist shot out and caught her a glancing blow on the side of her head, knocking her to the floor. On her hands and knees, her head reeling from the blow and blood trickling from a cut on her forehead, she glared defiantly up at her stepfather.

'I will not marry that . . . that stinking Lancastrian oaf!' she cried.

There was another yell of rage as Sir Hugh sprang towards her, a warning shout of 'Drayton, you'll slay the wench!' from Sir Henry, a scream from Cecily — and then darkness descended on Alys and she knew no more.

When she came to, she was aware of darkness, silence — broken only by a faint scratching sound — extreme cold, and the fact that her head ached dreadfully. Where am I, she thought, confused, what has happened?

She tried to sit up, but felt so dizzy and queasy that she fell back again on to . . . what? As her eyes grew used to the gloom, she realized that she was in the gatehouse tower room, where her young brothers were sent when they misbehaved. She was lying on an ancient, wooden bed, the mattress stuffed with mouldy straw, and covered only by two thin, woollen blankets. As for the scratching noises she could hear . . .

Rats, thought Alys, her skin crawling, for she had a horror of the filthy creatures. Groaning, she got slowly off the bed and made her way towards the door. It was locked, as she had suspected it would be. A mug of stale ale and a pewter plate with a hunk of dry bread lay beside the bed, but Alys had no appetite. Shivering, she climbed back on to the bed, her legs tucked underneath her, huddled under the inadequate blankets, and wondered what to do next.

He means to starve me, terrify me, and beat me, until I agree to marry Sir Henry, she thought. God knows how long he intends to keep me here! The straw rustled again, and for a moment her courage wavered. Could she really bear to stay locked up here, in this cold, dark room, with only rats and spiders for company?

Instinctively, her hand went to the bosom of her gown, to Tom's silver rose pendant. Oh, Tom, she thought, where are you? Come and save me, I need you! Perhaps Tom is in prison too, she thought, locked in some foreign jail, dreaming of freedom, and of me. The thought gave her courage. Tom would help me escape, if he were here, she thought. But as he's not, I must do it alone.

She racked her brains for what seemed like hours until she drifted into an uneasy doze. She was dreaming, fitfully, of Tom, and stables, and a long, jolting journey, when she heard footsteps on the stairs. At first she thought they were part of her dream, but then she heard the rattle of a key in the lock, the door swung open, and Dame Eleanor stood in the doorway, carrying a tray. Her plump face was creased with concern.

'Well, Alys, my girl,' she said as she advanced into the room, 'this is a fine old muddle, isn't it? My poor girl, my baby . . . '

She put the tray down and Alys was horrified to see tears pouring down her cheeks. She couldn't remember ever seeing Dame Eleanor weep before, not when her mother had wed Sir Hugh, not even when they had buried the baby twins. She put her arm round her old nurse and they hugged each other tight.

'You've upset your stepfather now, and no mistake,' said Dame Eleanor. 'He says you're to stay here till you come to your senses and accept Sir Henry.'

'That I'll never do,' said Alys calmly.

Dame Eleanor shook her head.

'He said you should be given dry bread and ale only, but your lady mother and I persuaded him to let us feed you, at least,' said Dame Eleanor. 'Your mother said Sir Henry would not wish to wed a skinny waif, who'd lost all her teeth from starvation!'

120

'I'm glad to see my mother showing so much spirit,' said Alys.

'She feels for you, as I do,' sighed Dame Eleanor, 'and bade me tell you she remembers you in her prayers. Oh, Alys, Alys, why must you be so headstrong? 'Tis true, Sir Henry is not the husband your mother would have chosen for you, nor I neither. But girls may not marry where they choose . . . '

'Why not? Mary did!' said Alys rebelliously. 'Sir Henry disgusts me. I would rather die than let him even touch me! Oh, Dame Eleanor, what can I do?'

Dame Eleanor thought for a moment, then she said slowly, 'Sir Henry is an old man, Alys, he must be past fifty.'

'So? Would you have me wed my grandfather?'

'No, no. I only meant, if you married him, he might not live long, and then you would be a rich widow and could wed whom you pleased!'

Alys opened her mouth to refuse, and then thought harder. What Dame Eleanor said was true. Sir Henry couldn't live forever. By the time King Edward and Tom came back to England to reclaim the throne for the House of York, Alys could be free again!

Then she imagined marrying Sir Henry, having him touch her, kiss her, share her bed, and shuddered. No, she thought, I cannot do it. Not even if that venomous toad were to keel over and die on our honeymoon, I couldn't bear him near me!

She had little appetite for the bowl of thick, wholesome pottage that Dame Eleanor had brought her, but forced it down under the old nurse's eagle eye. I shall need all my strength, whatever I decide to do, she thought. After Dame Eleanor had left she wrapped the meagre blankets around herself and began to think about escape.

Escape. That was what Tom would do, she was sure. But could she get out of the tower room, away from the Manor? And if she did, where would she go? It was mid-winter, and an icy, dangerous world for a girl on her own. It would be easier if I were a lad, she thought idly, I could . . . I could make my way up North to Tom's home, Broughton Hall in Yorkshire.

Slowly, very slowly, an idea began to form in Alys's mind. Supposing, she thought, just supposing I could get to Yorkshire, to Tom's family? Then, when he returns to England, they could send word to him at the Castle or the King's court, wherever he may be. Sir Hugh wouldn't think of looking for me there, as he might if I fled to the Castle or to Cousin Mary at Enderby Hall.

Alys began to feel excited, even hopeful. I'll do it, she thought. Somehow, I'll get out of here, take Joliet, and head north. Jack the stable-boy will help me, I know. He has no love for my stepfather, or Sir Henry. Why, he might even lend me his Sunday breeches and a jerkin! Under a heavy cloak, I could pass as a young squire, if it wasn't for my hair.

She tugged impatiently at her long dark plaits. They'll have to go, she thought, not without a pang of regret, for she knew Tom loved her shining mane of hair. Never mind, she thought, 'tis a good cause! I'll need a sharp knife, Jack's Sunday clothes, some money . . . but first, how do I get out of here?

Her spirits sank again. The door was securely locked, she knew, and she had heard Dame Eleanor remove the key when she left. Could she persuade Dame Eleanor to look the other way while she escaped? No, she couldn't. However much her old nurse might dislike her stepfather's treatment of her, she knew the good dame would never approve of her setting off on a journey, alone, over half of England, in the dead of winter!

Alys gnawed her thumbnail in frustration. If only I could get out of here, she thought. Just one key stands between me and freedom . . .

'Psst!'

Alys's head jerked up at the sound. Was it rats again, or . . .

'*Psst!*'

'Who is it?' she said cautiously.

' 'Tis I, Cecily,' came her sister's voice. There was the sound of the door unlocking, and then Cecily fell on her in a bear-hug. Alys was so surprised that she could only stare.

'Cecily! But . . . the key . . . Dame Eleanor . . . how came you here?'

Cecily grinned.

'I stole it when the good dame wasn't looking. Oh, Alys, 'tis shameful, the way our stepfather has treated you. How are you, were you badly hurt?'

'Bruised, mostly, and my head aches,' Alys admitted, 'but, Cecily, you are in great danger too! He'll beat you if he finds you here, you know that.'

'I care not. I've had enough of his bullying ways,' said Cecily stoutly. 'I want to help you, Alys. What can I do?'

'Well,' Alys said slowly, 'I'm going away, Cecily.'

'Away? Away where?'

'To Tom's family, in Yorkshire. I'm going to cut my hair, borrow clothes from Jack the stable-boy, and ride north as quickly as I can. Tom's family will shelter me, I'm sure.'

Cecily stared at her, round-eyed.

' 'Tis a bold plan, sister,' she said.

'That's why it will work,' said Alys. 'I'll need you to bring me a knife, to steal the key again so that I can get out, and to warn Jack to leave his Sunday clothes in Joliet's stall! Oh, and money . . . I shall need money . . . '

The two girls looked at each other.

'The chest in Mother's solar. I know where she keeps the key. And that money belonged to our true father, so 'tis ours by right,' said Cecily.

Alys had never admired her sister so much. She had already risked a beating, and was prepared to risk another. What would Sir Hugh do to her when he discovered that Alys had disappeared?

'Oh, sister,' she gasped, 'I know not what to say! How can I ask you to do this for me? How can I bear to leave you to face Sir Hugh's anger alone?'

Cecily grinned at her again.

'You won't have to,' she said. 'I'm coming with you!'

6

December 1470

Alys stared at her sister, hardly able to believe her ears. 'You're . . . you're coming with me?' she echoed, 'but, Cecily . . . '

'Why ever not?' her sister said briskly. 'It will be far safer for two of us than for you travelling alone, even if you *are* disguised as a boy. Less suspicious, too. We can tell anyone who asks that our parents are dead, and we're travelling to relatives in the North!'

Alys sat down on the edge of the sagging old bed, feeling rather as if she might burst into tears. It had been hard enough for her to decide to leave the Manor, leave her family and everything she knew, and travel to Yorkshire, but at least she would have Tom at her journey's end. For her young sister to be willing to face the perils and dangers of a midwinter journey, and an uncertain future, was bravery indeed.

'But . . . have you thought what this

means?' she asked anxiously. ' 'Tis a long and dangerous journey . . . '

'All the more reason for two of us to make it together,' said Cecily. 'Besides, what would happen to me if I stayed? I would be punished, beaten for sure, made to tell where you've gone, or perhaps even married off to Sir Henry myself! No, I'd rather take my chances with you, Alys!'

The two girls hugged one another warmly. Then Cecily said, 'When do you want to leave? I shall need a little time to warn Jack and get the money from the chest in Mother's solar.'

'I'll have to leave that to you,' Alys said. 'I can do nothing, locked up here.'

'Don't worry,' said Cecily. 'I shall be very, very careful. When I have spoken to Jack and have the knife and the money, I shall come to you again.'

Alys nodded.

'Don't take any risks. Better to wait a few days rather than have Sir Hugh discover our . . . '

'What's that?' cried Cecily suddenly. Both girls froze. There were footsteps, unmistakable footsteps, coming up the stairs!

'Quick,' muttered Alys, 'under the bed!

There's nowhere else to hide!'

Cecily thrust Dame Eleanor's key into her sister's hand and flung herself to the floor.

'Lock the door and hide the key,' she hissed desperately, 'or all will be discovered and we shall be lost!'

Alys tiptoed across the room, locked the heavy wooden door, and hastily flung the key into the darkest corner of the room. Glancing around, she saw that Cecily was well hidden under the bed. She sat on it and wrapped the blankets around herself, her heart hammering.

A few moments later the door opened and Sir Hugh stalked in, his key-chain dangling from his belt and his face like thunder. Alys couldn't help feeling afraid. She shrank back against the wall. Oh, God, she thought, is he going to beat me again?

'Well, girl,' barked Sir Hugh, 'have you come to your senses yet?'

Alys said nothing.

'Speak!' snapped her stepfather. 'Sir Henry Capshaw is offering you honourable marriage. 'Tis a fine match, he owns estates in Surrey and Kent, and a fine big house in London as well. You could even go to court! Sir Henry is well known to the Duke of Somerset, Queen Margaret's captain and favourite. What's more, Sir Henry seems to dote on you, for some reason. Agree to marry him, and you shall leave this unpleasant place . . . '

He looked around at the damp, mouldy walls where a couple of feeble candles guttered, at the broken-down bed with its thin covers, at Alys's white, stony face. As they stared at one another in silence, a rat scuttled across the floor and Alys had to stifle a scream.

'Come, my dear daughter,' Sir Hugh said, his eyes narrowing, 'be sensible. Wed Sir Henry, and we shall be friends once more!'

'Friends!' Alys cried. 'When were we ever friends? You just want to get rid of me, marrying me to the first Lancastrian to make an offer! I will not marry Sir Henry! I hate him! And I hate you!'

For a terrible moment, she thought that Sir Hugh was going to strike her again, but instead he just sneered, 'Very well, madam. You have made your choice. And here you stay, until you choose to obey your elders and betters. I will not have this defiance, do you hear me? Either you

130

marry Sir Henry, or you will remain here — until you die!'

'Then I shall die here,' said Alys woodenly.

Sir Hugh said no more, just turned on his heel and left the room, slamming the door and locking it behind him. A few moments later, Cecily crawled out from under the bed, her gown stained and damp, a spider's web adorning her curls.

'Ugh,' she shuddered, 'it was foul down there! But, Alys, do you wonder that I want to leave with you? Our stepfather is a bully and tyrant. I will live under his roof no longer!'

'Nor I,' said Alys, handing her sister the key she'd retrieved from the corner of the room. 'Cecily, it would be better if you did not risk coming here again until all the arrangements are made and 'tis time to leave. Don't forget, the money, a knife, and Jack! Oh, and dress warmly, sister, 'twill be a long, cold journey.'

'I know,' replied Cecily. 'Take heart, Alys. I will come for you as soon as I can, and we shall make our escape, I promise!'

When Cecily had gone, Alys lay back on the rough straw mattress, her heart pounding. I shall be free, she thought. Sir

Hugh will never find me, never beat or bully me again, and when Tom returns . . .

In spite of the cold and discomfort, she fell asleep smiling, and dreamed of Tom, of warm summer days and meetings beneath the Outlaws' Oak.

It was hard for Alys to be patient during the days that followed. She saw no one but Moll the kitchenmaid, who brought her food, indicating by signs that she had been forbidden to speak to Alys. She could hear the sounds of everyday life at the Manor, the maids drawing water from the courtyard well, the jingle of horses' bridles, shouts from Rob and Giles and squeals from the little girls, Dame Eleanor's raised voice. But all she could see from the narrow tower window was a grim, grey sky, drenching rain, and even once snowflakes.

She stayed in bed most of the time, huddled in blankets. One morning she awoke to find a large brown rat squatting on her chest. She flung it aside with a shudder of horror and it scuttled into a corner of the room with a squeak of protest. God and His Holy Mother protect me, Alys thought, how much longer must I stand this?

And then, one night, just when she had drifted into an uneasy, shivering sleep, she heard a sound at the door. It opened with a creak and in the doorway stood Cecily, wrapped in her warmest fur cloak and clutching something in her arms.

'Alys! Wake up! I bring you the knife, and I have the money here, too.'

Alys was wide awake in an instant.

'Oh, Cecily, 'tis good to see you,' she murmured through chattering teeth. 'I swear I shall lose my mind if I have to spend many more nights in this dreadful room!'

'Come, sister, hurry,' Cecily urged. 'Jack is waiting in the stables and has saddled Joliet and Beauty. He has brought his spare jerkin and breeches and a hood for you to wear, if you don't mind looking like a farmer's lad, he said!'

'As if I care about that!' said Alys, hacking at her thick plaits with the kitchen knife that Cecily had brought her. Her head felt light and strange when they had gone. For a moment, she looked at them regretfully. They were so long and thick. Her one beauty, she had told Tom once. Then she kicked them under the bed and ran her hands through the short, jagged crop that remained.

'I, too, am in disguise,' Cecily said. 'I gave an old gown of mine to Moll in exchange for one of her homespun kirtles. It's not over-clean, but it will serve! I told her 'twas a game, a bet, and I think she thought I was planning to creep out to meet a lover!'

In spite of herself, Alys giggled.

'Moll *would*!' she said. 'That wench has nothing on her mind but lovers!'

Stealthily, Cecily and Alys crept out of the tower room and down the stone staircase to the courtyard. It was damp and cool outside, but there was no frost, and in the courtyard nothing moved. Even the Manor hounds were asleep. The girls tiptoed across the stables and went inside. Some of the horses stirred uneasily at the unfamiliar sounds, and when Jack rose up from behind a wooden stall with a whisper of 'Lady Alys!' Alys nearly jumped out of her skin.

'Jack, is that you? Have you got the clothes?'

'Indeed I have. Here!'

Jack thrust a bundle that smelled strongly of horses into Alys's arms.

'Are you really determined to do this

mad thing, Lady Alys?' he demanded. 'I like it not. A gently-bred young woman like yourself, what do you know of the world out there? 'Tis a hard, cruel place, and you have hundreds of miles to ride!'

'I have to do it, Jack,' said Alys simply. 'The outside world may be hard and cruel, but it can be no worse than being locked in the tower room with rats and spiders until I agree to marry Sir Henry! And I would rather die than do that!'

Jack looked uncertain, then he shrugged.

'Perhaps you're right. I wouldn't know,' he said. 'Well . . . Godspeed, Lady Alys, Lady Cecily. Joliet and Beauty are saddled and ready for you, and the postern gate is open, 'tis quieter that way.'

He turned to leave, but Alys called him back, fumbling in the leather bag of coins Cecily had brought her and taking out a silver penny.

'Here,' she said awkwardly. 'For your trouble, and for the clothes. I shall not forget this, Jack. When Tom and I are wed, I'll send for you, and you shall take charge of our stables, up in Yorkshire!'

'God grant it may be so, lady,' said Jack in a choked voice. 'Fare well!'

Alys and Cecily didn't dare to mount

their horses until they had led them through the postern gate and away from the Manor. Joliet whinnied once, and Alys froze. But around the Manor, all was darkness and silence. In the shelter of the nearby woods, Alys slipped out of her gown, shivering, rolled it up and stuffed it into Joliet's saddle-bag. Dressed in Jack's loose, rough woollen shirt, leather breeches and jerkin, and her own riding boots, she turned to Cecily.

'How do I look?' she said, pushing her hair under Jack's thick hood. 'Will I pass as a lad, do you think?'

'For sure, if no one looks too closely,' said Cecily, sounding almost light-hearted now that the first part of their escape was complete. 'And as for me, I know I look like a peasant, or a serving-wench, and I certainly smell like one — phew!'

The girls divided the money they were carrying between them. Cecily had also put some bread, a mutton pasty or two, and some rather shrivelled apples into the horses' saddle-bags.

'For who knows when we shall next eat?' she said practically.

She and Alys remounted and headed east, Jack having told Cecily that the way to York was a few miles in that direction.

'And then, when we come to a village called Gallows Ford, and cross a river by a white bridge near an alehouse, we take the Great North Road,' she said.

For a while, the girls rode in silence. It seemed strange to be out at night, in a world of total darkness. No rushlights flickered in the peasants' cottages they passed, no one worked in the fields, no fellow-travellers rode along the way, no pigs or chickens rooted in the mud of the village streets. 'Tis like a world of ghosts, Alys thought, touching the silver rose pendant at her breast for comfort.

'We'll put as many miles between ourselves and the Manor as we can, to begin with,' she said out loud. 'Then, when we can go no further, we'll look for some decent inn or perhaps an Abbey guest-house for the night.'

'How many nights shall we be on the road, do you think?' Cecily asked.

'I don't really know. Tom said it was a week's riding, but that was for men on fine, swift horses. I don't want to push my poor Joliet too hard,' said Alys. 'We have plenty of money, we can travel as and when we please! But I shall feel happier when we are well away from the Manor.'

'So shall I. 'Twould be dreadful to be caught, and taken home,' said Cecily.

The night was fading into dawn when the two girls arrived at a large village and saw the white bridge, the alehouse, and the old gallows that Jack had described.

'This is where we begin to take the Great North Road, then,' said Alys, trying not to yawn. It seemed hours, days even, since they had left the Manor. The Great North Road proved easy to find, being wide and heavily-rutted from horses' hooves, farm carts, and carriages. Alys swung Joliet round and the little mare plodded gallantly forward. On and on they rode, until a pale, watery sun rose. Alys, dozing in the saddle, was jerked awake by a cry from behind her. When she looked around, she saw that Beauty had caught her hoof in a pothole and stumbled, throwing Cecily to the ground.

Alys flung herself from Joliet's back.

'Cecily, are you all right?' she demanded.

'I . . . I think so,' replied her sister, sounding half-dazed. 'Alys, I'm so . . . tired. I . . . I must sleep, just for a little while . . .'

Alys looked round. There was no sign of any village, nor even an isolated cottage or shepherd's hut, let alone an inn or abbey where they could seek shelter. She opened Beauty's saddle-bag and took out two pasties, one of which she handed to Cecily.

'Here,' she said, 'have something to eat! That will wake you up. Then as soon as we see anywhere suitable, we'll stop and rest, I promise.'

Cecily smiled wanly, but as she ate some colour returned to her cheeks and she remounted Beauty without protest. They rode on. The road still seemed deserted, and there was no sign of human habitation. Alys felt stiff and weary after so many hours in the saddle. This is a wild, lonely place, she thought.

'Look!' Cecily cried. 'What's that, ahead of us?'

Alys craned forward. Perhaps it was an inn? Or a cottage, at least, where the goodwife might sell them a mug of ale, a bowl of oatmeal, some bread and cheese? She urged Joliet on, only to find that the building Cecily had seen was no more than a rough wooden shelter, set back from the road, with a pile of hay at one

139

side and a few shrivelled turnips at the other.

'Someone keeps their animals here,' she said, dismounting, and noticing sheep-droppings among the straw. 'It's some sort of lambing-pen, I believe, with wooden walls to keep off the worst of the weather.'

'I don't care,' said Cecily sleepily. ' 'Twill serve, for now. I . . . I could sleep anywhere, I'm so tired . . . '

She slid from Beauty's back on to the dirty straw and was asleep in seconds. Alys tucked her sister's cloak round her, tied both horses' reins to the nearest wooden post, curled up beside Cecily, and fell asleep.

'Oy! *Oy!* What be ye doin' then?'

Alys groaned as something hard and sharp stabbed into her ribs.

'Wha-at? What's . . . ?' she gasped, waking up to find a huge, beetle-browed man in a peasant's grubby tunic and breeches jabbing at her body with a pitchfork-handle. Beside her, Cecily stirred uncomfortably.

'Well? Who are ye? And why are ye sleepin' here, wi' the beasts o' the field? 'Tis my lord's land, and he'd have summat ter say, could he see yer!'

Alys scrambled to her feet, shaking the straw out of her hair and clothes, and trying not to panic. The brawny peasant looked as if he was quite capable of stabbing both her and Cecily with the business end of his pitchfork.

'I . . . I'm sorry,' she faltered. 'My sister and I were so tired, we needed somewhere to shelter, and this was nearest . . .'

Just then Cecily woke up, saw the peasant's ugly, suspicious face looming over her, and jumped to her feet with a cry.

'Who is this? What's happening?'

Alys squeezed her hand.

'Don't worry. I was just explaining to the, er, gentleman . . .'

The fat peasant gave a snort of laughter, or disgust, it was hard to tell which, and spat noisily into the straw.

'Gentleman? I be no gentleman! And you, who be you? Outlaws? Runaways? My lord doesna want your kind on his land, a-robbin' and a-thievin'!'

Alys drew herself up to her full height.

'My man,' she said grandly, 'we are neither robbers nor thieves, just travellers fallen on hard times and taking a rest! We shall move on, now. Thank you for your

141

hospitality! Come, Cecily!'

The fat peasant watched sullenly, pitchfork at the ready, as the girls untied Joliet and Beauty, mounted, and rode away. Alys glanced back once and saw him standing in the middle of the road, scratching his head. In spite of herself, she started to giggle, and Cecily joined in.

'D-did you see his face, when you called him a gentleman?' Cecily laughed. 'I'll wager no one had ever called him that before!'

'No, nor ever will again!'

Refreshed by their sleep, the girls rode on. It was a mild, dry day. Now that she felt less tired, Alys felt her spirits rising, and she looked about her with interest. Not that there was much to see, just workers in the fields, a goosegirl with her flock, smoke spiralling up from the occasional cottage, a small troop of horsemen jingling past, a barefoot friar in a rough homespun habit who said, 'God's greetings to you, young sir, young lady,' as he passed them by. After another hour's riding they took a break and ate their remaining bread and apples. A church bell rang in the distance and Alys said, 'I think we should look for a room for the night in the next village. Alehouse, inn or abbey, it matters not. We have money, we can pay for a clean bed and a good meal.'

The short winter's day was almost over when they finally came to a sizeable village. There was an alehouse on the main road, with the usual bundle of twigs hanging outside. It was no more than a large cottage, with a pig grunting in its pen outside and a lean-to shed with a few scrawny cattle, but Alys and Cecily were too tired to care. They dismounted, and went in.

It was a long, low room with three or four wooden tables. A slatternly girl with greasy black hair and a pockmarked face carried mugs of ale to a group of rough-looking peasants. A fat priest sat at another table, his face almost hidden in a bowl of something that steamed and smelled savoury. Alys's stomach contracted. It seemed a week since she had tasted hot food. A couple of mangy dogs sniffed round her legs as she strode forward, trying to look braver than she felt. The crowd of men fell silent as she approached, and even the fat priest stopped wolfing his food for long enough to stare at her.

'Are you the alewife? The landlady?' she asked the black-haired girl.

'I might be,' she said. 'What d'yer want?'

'Stabling, food, and a bed for tonight for myself and my sister,' said Alys briskly.

'Hmm,' the woman said. 'Have yer any money?'

Alys turned to Cecily, who took a few coins out of her leather money-bag and handed them to the alewife, who examined them carefully, bit them, and stuffed them into a greasy pouch at her waist.

'Upstairs,' she said, jerking her head towards a wooden ladder at the other side of the room. 'There's mutton pottage, bread, cheese and ale, if that's not too humble fare for yer.'

Alys nodded.

'First,' she said, 'can someone take care of our horses?'

'Sim will,' said the alewife, 'but it'll cost yer!'

Cecily gave her another coin, and a scab-faced youth slouched out into the yard. The priest had returned to his meal, but the other men's eyes followed Alys and Cecily as they climbed the wooden ladder. They found themselves in a dark loft room with two rickety stools and a number of grubby, straw-filled mattresses, on one of which someone was already snoring.

'Dear God,' whispered Cecily, 'what sort of a place is this?'

'Better than the cold ground, on a winter's night!' said Alys. 'The fireplace is just below us, so we shall be warm, at least. And that pottage smelled good!'

It tasted good, too, as both girls discovered when the alewife served them a bowlful. The bread was half-straw, the ale watery, and they had to trim mould off the cheese, but Alys was too hungry to care. She was just draining her mug when one of the men came over to their table.

Alys stiffened, not liking his looks. A scar puckered his left cheek and when he spoke she noticed that most of his front teeth were missing.

'And where are you bound, my fine young traveller?' he enquired silkily. 'You and your . . . er . . . sister?'

'North, to Yorkshire. We have relatives there,' said Alys.

'Relatives, eh? Would you believe that? I'm a Yorkshire-man myself,' he said, grinning. 'Perhaps I know your relatives?'

Alys doubted it very much. Even if he

was from Yorkshire, which she didn't believe, he was far too dirty and disreputable to be any acquaintance of Tom's family.

'Their name is Taverner, of Broughton Hall,' Cecily said in a quavering voice. Alys pressed her hand comfortingly under the table.

'Taverner? Taverner? I believe I have heard the name,' he said airily. 'But you seem full young to be alone on such a long journey, and in winter too. You and your sister . . .'

He looked meaningfully at Cecily, who blushed. He thinks we are runaway lovers, Alys thought.

'I'm eighteen years old, good sir,' she lied, trying to deepen her voice and assume an air of manly bravado. 'And, as for the winter journey, my sister and I had no choice. Our parents died within a week of one another, God rest their souls, and we had nowhere else to go.'

'Died? Within a week of one another?' said the greasy-haired alewife, hearing this. ' 'Twasn't plague, was it? Or the pox? Or the sweating sickness?'

Even the scar-faced man had backed away in alarm, and Alys heard one of the other customers mutter, 'We want no plague-bearers here!'

'No, no,' she said soothingly. 'Our father was a merchant in London. He was struck down by . . . by a visitation from God. He just dropped dead in the street, God rest him.'

The alewife and the scar-faced man crossed themselves.

'And our mother, she died of a broken heart, just days later,' added Cecily helpfully. 'Now we are alone in the world apart from our relatives in Yorkshire, so we ride to join them.'

The scar-faced fellow had shambled off to join his cronies, but the alewife lingered, looking friendlier and less suspicious than before.

'Take my tip, young sir,' she said, leaning across the table towards Alys and speaking in lowered tones, 'you'd do better to wait awhile here, until another party of north-bound travellers pass through, and you can go on with them. 'Tis not safe to be out riding, in the dark and the winter cold, two young sprigs like yerselves. There's outlaws about, real bad 'uns. Cut yer throat for a silver penny, some of 'em would!'

For a moment, Alys's courage failed her, but she managed to square her shoulders and smile.

'Thank you for the warning,' she said graciously. 'But we need to press on with our journey. We may catch up with some other travellers later. Our horses are fleet-footed and I think we can outrun any cut-purses who might threaten us. Besides, I am armed!'

She slapped her thigh, where she kept the sharp kitchen knife Cecily had brought her to cut her hair with, hoping that it would pass for a dagger. Aye, and I'd not hesitate to use it, too, if anyone tried to rob us, she thought.

The alewife shrugged.

'Suit yerselves,' she said, gathering up their empty bowls and mugs.

Cecily yawned suddenly.

'Let's go to bed, er, brother,' she said sleepily. 'We have another hard day's riding tomorrow.'

Wearily, the girls climbed the ladder to the dingy loft room, where their sleeping companion still snored and twitched on one of the lumpy mattresses. Alys tucked Jack's jerkin around her money pouch and laid her head on it for a pillow, wrapping herself in her warm cloak and trying not to hear the rustlings and scuttlings in the straw that meant mice — or rats. There were certainly plenty of fleas, she thought crossly, scratching. Oh well, 'tis better than sleeping on the cold ground, and, God willing, we shall find more comfortable sleeping-quarters tomorrow . . .

Within moments, she was asleep.

When she awoke, she and Cecily were alone in the room. It was colder, much colder, and there was no sound from the alehouse below. Alys yawned and stretched, flinching as her aching thigh-muscles protested. She had never ridden Joliet all day before. Oh, well, she thought, I suppose I shall get used to it.

Another coin brought them a breakfast of rather stale bread, ale, and a little salt fish. Then they set off, and Alys was pleased to note that at least Beauty and Joliet had been properly cared for. The little mare positively pranced as she stepped out along the frost-hard path with delicate hooves.

'Dear Joliet,' Alys said out loud, patting the chestnut neck, then turning to smile at Cecily, who smiled back — and then groaned.

'What's amiss?' Alys called.

'Nothing,' replied her sister, teeth gritted. 'Or . . . 'tis just the road is so hard today after last night's frost, and my bottom so tender after riding all day yesterday . . . ouch!'

'I know,' said Alys sympathetically. 'When I tried to get up this morning, my legs . . . what's that?'

There was a rustling noise ahead of them and Alys reined Joliet in, alarmed. Within seconds, it seemed, they were surrounded by a group of ruffians, armed with wooden staves and knives. Cecily screamed. One of the men grabbed Joliet's bridle roughly and the little mare reared up in fright, almost unseating Alys.

'Who are you? What do you want?' she cried.

One of the peasants, a tall one-eyed fellow with a straggly beard, laughed unpleasantly, and Alys felt the chill of sheer terror.

'What yer got?' he said insolently, running dirty, calloused hands over Joliet's coat, Alys's leg, and the saddle-bags. Oh, God, Alys thought, our money, he's going to take our money, all we have in the world! She could hear Cecily whimpering with fear behind her, as two of the outlaws went to grab Beauty.

'Let us go!' she cried, with all the courage she could muster.

'Or what?' said the one-eyed man, with a sinister chuckle. 'Oh, no, young sir, not till you've paid us a . . . toll fee, shall we say, for letting you use the Great North Road!'

Alys dug her heels desperately into Joliet's sides, but the little mare couldn't move with two outlaws tugging at her bridle. Then Alys remembered the knife at her belt, slid her hand down to grasp it, slashed at the filthy hands clutching at her legs, the saddle-bags, Joliet's bridle . . .

'Take that! Let me go!' she yelled, slashing at random.

'Aaaagh!' screamed one of the outlaws, falling back, blood spurting from his wounded hand.

'Damn you and your fancy ways!' roared the one-eyed man, rushing at the plunging, rearing Joliet, his stave at the ready. Alys heard a terrified whinny from her mare, a scream from Cecily, and then there was a blinding pain and she plunged down, down into blackness.

7

January 1471

'Tom! Tom!' Alys cried desperately.

She was in some sort of clearing in the woods, and Tom was striding along the path just ahead of her. She tried to run after him, calling his name, but somehow her legs didn't work properly. Perhaps it was the long cloak she wore, getting in the way. Although she screamed his name he didn't seem to hear.

She was terrified. Someone was chasing her, a huge, burly ruffian with a scarred face and a wooden stave, who laughed horribly as he demanded a toll fee, a toll fee for the Great North Road . . .

Alys whimpered, struggled . . . and woke up.

A cool hand was placed on her hot forehead and a gentle voice said, 'Lie still, my daughter. You are quite safe here. 'Twas only a bad dream, brought on by your fever.'

Alys opened her eyes, blinking in the

candlelight, and looked around her in bewilderment. She was in bed, warmly wrapped in rough linen sheets and a fur rug, in a tiny cell-like room with stone walls. Beside her bed sat a sweet-faced elderly nun in a spotlessly clean, though much-darned, grey habit. She smiled and held a cup to Alys's lips. The drink tasted of honey and herbs, and was not unpleasant.

'Where am I? What is this place?' she asked faintly. 'And . . . who are you?'

'I'm Sister Benedicta, and you are in the infirmary of St Ursula's Convent, ten miles from Bedford town,' said the nun.

Alys eased her aching head on the pillow, wincing in pain. There's something I should remember, she thought vaguely, but her head felt rather as though it was filled with straw, or sheeps' wool. A name came to her.

'Cecily?' she enquired.

'Your sister is well. 'Twas she who brought you to us, she and the King's messenger,' said the nun, patting her arm kindly. 'Sleep is the best medicine for the hurt you have suffered.'

When Alys awoke again, it was full daylight. Her head felt much less muzzy and the figure sitting beside her on the stool was Cecily. She was biting her lip anxiously, and looked as though she had been crying.

'Oh, Alys! Sister, do you know who I am?' she cried in a choked voice.

'Of course I do,' said Alys, feeling bewildered and rather cross. 'You are Cecily Sherwood, my sister. I am here in this convent . . . where is Sister Benedicta?'

Cecily didn't reply, being too busy mopping her streaming eyes.

'Oh, Alys,' she sobbed, 'I . . . I thought you were going to die! Those awful men! When that great lout hit you, and you went down like . . . like a poleaxed ox, I truly thought he had killed you!'

Alys sat up, remembering.

'Yes! They attacked us, tried to steal our money, I slashed at one of them with my knife . . . '

'You fought like a wildcat, sister,' said Cecily admiringly. 'But no one could have held out against so many attackers.'

'Then what happened?' Alys demanded.

Cecily was silent for a moment and seemed unable to meet her eyes.

'Well?'

'They . . . they stole the horses . . . ' she faltered.

Alys swallowed hard. 'The horses,' she echoed. 'Saddle-bags and all, I suppose?'

Cecily nodded.

'I . . . see,' said Alys slowly. 'So that means we have lost everything, everything we own in the world, including Joliet and Beauty.'

'Yes,' said Cecily in a small voice, 'but, Alys, it could have been worse! We have our lives, and we have each other!'

Alys sank back upon her pillows, hardly able to take in the full horror of it all. Yes, she and Cecily were alive, and safe here in the convent, but how were they to continue their journey with no horses and no money?

'Go on,' she said in a deadly quiet voice, 'what happened then?'

'I . . . I don't know what they'd planned to do to you, or to me,' Cecily said with a shudder, 'but a King's messenger came thundering along the road on a beautiful bay stallion, and the outlaws scattered. He . . . he was really kind, Alys. He said 'What's amiss here?' and when I explained what had happened, he said he would escort us to the convent, where we would be safe. He slung you across the saddle as if you were no bigger than Joanna or Katherine, I climbed up behind to hold you safe, and we came here!'

'So I owe my life to one of King Henry's messengers,' murmured Alys.

'Yes, isn't it strange? He was a gentleman and a true Christian,' said Cecily. 'Sister Benedicta is the infirmaress here. She takes care of the sick, both nuns and travellers. When she took off your shirt and breeches and discovered you were a girl and not a boy, there was a fine to-do!'

'And you said?'

'I stuck to the story we told the alewife in that awful tavern,' said Cecily. 'That we were going north to relatives, and thought it safer to travel as brother and sister.'

Alys nodded slowly.

'You did well,' she said, 'and I can see I owe my life to you and the good nuns, as well as the Lancastrian messenger.'

Cecily leaned over suddenly and clasped her sister's hand.

'Whatever are we going to do, Alys?' she said.

Alys shook her head.

'We must go on,' she said, 'on foot, if we

have to. 'Twill take much longer than I had planned, and I think we should do as that alewife suggested, and join another party of northbound travellers, even though we have nothing left to steal. I don't want to meet any more outlaws!'

Cecily shivered.

'No . . . oh, no, that was terrible!'

Just then, the infirmaress, Sister Benedicta, bustled in, her rosy face creased with smiles when she saw Alys.

'Sitting up and taking notice, the Lord be praised!' she said, crossing herself. 'Now, all we have to do is feed you some of Sister Margaret's good soup and you will soon be on your feet, Alys.'

'Thanks to your skill, Sister Benedicta,' said Alys gratefully.

'Tut, 'twas nothing,' said the nun. 'I've some skill, perhaps, but you were in the Lord's hands, child, as we all are.'

Cecily caught at the old nun's arm.

'We've . . . been talking about what to do next,' she said nervously. 'I mean, when Alys is better . . . '

'Oh, yes, your journey north,' nodded Sister Benedicta. 'Reverend Mother and I have been discussing it, and we think it would be best if you travelled on with

157

Dame Margery Salter, who is staying in our guest-house. She is going to Bedford to keep house for her brother, a wool merchant whose wife has recently died, God rest her. Dame Margery is travelling in a party, with two maids, another merchant with his wife and son, and a couple of apprentice-lads big and strong enough to keep any robbers at bay! Reverend Mother spoke to Dame Margery of you, and the good dame has agreed . . . '

'But we have no horses,' murmured Cecily, rather overwhelmed by this.

'It's no matter. You're both lightweight enough to ride pillion behind Dame Margery or one of the apprentices,' said Sister Benedicta. 'She has agreed to wait until Alys is recovered before she sets off. She has had a weary journey and is glad to rest awhile with us. Now, Mistress Alys, drink this, and try to sleep again.'

Alys, who had been going to object, or at least ask questions about the unknown Dame Margery, found herself meekly drinking another cupful of Sister Benedicta's honey-flavoured medicine instead. The next time she woke, Cecily was beside her, and a tiny, beady-eyed middle-aged woman, neatly dressed in a housewife's russet gown and kirtle, was bending over her.

'So you're Alys, the wench who dresses like a lad and fights like an alleycat!' was her brisk greeting.

'Er . . . yes, that's me,' Alys agreed.

Dame Margery nodded thoughtfully, her black eyes twinkling.

'Good. Good. I like a wench with spirit,' she declared. 'Mind you, 'twas foolhardy to try to travel alone in winter. I don't know what you were thinking of! Even when my poor brother sent for me, I waited until I'd a sturdy crew of travelling companions before I set off across the country. I don't care for the country, mind, never did. City life is what suits me. Now I've to see how I settle to life in Bedford town, and what sort of pie's nest my sister-in-law left behind her when she went to meet her Maker, poor soul. There are seven children in that house, Mistress Alys, and my poor brother with no more idea of caring for little ones than a cage-full of lions! Not that my sister-in-law was much better. A feeble wisp of a woman, I thought her, always ailing. I never could abide that type. My brother should've wed a stout, sturdy girl with some idea of how to run a merchant's household . . . '

Suddenly she stopped talking and peered inquisitively at Alys.

'Could you run a household, young woman? You and your sister?' she enquired severely.

Alys met her gaze fearlessly.

'My sister and I were trained by our mother and our old nurse to take our places, one day, at the head of a gentleman's household,' she replied.

'Indeed?' said Dame Margery. 'So can you sew and spin and mend, care for children, oversee the brewing and the baking, nurse the sick?'

'Yes,' Alys said. 'Yes, I believe I can, and my sister too.'

Dame Margery's wrinkled-walnut face broke into a smile.

'I knew it,' she said. 'As soon as the good nuns told me your story, and how fiercely you defended yourself against those vagabonds, I knew you'd be a girl after my own heart. Ride with us to Bedford, and welcome! I shall have need of a couple of useful pairs of hands to sort out that household, I'll be bound. I brought two maids with me from London, but Mary does nothing but snivel and whinge for some lad she left behind, and Tibby is a good girl, but slow-witted. If you and your sister are willing to help with whatever we may find at my brother's house . . . '

'We are. And neither of us is afraid of hard work,' said Cecily.

Three days later, the party set off from the convent on the road to Bedford. Since she had nothing else to wear, Alys was still dressed in the rough shirt, breeches and jerkin she had bought from Jack. She rode pillion behind one of Dame Margery's apprentices, a thickset lad about her own age, who blushed and stammered when she, or anyone else, spoke to him. Cecily, meanwhile, rode behind Dame Margery.

The apprentice's horse was a plodding beast, sound enough, but without much spirit, and Alys felt tears springing to her eyes as she thought of her high-stepping, affectionate little mare Joliet, her smooth chestnut coat, liquid brown eyes, and soft muzzle. She was a lady's riding-horse, not to be harnessed to a plough or cart. I pray she will not be ill-treated, Alys thought, sniffing. Those scurvy knaves will have no idea how to care for her. Perhaps they'll sell her. I hope she finds a good home, someone to love her as I did. Oh, Joliet, I shall miss you!

She dashed the tears away with the sleeve of her shirt and pulled Jack's hood round her face to hide her reddened eyes. I'm supposed to be a lad, she thought, and strong lads don't weep. But every time she remembered the gentle mare's whickers of welcome, or the soft muzzle pushed into her hand as she searched for some titbit Alys had brought her, her eyes filled. I shall never see you again, poor Joliet, she thought sadly.

Her spirits rose a little as the party rode into Bedford, and she looked around her with interest. It was a busy, bustling town, the streets crammed with riders, carts, a pack of squabbling hounds, merchants and priests and goodwives with plaited rush baskets over their arms. And the noise! For a moment, Alys shrank back as she became aware of the clanging of church bells, the grunting of hogs and the squawk of chickens, the cries of shop-keepers to 'come buy', the yells of a street-vendor carrying a tray of hot pies, the wailing of a baby, the shrieks and giggles of children getting under every-one's feet.

'Tis a wonder city folk aren't all deaf, indeed, she thought, remembering what Tom had said about London. Thinking of him, her hand went instinctively to the silver rose pendant beneath her shirt. I won't forget you, my only love, she said, under her breath. And I will come to you one day, I swear I will!

They turned into a side-street which was slightly quieter. Dame Margery dismounted and rapped loudly on the door of one of the houses, whose upper storey leaned right out over the street, so that it was possible for neighbours across the road to shake hands from their bedroom windows.

There was no reply, though Alys thought she heard a child cry, indoors. Dame Margery knocked again, even more loudly.

'In faith,' she said, sniffing, ' 'tis worse than I thought! No doubt my brother is in his counting-house, or out buying fleeces, and his servants grown slatternly and neglecting their duties. Well, I shall see to that!'

I'm sure you will, thought Alys,

exchanging grins with Cecily. Neither of them could imagine lazy servants lasting long in any household run by Dame Margery!

The front door creaked open and a red-faced man in a filthy smock peered blearily out at them.

'Maister's not 'ome,' he declared, squinting. 'Who be ye, then?'

Dame Margery leaned forward, sniffed the unmistakable stench of sour ale on his breath, and drew herself up to her full height. She was smaller even than Cecily, but at the look in her eye, the man stepped back in alarm.

'This *is* John Stillington's house? John Stillington, wool merchant and citizen?' she demanded.

'Aye, that it be. John Stillington's my maister,' said the servant uneasily.

'I am his sister, Dame Margery Salter, widow, come to set his household to rights. By Our Lady, I can see I'm needed!' she said. 'You, my good man, are drunk! If you want to keep your job, I suggest you go to your bed and sleep it off, and don't let me see you in that disgusting condition again! Come, Mary, Tibby . . . Alys, Cecily, Peter and Tamkin, there is work to do here!'

And there was. When, later, Alys looked back on her first few days in the house, she could remember back-breaking work, poor food, half-wild children, and sullen servants who had clearly never met anyone like Dame Margery in their lives. John Stillington might be a prosperous wool merchant, but his home and his children were as filthy as the poorest peasants. He was a tall, stooping, grey-haired man, quite unlike his whirlwind of a sister.

'Dear God, man, how could you let your home get into such a state?' Dame Margery cried, looking round at the rotting tapestries, greasy tables, filthy rugs, and staircase thick with dust.

' 'Twas my poor Elizabeth, she couldn't . . . she was so sickly after young Joseph was born . . . ' he said.

Dame Margery tutted.

'Well, you should have got some strong, sensible woman to take charge . . . '

'That's what I have done, sister,' he said mildly.

Dame Margery shook her head and carried on. She dismissed the worst of the servants, including the drunken steward, the cook and two kitchen-boys so dirty and pockfaced she refused to eat anything they had prepared. She also dismissed the nursemaid whose idea of caring for the seven undersized Stillington children was to feed them thin gruel when she thought of it, and slap them half-senseless if they cried. After one horrified look at their ragged clothes and skinny little bodies crawling with lice, Dame Margery had put them in Alys and Cecily's care.

'Clean them up, feed them, dress them decently, and try to make them look less like young savages,' she said roughly, but her eyes were kinder than her words.

Tender-hearted Cecily's lips trembled as she looked at her new charges. Alys suddenly remembered the round, rosy faces of her young stepsisters, well-fed and warmly clad. These children, scabby-faced and runny-nosed, were barefoot and dressed in ragged garments that fitted where they touched. The baby, puny and yellow-skinned, was wrapped in no more than a bit of old sheet.

'He needs milk,' Elizabeth, the eldest girl, said in a frightened whisper. 'But when I asked Bessy, she slapped my legs . . . '

'No one shall slap you any more,' said

166

Alys, but the child obviously didn't believe her, for she cowered and flinched when Cecily tried to put her arms round her. The younger children just stared, round-eyed, and the baby set up a weak, fretful wailing.

'Dear God, Cecily,' said Alys, through clenched teeth, 'where do we start?'

Cecily drew a deep breath.

'First, warmth,' she said practically. 'We must have a fire in the nursery, these poor mites are half-frozen! We'll heat a big tub of water, wash them, and burn the rags they have on. There must be more clothes somewhere, and blankets too.'

Cecily flew about, collecting wood from the store in the yard, lighting a fire, heating water. Alys, exploring, found two dusty chests of children's clothes, and some grown-up garments that could be cut down for the older girls. Together, the girls washed the children, dressed them, then used the water to wash the filthy bed-linen, and last of all, the nursery floor. Then, damp and exhausted, Alys went downstairs to see what could be found to make a nourishing supper for them. She found Dame Margery wrapped in a huge apron, stirring a pot of something savoury over the kitchen fire.

'Did you ever see such a household, Alys? What would have happened if we had not come?' she said. 'This', she indicated the pot, 'is rabbit stew. Stringy old rabbits and withered vegetables were all that foolish Tibby could find in the market. There's no flour in the bins to make bread. Mary had to buy some, and poor stuff it looks to me . . . '

'It will be a better meal than those children have eaten in weeks,' said Alys. 'We've got them cleaned up, Dame Margery, and Cecily is braiding the girl's hair. We'll need to find a wet-nurse for the baby, he needs milk . . . '

'Woman nex' door, Mistress Compton, she'd a baby in arms,' put in Tibby, Dame Margery's maidservant. 'I saw her in market. She'd mebbe give this little 'un suck, an' all.'

Dame Margery nodded.

'See to it, Alys,' she said. 'Or . . . no, I'll speak to Mistress Compton, while you feed the children.'

Alys, toiling wearily back to the nursery with bowls of savoury rabbit stew, thought that she had never felt so tired in her life. Dame Margery was right, she thought, we arrived not a moment too soon!

'Come, children,' she said brightly, as she went into the nursery, warm and cheery now, with a glowing fire. 'I've brought you some supper!'

Elizabeth came forward hesitantly, but the others huddled in a corner like frightened kittens. Poor little mites, Alys thought, they've never known true kindness. Sighing, she handed a spoon to Cecily and the girls began the long, slow task of coaxing the children to eat.

Two or three weeks of back-breaking work turned John Stillington's neglected house into a comfortable home, 'fit for a Christian family' as Dame Margery said proudly. It was a bleak, snowy evening, and she, Alys and Cecily sat as close as they could to the fire, stitching yet more clothes for the children. Although she was grateful to Dame Margery and her brother, and was beginning to feel fond of the children, Alys was also starting to feel restless. The never-ending sewing bored her to tears. If only I still had Joliet, she thought longingly, a good gallop through the forest would blow the cobwebs away.

She heaved a sigh and Cecily looked up. 'What is it, Alys?'

Alys immediately felt guilty. After all, she thought, without Dame Margery, Cecily and I would be begging in the snow for our bread! And I would not wish to be travelling north in this weather, anyway. But oh, Tom, Tom, where are you? Shall I ever see you again?

'Oh . . . nothing,' she said, picking up the nightgown she was hemming and stabbing the needle into the fabric, pricking her thumb in the process and letting out a squeal of pain.

'You don't care for sewing, Alys?' twinkled Dame Margery.

'Well . . . well, er, not as much as Cecily does. And she's far better at it than I am,' Alys admitted.

'Give it to me,' said Dame Margery. 'You might run upstairs to the nursery, and see what the children are about. Tibby and Mary are with them, and Mistress Compton took Sally and the baby with her next door. My legs aren't as young as yours!'

Alys needed no second telling. She laid down her sewing and ran up the newly-polished wooden staircase to the nursery, marvelling at the difference Dame Margery's orderly housekeeping methods

170

had made. Meals were tasty and served on time, rooms and closets swept, laundry washed, bread baked, and the children were beginning to lose their pinched, fretful look and romp and play just like any other children. Little William had even given her and Cecily a hug last night as they tucked him up in bed with his brothers. Yes, all's well here, thought Alys, with a sudden glow of satisfaction. And we have helped to make it happen, Cecily and I! Perhaps, in a few weeks, when the days are a little warmer, I could mention our journey north to Dame Margery . . .

She opened the nursery door and peered inside. Mary, the maid, sat by the fire with little Elizabeth, showing her how to make neat stitches with thick woollen thread. Judith, her younger sister, watched, while Edward and young John played with a mongrel puppy in a corner of the room. Tibby was bending over the boy's bed. At first, Alys thought she was tidying it, but then she saw young William lying under the covers.

'Oh, Mistress Alys, I'm right glad you come,' babbled Tibby. 'Young William here, he won't wake up, I be afeared for 'en!'

'Why, what's wrong?' said Alys, more puzzled than alarmed. 'Did he eat too much supper and give himself a belly-ache? He seemed well enough last night.'

Tibby shook her head, and there was fear on her usually placid face.

'I'm afeared,' she repeated.

Swiftly, Alys crossed the room and bent over William, laying her hand on his forehead. It was burning hot, and the little boy's breathing was laboured. Alys's heart began to pound. She could tell that something was badly wrong. She pulled the covers aside and drew back William's shirt. His chest was a mass of scarlet spots. Alys gasped.

'Oh, what is it?' cried Tibby.

Alys shook her head.

'I know not. Some spotted fever. Pray God 'tis but a childish ailment, and nothing serious! Mary, run down and tell Dame Margery that William is sick. Then . . . then bring a basin of water, and some clean rags. We must try and get his fever down, poor mite.'

With a frightened look at William, Mary fled, her apron over her nose and mouth. Alys felt almost as frightened herself. She wished she had the kind nun, Sister

Benedicta, to consult, or even Dame Eleanor at the Manor with her foul-tasting cures. What had she given Joanna and Katherine when they fell ill of a fever? She couldn't remember.

Dame Margery came in, followed by Cecily and Mary, who lingered in the doorway, peering into the nursery with frightened eyes. The other children fell silent. Dame Margery took one look at William and nodded.

' 'Tis the scarlet sickness. God forbid they should all take it,' she muttered. 'It can kill little ones, especially feeble little ones like these . . . '

'What can we do? Is there any cure?' said Cecily fearfully.

'Some swear by honey-water, others say that if you place a four-leaf clover, picked by the full moon, on the pillow, the child will recover,' said Dame Margery. 'We can but care for him as best we may and . . . Alys, run next door and ask Mistress Compton if she can keep Sally and Joseph alongside her little ones. Say we've sickness here, fever . . . '

And so the nightmare began. William, his eyes bright with fever and knowing no one, tossed and turned and babbled nonsense, his thin little body pouring sweat and his skin seeming to peel away in great strips. Alys, Cecily and Dame Margery took it in turns to sit with him, sponging his forehead, trying to force nourishing broth between his lips, soothing him when he cried out in pain. Meanwhile, there were the other children to care for, meals to cook and linen to wash. John Stillington, a posy of herbs held to his nose as a precaution against infection, stood in the doorway as his sister and her helpers fought to save his little boy's life.

'I shall pray for him, for you all,' he called.

'Useless great lump. Just like a man!' scolded Dame Margery, but although her voice had lost none of its briskness, her eyes were anxious, for Elizabeth and Judith were complaining of sore throats, and when Cecily undressed Edward for bed she saw the tell-tale red spots on his body too.

Alys was snatching a few hours much-needed sleep when there was a pounding at her door. She was awake in an instant.

'What is it?' she cried, and Dame

Margery burst in, her hair in two long, greying braids down her back and a swaddled bundle in her arms.

' 'Tis the baby ... 'tis Joseph,' she gasped. 'Mistress Compton has brought him home. She said he seemed listless, and wouldn't take his milk, and now ... '

She unwrapped the tiny, waxen body from its garments and put a finger to the child's pale lips. It did not move.

'Does ... does he still breathe?' muttered Alys, her teeth chattering.

Dame Margery laid the baby down on the bed, her eyes full of tears. She shook her head sadly.

'He's gone, Alys. Gone to join his mother and the blessed saints in Paradise, poor, innocent creature!'

Alys stared for a moment at the pale little body. Dead, she thought. Dead before he even had a chance to live, like my mother's babies, poor little things!

Dame Margery had gathered the baby's body in her arms.

'I must tell his father,' she said. 'Alys, go up to the nursery and tell Cecily to come down and get some rest.'

Alys nodded wearily and began to climb the stairs. That poor baby, she thought, too small and weak to survive a fever . . . and the others, William, Elizabeth, will they die too? Will they all die?

She crossed herself as she opened the nursery door, and then couldn't help smiling as she saw Cecily, fast asleep in her chair. Young William seemed to be breathing more easily, although Elizabeth tossed and turned restlessly still.

'Cecily,' Alys whispered, 'go and get some rest! I'll watch the children.'

Cecily did not stir, so Alys went over and shook her gently. Her skin felt burning hot. Fear gripped Alys like a vice. Surely Cecily hadn't taken the fever too? But then her sister's eyes opened. They looked unnaturally bright.

'Why, Alys,' she said, in a high little voice quite unlike her own, 'what do you here? 'Tis hot! 'Tis so hot . . . I feel strange!'

She tried to rise, swayed, put out a hand to steady herself, swayed again, and before Alys's horrified eyes, pitched forward on to the floor.

8

February 1471

Alys sat beside the bed where her sister tossed and muttered, her hair matted with sweat and her eyes fever-bright. Now and again she moistened Cecily's dry, cracked lips with a little wine, and laid fresh, cool cloths against her burning forehead. The stuffy little room smelled of woodsmoke and sickness, but Alys was too exhausted to care. For seven long days and seven long nights she had hardly left her sister's side. She felt as though she had been in that room for ever, changing Cecily's sweat-soaked linen, forcing honey and parsley juice between her lips, soothing her cries of pain, and willing her to get well.

'You *shall* not die, Cecily! I won't let you die,' she murmured, over and over. 'And when you're well, we're going to Yorkshire, to Tom's house. Tom and I are going to find you the handsomest knight in the North of England to be your husband. I promise, Cecily. If you'll only get well . . . '

Sometimes, during the long, dark nights, she fancied that Cecily knew she was there, even in the depths of her fever. She sat for hours holding the hot, limp hands in hers. Once, she thought she felt an answering squeeze of her fingers. Mostly, her sister seemed to be in another world, pain-racked and fever-filled. Alys thought about the Manor, about growing up with Cecily. They had squabbled sometimes, as sisters do, but they had always been there for each other, enduring Dame Eleanor's scoldings, their mother's remarriage, beatings from their stepfather, comforting each other . . .

'I never knew . . . I never realized how much I love her,' she had wept to Dame Margery, when Cecily first became ill.

'I know. I know. 'Tis hard, to lose a loved one. My own dear sister died in childbed when she was little older than Cecily,' Dame Margery sighed. 'God rest her soul. 'Tis a cruel world, Alys. But while there's life, there's hope, and Cecily is strong. We must pray that she recovers.'

Dame Margery herself was thinner than ever, worn out with nursing the children while Alys cared for Cecily. The maidservant Mary had fled in terror of catching the sickness herself, and was assumed to have run away to London. That only left Tibby, good-natured and willing, but slow. Mistress Compton next door sent word that they had the fever there too, and little Sally, John Stillington's two-year-old daughter, died not long after her baby brother, along with two of Mistress Compton's brood.

'Praise be, the other children seem to be recovering,' Dame Margery told Alys, dabbing her eyes. 'William is thin and fretful, but his fever is gone. Elizabeth ate some chicken broth today, and young Edward was always less ill than the others. John and Judith have not yet sickened, I pray they may escape altogether.'

John Stillington was even persuaded to send for a physician to see if he could help. He came, a thin, stooped figure in a dirty black robe patterned with moons and stars, foul-breathed and unkempt.

'Hmm,' he said, peering short-sightedly at Cecily. 'Under what sign was the maiden born? When is her birthday?'

'October,' said Alys, amazed that he should ask such a question. She had hoped that this learned man, who was being well-paid for his trouble, would be able to offer sensible advice, maybe mix up a herbal potion to soothe Cecily's fever or an ointment for her burning skin. Instead, he peered and poked and prodded, murmured a lot of gibberish about the Moon's aspects and Virgo rising, and finally suggested that Alys find a pair of toads and place them beneath Cecily's bed to draw the fever downwards.

'And she must neither ear nor drink while they are there, for 'tis well known that toads poison the air all round them,' he said gravely.

Dame Margery and Alys exchanged glances, and neither was sorry to see him go.

'Toads, indeed!' sniffed Dame Margery. 'The man's a quack, with no more knowledge of nursing the sick than . . . than a sheep!'

'Indeed, no,' sighed Alys.

She did her best to make Cecily comfortable, persuading her to sip wine for strength and nourishing broth to build her up. And then, one night, the crisis came. Cecily had been especially restless, crying out in pain and throwing off her bed-covers, muttering that she was 'on fire, and burning up!'

'Hush, Cecily, hush,' Alys said automatically, wiping the hot forehead again and pulling the covers back over her sister. Everyone knew that night air was unwholesome, especially for the sick. Cecily began to cough and choke, every breath an effort. Tears rolled down Alys's cheeks at the sight of her sister's suffering. When the painful, hacking cough eased a little, she held a cup of wine to Cecily's lips. Cecily took a sip, but most of the liquid seemed to run out from between her parted lips and down her neck, staining her nightdress like blood.

There's nothing more I can do for her, Alys thought bleakly. Perhaps I should have gone out searching for toads to place under her bed, or a four-leaf clover, picked beneath the full moon. I've tried everything else I know, everything Dame Margery knows, and still my sister is dying!

When a voice called her name, she thought at first that she was dreaming. Light-headed with exhaustion, she looked up and saw that Cecily was smiling at her.

'Alys?' she said. 'What has happened? I feel . . . '

'Hush,' said Alys, her heart in her mouth. 'You have been very ill, Cecily. You took the fever, from the children, don't you remember?'

Cecily sank back among the pillows with a little sigh. The hectic flush was gone from her cheeks and the fingers that felt for Alys's were icy cold. With an exclamation, Alys pulled the covers over her sister and rushed to bank up the fire. When she returned, Cecily was lying on her side, a faint smile on her pale lips. The harsh, painful breathing had quietened and beads of sweat stood on her brow.

Oh, no, Alys thought, this is the end . . .

She laid her head down on her folded arms and began to cry.

Just then the door opened and Dame Margery bustled in.

'What's to-do here? Alys, are you asleep?' she cried. Then she bent over Cecily with an exclamation. Alys raised tormented eyes from the bed.

'Is she . . . is she . . . ?' she murmured, unable to say the word.

'Is she what?' came Dame Margery's reassuring voice. 'The fever has broken, praise be! Look how cool she is, how pale her skin! This is just how it was with William, and young Elizabeth. She has turned the corner now, thanks to your good nursing, Alys!'

Alys stared at Dame Margery as though she couldn't believe her eyes.

'You . . . you mean she isn't dead? Isn't dying? But I thought . . . '

Dame Margery put her arms round her.

'Dead? Dying? Of course she isn't! I tell you, she will recover! Look how sweetly she sleeps!'

Through a blur of tears, Alys saw that her sister was, indeed, not sleeping the restless sleep of fever, but refreshing, natural sleep. Thanks be to God and His blessed Mother, she thought gratefully. The crisis is past, and Cecily will live!

'How . . . how are the children, Dame Margery?' she asked.

'Fairly,' said Dame Margery. 'There is still no sign of sickness on John and Judith, and the others are recovering fast. I never saw such appetites! But, Alys, you must rest now. Tibby will sit with Cecily, and I have a new maid-servant, Lizzy, to help me. I hope she will be more loyal than that feckless Mary! Come, child, to bed with you, or I shall have you sick, too!'

Alys didn't need telling twice. Now that she knew Cecily was going to be all right, she realized how tired she was, so tired that all she wanted to do was fall into bed and sleep and sleep and sleep. She hardly felt Dame Margery's arms go round her, helping her from the sickroom to her own bedchamber, where she peeled off her stained gown and grubby shift, dressed her in a fresh nightdress that smelled of dried herbs, and tucked her in between blessedly cool, scented sheets.

Alys slept. She slept so long and so deeply that she couldn't remember where she was or what had happened, when she woke up. A pale, wintery sun was creeping through the window as she lay blinking drowsily and wondering whether it had all been a foul dream — sickness, a dead baby, Cecily . . .

Dame Margery's new maid, Lizzy, a bouncing rosy-cheeked wench with arms like hams and a gap-toothed freckled face, came into the room with a mug of spiced ale, bread, and a dish of stewed plums.

'Here you are, my dear. Lord, but you've slept! Not that it's any wonder, the time you've had with them bairns and your poor sister,' she said cheerfully. 'Come, eat, you've got to keep your strength up.'

'How is my sister? How is Cecily?' Alys demanded.

'Weak as a newborn kitten, dearie, but she'll live,' said Lizzy reassuringly. 'That scarlet sickness is a terrible thing, I had 'un as a bairn, and two of my brothers died of 'un. Makes you weak for a time, it does, but don't you fret, your sister'll be as good as new in a week or two. Young William, he was first to go down with 'un from what I hear, and now he's as rampageous as any young lad ever was! Come on, sup your ale, my dear, and try these plums, they're sweetened with honey and cinnamon . . . '

Alys suddenly realized she was ravenously hungry. She'd had neither time nor appetite for her meals when she was tending the children and Cecily.

'And the other children? Elizabeth? Young Edward? How are they?' she asked as she sampled the good, fresh bread Dame Margery had sent up.

'Pale and feeble, but mending fast,' was Lizzy's reply. ' 'Twas a shame the baby died, and the other little lass too, but 'tis a miracle that five of the children were spared. I've seen these fevers sweep through a nursery-full of bairns and carry 'em all off, one after another. Master John Stillington is a lucky man. Luck, and good nursing, that's what saved 'em. I only hope he's grateful to you, Mistress Alys!'

'Grateful? To me?' echoed Alys, bewildered. To her, John Stillington was a shadowy, colourless figure. She gave little thought to him one way or another!

'Yes, you and your sister and Dame Margery between you saved those children's lives,' said Lizzy. 'I've eyes in my head, Mistress Alys, and I'm a local girl. There was tales told about Master Stillington's household long before Dame Margery arrived to take charge — and not before time, either! The steward, he was a drunken oaf, and Bessy the nursemaid no better than she should be, leaving the bairns half-starved. I tell you, Mistress Alys, I wouldn't have cared to take it on, like Dame Margery did, no, nor you neither, and you not even kin to the family . . . '

'Dame Margery has been kind to us. It was the least we could do,' Alys protested, blushing.

'Well, if it weren't for you, those bairns 'ud be dead,' said Lizzy bluntly. ' 'Twas your good food and care gave 'em the strength to fight the fever, I don't doubt. Master Stillington has plenty to thank you for, if he's a mind to!'

Alys drained her mug of ale and said nothing. Lizzy is right, though, she thought, without us, the children would have died. 'Tis good to know we helped to save their lives!

As soon as she had dressed, she went to see Cecily. She found her sister sitting up in bed, drinking chicken broth. She was white and thin, but her eyes lit up when she saw Alys. The two girls clung to one another for a moment and Alys tried hard not to weep. I seem to do nothing but weep these days, she told herself crossly.

'Thank you for looking after me, Alys,' said Cecily. 'Dame Margery told me you never left my bedside. That was good of you . . . '

'Oh, nonsense, you'd have done the same for me,' said Alys, rather ungraciously. 'I was afraid for you . . . '

'I know. Dame Margery told me that Sally and the baby, and two of Mistress Compton's little ones died, God rest their souls,' said Cecily seriously. 'But the other children are mending, I hear. Young William has been in to see me already! I shall be sad when we have to leave the children and go north again.'

'Don't think about that yet,' said Alys, wondering how long it would be before Cecily was strong enough to travel. Now that the fever had passed and she could make plans again, she couldn't help wondering how they were to get to Broughton Hall. Without horses, they would have to walk, but how were they to manage without money? Perhaps if we stay in nunneries, or offer to wash the pots in taverns, she thought, but without much hope. We could sleep in barns or under hedgerows, like beggars, but we shall need a few pennies for food. Unless we steal it . . .

Round and round went her thoughts, as she cared for the children, helped with the cooking and baking and brewing, sewed and stitched and mended, and watched Cecily grow strong and well again. The fever had changed her, though. She had lost weight, and was almost as tall as Alys. She's not my little sister any more, Alys thought.

Then, one day in March, when daffodils danced in the garden and everyone from the kitchen boys to Dame Margery tripped around light-hearted, feeling that the long dreary winter days might be ending at last, Lizzy came into the nursery with a message for Alys.

'The master wants to see you,' she said.

'Master John wants to see me? But why?' Alys asked. He didn't usually take any notice of her, or Cecily, and he had certainly never asked to see her before. Perhaps he wants us to leave, Alys thought fearfully as she tidied her hair and tried to hide a grease-spot on her gown. She and Cecily were in a strange position in the Stillington household. They worked too hard to be guests, yet they were not exactly servants, like Lizzy and Tibby.

John Stillington sat in his great carved chair on the raised platform at one end of the hall. Dame Margery sat beside him, an inscrutable expression on her face. Remembering her manners, Alys dropped a polite curtsey.

'You wished to see me, Master John?' she said formally.

'Er . . . yes,' the wool merchant said, peering at her in his short-sighted way.

189

Not for the first time, Alys wondered how a prosperous and successful man could seem so vague and almost dim-witted.

'Yes, Lady Alys,' he said. 'I sent for you so that I could thank you. My sister, here, has told me what you and . . . er . . . er . . . '

'Cecily,' hissed Dame Margery, loudly enough for Alys to hear.

'Er . . . yes, Cecily. What you and Cecily have done for my family,' he went on. 'You nursed my children, William, Elizabeth and young Edward, through the fever, at great risk to yourselves. You shall know my gratitude.'

'Sir,' Alys protested, 'I could do nothing else! You and your sister were good enough to take us in when we were cold and hungry and had lost everything we owned in the world to outlaws. Caring for the children was the least we could do!'

'Nevertheless,' said Master John, 'I am grateful. Dame Margery tells me you have helped run my household, too, ever since you came.'

'I would have been lost without them,' added Dame Margery.

Alys felt a glow of pleasure. She and Cecily *had* worked hard.

'I understand you were travelling north, to relatives in Yorkshire,' Master John went on.

'That's right,' said Alys, her heart beating fast. 'Our . . . er . . . our relatives live in Broughton Hall, not far from York.'

Master John nodded.

'Well, my friend Ned Herring, who, in spite of his name, is a wool merchant like myself,' he chuckled, leaving Alys amazed that he had actually made a *joke*, 'will be travelling north to Stamford next week. He has agreed to take you with him, and I am prepared to give you a purse of money for your journey onwards, in recognition of all you have done for me and mine!'

Alys felt stunned. She had certainly not expected such generosity. Master Stillington had seemed a dry old stick, with no strong feelings for anyone, not even his children. It was Dame Margery who had wept over the still little bodies of Sally and Joseph, Dame Margery who had rejoiced with Alys and Cecily when the other children recovered. John Stillington had left his children to the none-too-tender mercies of Bessy, the cruel nursemaid, so Alys had assumed he didn't care.

Now it seemed that she was wrong.

'Why . . . why, that's very generous of you, sir,' she faltered, dropping another curtsey. 'I . . . I didn't know how we were to continue our journey, with no horses and no money.'

'Ned Herring has a train of pack-ponies,' said Master John. 'And there is sure to be someone York-bound from Stamford. You will not need to travel alone.'

Alys shook her head, still finding it hard to believe that she was being offered a solution to all her difficulties. Impulsively, she flung her arms around Dame Margery, hugging her tight.

'How can I ever thank you?' she exclaimed.

'Enough, child,' tutted Dame Margery, straightening her head-dress, which Alys's hug had knocked askew. 'I'm sorry to be losing you, and your sister. 'Tis true what my brother says, you've been a great help to me. Tell me, can you write?'

'A little,' said Alys, bewildered. 'My brother's tutor showed Cecily and me how to read, and some writing too, though I have little chance to practise the art. Why do you ask?'

'Because, when you get to your relatives

in Yorkshire, I want you to write me a letter,' said Dame Margery. 'Then I will know that all is well with you. No more fevers, or brawls with vagabonds along the way!'

Alys blushed.

'Of course I will send word, I promise,' she said.

The next day, Alys and Cecily met Ned Herring, a bluff, hearty man, over six feet tall and built like a barrel, and liked him at once.

'I had not thought to travel in such fair company,' he roared, pinching Cecily's cheek, but so good-naturedly that she could not take offence. 'I've a couple of sturdy fellows travelling with us, too, so ye need not worry about beggars or outlaws, young ladies, Ned Herring is a match for 'em all!'

'I don't doubt it,' grinned Alys, thinking that it would be a brave outlaw indeed who would dare to tackle a man of Ned Herring's size and build.

The whole Stillington household turned out to see Alys and Cecily leave. There were tears in Dame Margery's black eyes, Tibby wept openly, and little William set up such a roaring that Lizzy threatened to take him inside. There was a lump in Alys's throat as she kissed all the children and hugged Dame Margery, while Cecily dabbed at her eyes.

'Fare well Alys, Cecily, God go with you both. Don't forget to send word when you're safe in Yorkshire,' cried Dame Margery, as the girls mounted their sturdy little ponies and rode away, accompanied by one of Ned Herring's burly apprentices.

'Fare well!' cried Alys, while Cecily could do nothing but weep. However, by the time they had joined the long, slow line of pack-ponies and made their way out of Bedford town and towards the Great North Road, Cecily had cheered up and begun to look around her with interest. The ponies, slow patient beasts loaded with bolts of good woollen cloth, picked their way carefully along the rutted pathways. The sun shone, a gentle breeze blew, and Alys felt excitement begin to uncurl, deep within her. At last, she thought, at last we're travelling north again, and every mile brings me closer to Tom's home! My love, my darling, will he be there? Does he think of me, remember me, as I think of him?

The silver rose pendant lay warm against her skin, beneath the blue gown Dame Margery had given her. Travelling with Ned Herring, she felt no need to disguise herself as a boy, though she kept Jack's shirt, jerkin and breeches rolled into a bundle in her saddle-bag, just in case!

She turned to say something to Cecily when she heard a booming bass voice raised in song.

'Hey, ho, fair Spring is here
Men and maids, be of good cheer,
With a lusty wench and a barrel of beer,
Sing ho, sing hey!'

Alys couldn't help giggling, and Cecily joined in. A moment later Ned Herring rode up alongside them, still singing, his round red face wreathed in smiles.

' 'Tis a fair day for a journey,' he observed. 'We'll spend the night in a tavern I know. The landlord's a rogue but an honest one, unless you young ladies would prefer to stay with the nuns? I believe there's a small religious house not far from the road, not that I've had any use for it, you understand, holy women not being my style!'

He winked and grinned at Alys, who smiled back.

'I'm sure the tavern will be fine,' she assured him.

'It's agreeable to feel safe and protected on the road, isn't it?' Cecily observed. 'I wish Ned Herring was travelling further than Stamford, on to York perhaps.'

'Oh, we'll soon find another party of northbound travellers,' said Alys easily. 'This is a busy road, look how many parties have passed us, just this morning.'

It was true, the Great North Road did seem busy, with wool-trains like their own, lone riders on fast horses, a group of nuns singing a psalm as they walked along, a pedlar loaded with ribbons and laces, a drover and his lad with a flock of sheep. Once, a group of mounted soldiers rode southward, spurs and swords jingling. Alys looked at them with a pang, wondering whose men they were with the red-and-gold blazon on their shields. One of them, blond-haired and with blue eyes, stared and smiled at her. Alys lowered her eyes modestly, but her heart was thumping. He didn't really look like Tom, but there was something about him, a quirk of the eyebrow, something in his smile, that reminded her, and she felt a stab of longing. God keep you, my love, wherever you are, she thought.

They spent a comfortable night in the tavern Ned Herring had recommended, where the landlord's wife was a motherly soul who tut-tutted over the two girls travelling all the way to far-off Yorkshire.

'Riding to strangers in the North Country!' she marvelled, never having left her native village in her life. 'I wish you Godspeed, my dears. I've roasted my best fowl today, so make a hearty breakfast, won't you?'

How kind people can be, Alys thought.

Both she and Cecily were stiff and saddle-sore when they rode into Stamford that evening. It was a fair small town, the buildings of honey-coloured stone which Ned Herring told them was the local style. This time they put up at a much larger, wayside inn, the courtyard a bustle of ponies, barking dogs, busy stable-lads and shouting servants. The landlady, a harassed-looking woman with a baby at her hip and another child clinging to her skirts, showed the girls to a small, but clean bedchamber under the eaves, after they had taken leave of Ned Herring.

' 'Tis the Market Fair tomorrow, that's why we're so busy,' she explained wearily.

'When you've rested and supped, ladies, you might care to go out and join the merrymakers. 'Tis safe enough, if you don't stay out too late; there are fights and broken heads late at night when the apprentices have been drinking all day! They say there's a troupe of travelling players; mummers, tumblers, jugglers, I know not. Gypsies, most like, from some far-off heathen place . . . '

'Thank you, but we're journey-tired. We'll sup quietly in our room, and then rest for the night,' said Alys, looking at Cecily's white face.

'As you wish,' said the landlady. 'I'll send the girl up with your supper.'

After a good night's sleep, both girls felt refreshed, and decided to take a look at the Market Fair before asking at the tavern if there were any more northbound travellers.

'In truth, I'm impatient to get to Yorkshire now,' Alys admitted. 'It could be another week's riding, and, oh, Cecily you don't know how I long for news of Tom!'

Cecily squeezed her hand sympathetically.

Stamford was teeming with people and animals, its narrow streets crammed with a chattering, mostly good-natured throng. With no real idea where they were going, the girls followed the crowd until they came to an open square, where a stage was being erected with much hammering, cursing, and helpful comments from the bystanders. Alys heard music coming from one side, and attracted by the sound, wandered over to see who was making it.

A girl, about her own age or perhaps a little older, sat strumming a stringed instrument and singing in a low, sweet voice. Alys couldn't understand the words, but the sad tune and the feeling in the young singer's voice brought tears to her eyes. When the song finished, she couldn't help clapping.

'Why, thank you!' said the girl, jumping up and spreading her scarlet skirts in an exotic curtsey. She was small, slim and dark, with inky-black hair and a nut-brown skin. She looked and sounded foreign.

'That was beautiful, mistress,' said Alys, and Cecily, behind her, nodded. 'Where did you learn to sing like that? You're nor from around here, are you?'

The girl laughed, a sound like chiming bells.

'Indeed I am not,' she grinned, showing milk-white teeth. 'Today Stamford, tomorrow Lincoln, then York, then it's the wide world for Katrin . . . '

'Katrin. Is that your name?' said Cecily, intrigued by the foreigner's beauty and talent.

'It is. Katrin the singer. My name is known from fair France to wild Ireland. King's court, palace, or Market Fair, 'tis all the same to me,' she said.

'But where were you born? Who are your family?' Alys enquired.

Katrin shrugged.

'Born? By the side of the road somewhere, I know not. My mother didn't survive the experience long enough to tell me of it,' she said carelessly. 'And, as to my family, 'tis all around me. Players and gypsies, they are my family and always have been. Now, if you'll excuse me, young ladies, I have work to do!'

She smiled, curtseyed again, and disappeared into the crowd.

'We must come out later and hear her again,' chattered Cecily, as she and Alys moved through the crowded booths of the market. Everything from live fowls to cheeses, ribbons and cloth to gingerbread

200

men, seemed to be on sale, and pedlars, farmers' wives and stallholders competing with one another to see who could shout the loudest!

'I'd like that. Her voice was beautiful. She . . . ' began Alys. Then she stopped, looked, stared . . . and looked again.

'Alys? What's amiss?' said Cecily curiously.

Alys turned to her sister, her face chalk-white.

'Cecily,' she muttered through chattering teeth, 'look, over there. Who's that?'

Cecily looked. There, pushing their way impatiently through the crowds, unmistakable in travel-stained jerkins, were two men she had hoped never to see again. Their stepfather's cronies, the Lancastrian spies, the weasel-faced Frenchman and Robert Saville!

9

March 1471

Alys's first thought was to turn and run, to put as much distance as she could between herself and Cecily and the two Lancastrians. Her heart was pounding and her legs seemed to have turned to jelly. White-faced, she ducked down behind the brightly-painted booth of a gingerbread-seller. A moment later, Cecily joined her.

'It . . . it *is* them, isn't it?' Alys muttered through chattering teeth.

Cecily peered out cautiously.

'Yes, it's Saville and his crony, right enough. I'd know that weasel-faced Frenchman anywhere!' she said viciously. 'Oh, Alys, I'm scared! How could they possibly have known where we were? We've come so far, been through so much . . . I swear I would die if we were dragged back to the Manor now, to face one of Sir Hugh's beatings . . . '

'Not to mention my so-called husband-to-be, that fat oaf Sir Henry Capshaw,' said Alys, her teeth gritted. 'You're right, Cecily, they must not catch us. They must not even see us or suspect that we have seen them. We shall have to go back to the inn at once, and decide what to do from there. There may even be a party of travellers going north today. We could join them, and be away long before Saville and his friend start asking at the inns for us!'

Stealthily, the two girls crept away from the marketplace, using all the back-alleys they could find, glancing behind them every few moments to make sure they weren't being followed. When they reached the inn they looked around carefully, but Robert Saville and the Frenchman were nowhere to be seen. They hurried up the stairs to the little room under the eaves and collapsed on the rough, straw-stuffed mattress, feeling weak with relief.

'We're safe enough here, for the moment at least,' said Alys. 'Oh, Cecily, I can't tell you how I felt when I saw those two. I thought my heart was going to stop beating!'

'Thank God they didn't spot us first,' said Cecily fervently. 'Or it would have been all up with us, and we'd be bound in the back of some waggon and on our way back to Hertfordshire by now!'

'Aye, 'twas a lucky escape,' said Alys, frowning.

'What is it, sister?' Cecily asked.

Alys was silent for a moment. Then she spoke.

'Cecily,' she said thoughtfully, 'we're being foolish. Foolish, and wrong!'

'Wrong?'

Alys grabbed her sister's hands.

'Don't you see? Saville and Weasel-face aren't looking for us! They never were!'

'But how can you know that?'

'Because there's no way, no possible way, that they could have known we would be in Stamford today! Think about it, sister. The only person at the Manor who knew where we were going was Jack the stable-boy. Even if our stepfather suspected him, and beat him until he confessed, all that he could say was that we were heading for Yorkshire on horseback. If we hadn't had our horses stolen by those outlaws, if you hadn't had the fever, we should have been there weeks ago! If Sir Hugh had really troubled himself to send someone to look for us — and it's my belief he would be more likely to say 'good riddance' to us both — he would send them to Yorkshire, not Lincolnshire!'

'Then why are they here?' Cecily demanded.

'Who knows? But we *do* know that they are spies for Henry of Lancaster and his cause. Perhaps there is trouble in the North, some rising in favour of King Edward and the Yorkists, and Saville has been sent to these parts to spy!'

'I do believe you're right,' said Cecily slowly. ' 'Tis far more likely that they are here on Lancastrian business than that they're hunting for couple of runaways, and girls, at that!'

'I still think we should leave Stamford as soon as we can, though,' Alys added. 'While we are here, there's a chance they'll see us, and who knows what they might do? Sir Henry would reward them well, no doubt, if they returned me to him, bound and helpless.'

She began to tie up her few belongings into a bundle.

'Come, Cecily,' she said, 'let's go downstairs and see if we can find anyone going north to York. Or even Lincoln, Ned Herring said that Lincoln was the next large town. Someone might be heading

Lincoln-wards . . . '

'That singer was,' said Cecily.

'Singer?'

'Yes. What was her name? The foreign girl playing that strange-looking lute, with black hair and the beautiful voice.'

'Katrin!' said Alys. 'Yes, Katrin the singer! Lincoln, York, and the whole wide world, didn't she say? If we could travel with her, then even if Saville gets word we have been seen in Stamford, he'll not look for us with a troupe of travelling players! I pray we can find her, and that they will let us go with them! Wait, Cecily, before I go out again I'll put on Jack's jerkin and breeches again, and hide my hair beneath a hood, just in case.'

But the girls were lucky. When they went back to the market square, there was no sign of the two Lancastrians. After a few moments' anxious hunting they caught sight of Katrin sitting on a low wall, petting an enormous, strange-looking hound with rough yellow-brown fur and a great plume of a tail. She looked up at them, her eyes widening at the sight of Alys's breeches and hood.

'We meet again, young demoiselles — or should it be sir and mademoiselle?' she said. 'I regret, the performance is over for today. We are moving on, up to Lincoln town.'

'Y-yes, Mistress Katrin,' said Alys, feeling nervous. 'We . . . er, my sister and I want to go north. To Lincoln, and from there to York. Today, if possible.'

Katrin's eyebrows rose and she looked them up and down.

'Hmmm,' she said thoughtfully. 'You are in a hurry, aren't you? More of a hurry than you were this morning?'

'Yes. We . . . er . . . we need to leave sooner than we expected,' said Cecily.

To the girls' surprise, Katrin bent down to the yellow dog.

'What do you think, Rough? *Que penses-tu?*' she said, fondling the great beast's ears. 'Are these two rogues, vagabonds, thieves perhaps, who have made Stamford too hot to hold them?'

'Indeed we are not!' Cecily began indignantly, but Alys hushed her. Katrin continued to watch them, her black eyes expressionless. Then, quite suddenly, the great dog got up, shook himself and walked over to present a huge paw to Alys, and then to Cecily, in turn! Both girls shrank back at first, he was so big, and

207

fierce-looking, but then Alys seized his paw and shook it solemnly. After a moment's hesitation, Cecily did the same.

'Rough likes you, it seems,' Katrin said thoughtfully. 'Animals are better than people at deciding whom to trust, I find. We shall have to ask Hal, who heads the players, whether you can come with us, but as far as Rough and I are concerned, you're welcome! Now, what are your names?'

'I'm Cecily,' said Cecily.

'And I'm Alys. We're sisters,' said Alys.

'Cecily. And Alys, the maiden who dresses like a lad,' said Katrin dryly.

Alys felt herself blushing.

'Aye . . . well . . . these clothes are borrowed,' she explained. 'We thought it safer to travel as brother and sister at first.'

'It may be so. But if it is, you must choose another name than Alys!' said Katrin.

Alys grinned, liking the foreign singer more and more.

'When we're away from Stamford, I'll decide,' she promised. 'Either I'll put on a gown again, or call myself Peter or John or Matthew!'

Katrin slid down off her wall and,

followed by Rough, threaded her way through the crowds to where a tall man with a shock of yellow hair and a clean-shaven face seemed to be arguing with another, a plump fellow with sleek jowls, whose velvet doublet and chain of office proclaimed him mayor or perhaps alderman.

'Come, man. Pay us what you owe, what you promised,' said the yellow-haired man patiently.

'Times are hard. Stamford isn't a rich town, you know,' complained the other in a whining voice.

'Times may be hard, but there's one who doesn't starve himself,' muttered Katrin, with a pointed look at the man's large belly. Then, at a signal from the yellow-haired man, a huge, ugly fellow with arms like ham-shanks and a threatening expression stopped packing the stage and scenery into a waggon and moved forward to stand beside him, dwarfing him. The Mayor, if that was what he was, took one look at the beetle-browed giant, and went pale.

'Of course, of course. 'Twas a fine performance,' he muttered, shoving a leather money-bag into the blond man's outstretched hand. 'Thank you, Master . . . er . . . Hal. A fine performance . . . Stamford is honoured . . . '

Still muttering, he backed hastily away. The giant went back to his work and the yellow-haired man turned his attention to the three girls.

'Why do these so-called respectable citizens never agree to pay what they owe, until Ludo there looks at them?' he muttered, half to himself. 'Well-a-day, Katrin, what have we here? A likely lad and a fair young wench? Or . . . ?' he peered more closely at Alys.

Alys faced him fearlessly. He was older than she had thought at first, there were lines round his eyes and grey in his yellow hair. He looked weary, as if he had seen everything there was to see in the world, and had not been impressed. But it was a kind face, a face to trust.

'We are northbound travellers, good sir,' Alys said, 'and we'd like to leave with you, today. There's safety in numbers, we believe . . . '

'Indeed,' said Hal coolly. He looked at Katrin, who nodded.

'Rough likes them, Master Hal,' she said. Alys noted the respectful way she

210

spoke to him, and she had the feeling that Katrin didn't respect very many people.

'We don't take passengers,' said Hal warningly. 'If you come with us, you'll need to earn your keep. What can you do?'

'They are young ladies, perhaps they can sew?' Katrin put in.

Hal's serious face broke into a smile.

'Can you?' he asked. 'Our costumes, the ones we use in our plays, are almost falling apart, and we've no skilled needlewoman among us . . .'

'I can,' said Cecily. 'I'll happily mend your costumes for you.'

'And you?' Hal said to Alys, whose heart sank at the thought of spending even more time plying her hated needle. 'Twould be like being back at the Manor, or with Dame Margery, she thought desperately.

'My sister is better at other things,' said Cecily, with a giggle. 'She can cook, take care of children, nurse the sick . . . oh, and she has some musical skills . . .'

'Have you really?' said Katrin eagerly. 'Do you know English songs, Alys? I have learned a few, but I'd love to know more!'

'Then — Alys, is it? — shall teach you,' said Hal. 'Right, that's settled. We shall be ready to leave when Ludo and the lads have finished packing up this last waggon.'

'Who is Ludo?' Alys whispered to Katrin, as the three girls waited for the last of the bundles, wooden swords and shields, and brightly-painted pieces of scenery to be loaded on to one of the carts.

'Oh, don't mind him, he's harmless,' said Katrin carelessly. 'Hal just uses him to frighten people when they won't pay. He's useful to have around, strong as an ox but as gentle as a baby, and he adores Hal, for Hal is kind to him. 'Twas Hal who rescued him from some side-show. He was kept by an unkind master who used him to wrestle with bears or wild dogs or any fool or drunk who cared to challenge him. He was kept half-starved, like a brute beast, for his owner thought that made him more ferocious!'

'How terrible! The poor man! But why did he not escape?' said tender-hearted Cecily.

'He's simple in the head and cannot speak, only grunt,' said Katrin. 'How could he take care of himself? Anyway, Hal bought him, and now he lives with us, part of our family.'

'Hal seems a good man,' said Alys.

'He is. One of the best,' said Katrin. 'Then there's Walter, another one of the players, he's young and fair and takes all the girls' parts like Maid Marian and the Lady Guinevere, and the Bohemian tumblers, Joe, Joe and Matilda. Those aren't really their names, but none of us can get our tongues round their real names, and they speak neither English nor French, so all we do is smile at one another. Then there's Juan from Castile and his wife Juanita, and Carlos who taught me to play the *guitarra* . . . '

'The what?' said Alys and Cecily together.

'The *guitarra*, the instrument you saw me playing this morning. 'Tis plucked and strummed like a lute, but not quite the same, 'tis some new-styled instrument from Italy, or Castile perhaps, I don't think even Carlos knows, but it has a fair sound . . . '

'Indeed it does. I love music and singing, dancing too,' said Alys eagerly. For a moment, she imagined she was back at the Manor, listening to the minstrels play a merry tune at the time of the harvest-home, with Tom Taverner's warm hand in hers, and his sea-blue eyes gazing

213

down on her. That was the night of our very first kiss, thought Alys, with a sudden pang of longing. And here I am, among strangers, even though they are kindly strangers, and you, my own true love, where are you?

'Don't be sad, Alys,' said Katrin in her singsong voice.

'Sad?'

'There's sadness in you. Sadness, and love-longing, I can feel it. But you have no need to fear, all will in the end be well.'

Alys felt the hairs rise on the back of her neck.

'Can . . . can you tell fortunes, also, Mistress Katrin?' she asked breathlessly.

Katrin laughed

'I can . . . and I can't,' she said teasingly. 'You need not be a fortune-teller to know what it means when a young girl sighs, and looks wistful, as you did just then!'

Hal strode up to them, his fair hair ruffled by the keen wind which had just sprung up.

'We're all packed and ready to leave. A waggon, two carts, and two ponies,' he said. 'Come, Katrin, call that great hound of yours to heel, and we'll be off. It's farewell to Stamford and on to Lincoln.

Let's hope its citizens will give us fair welcome!'

The party made faster progress than Alys had expected, as they were used to walking. She and Cecily, being less hardened, took it in turns to ride in the jolting carts with the scenery and the players' belongings, though after being tossed around against the rough wooden sides, Cecily whispered to Alys that she would rather walk! At night they slept under the waggon, wrapped in their cloaks, huddled together for warmth, with Rough's big furry body providing both extra warmth and protection. Cecily was given a pile of tattered garments to mend, and Alys made a tasty stew out of two rabbits, some turnips and dried beans that Hal provided. The beans came from a sack in the cart, and if Alys suspected that the rabbits were poached, and the turnips stolen from one of the many farms they passed, she was too hungry to care!

After they had eaten, they sat round the embers of the fire, and Carlos and Katrin took turns to play the *guitarra* and sing. Carlos sang passionate melodies from his native Castile, Katrin sad, lilting songs from Provence and France. Both she and

215

Alys were quick learners, and on the second night they sang together, in English, the beautiful old song, 'Summer is a-coming in', their voices dipping, soaring and blending in perfect harmony. When they had finished, everyone clapped, Cecily loudest of all.

'In faith, you have a lovely voice, Mistress Alys,' said Walter, the young actor, admiringly. 'Katrin, you have a rival at last!'

Alys felt embarrassed. She already thought of Katrin as a friend, and wanted no rivalry or jealousy to come between them.

'Nonsense,' she said, 'I am but a beginner! I know nothing compared to Katrin. And think how wonderfully she plays! When I pick up the *guitarra*, it makes a sound like ... like a hog being slaughtered!'

Everyone laughed, including Katrin, and Alys relaxed again.

The girls' first sight in Lincoln town was a shock. No one had told them it was such a fair city, the cathedral and castle perched high on a hill, with a steep cobbled street lined with shops leading up to it.

'Goodness, Lincoln folks must be able

to fly!' gasped Cecily, dazzled, as they began the long climb to the castle yard where the players were planning to perform 'Robin Hood and Maid Marian', a lively, romantic tale that always went down well with the crowd. Ludo and the other men quickly set up the stage, and Alys helped her sister put the finishing touches to some of the costumes. Walter, as Maid Marian, wore a pink silk gown that had definitely seen better days, and a blonde wig that looked more like straw than hair. The first time she saw him, Alys couldn't help going off into a fit of giggles, and then wished she hadn't when he blushed dark red.

'Don't mock me, Alys, please!' he begged. 'You don't know what it's like, being fair of face like me, always forced to play the woman's part, while Hal is always the hero and Carlos or Juan the wicked villain!'

'I didn't mean to mock. And 'tis not you, Walter, 'tis the clothes,' she said truthfully. She liked Walter well enough. He was a silent young man rather given to sitting moodily in corners reciting his lines, while the other men did the heavy work, but he had always been nice to her, and even praised her singing!

'Could you not get a better wig? That one looks like a pie's nest! And I know when my sister was mending your gown, she said it was more hole than cloth in some places!'

'And where would I get a good silk gown? Only if we play to rich lords and ladies, in a castle or manor-house, and they have old clothes to spare,' said Walter sulkily.

Oh, dear, thought Alys, I've offended him. She didn't want to upset Walter, or any of her travelling companions for that matter, so she smiled kindly at him and said, 'Tell me about yourself, Walter! How do you come to be an actor? And what sort of parts do you want to play? Have you asked Hal? Perhaps you could play a gallant knight with sword and shield, set to rescue a fair lady from her evil guardian?'

'Oh, Alys, that's a wonderful idea,' cried Walter eagerly. 'Do you . . . do you know any stories like that? If we went to Hal, you and I together, and told him that we had devised a new play, he might listen to us! He often says he is weary of Robin Hood and Lancelot and the same old tales . . . '

It took Alys no more than a few moments to make up her story — not surprisingly, since it was her own!

'We could have a fair young maiden, forced by her wicked stepfather to marry a fat, ugly old knight, and rescued by her true love . . . ' she said.

Walter looked at her as though she had given him a gift beyond price.

'Oh, yes!' he breathed. 'Come, Alys, let's go and find Hal this minute, and see what he says!'

He held out his hand to help her to her feet, and didn't let it go. Alys felt embarrassed. It seemed ill-mannered to snatch her hand away, but she didn't want to face Hal hand-in-hand with Walter, as if they were sweethearts. She didn't care for the feel of Walter's hand anyway — so soft, so white, it was rather like holding hands with Cecily.

'Well? What is it, Walter?' Hal said, not unkindly, when they approached him. He was sitting at the back of one of the carts, painting a bright green tree on a piece of scenery.

'I . . . I've had an idea. Well, it was Alys's idea really. Well, both of us . . . ' stammered Walter, blushing again.

Hal raised one eyebrow.

'Yours and Alys's? Let's hear it then!' he commanded.

'It's . . . it's an idea for a new play. You said, you often say you're tired of the same old stories, well, we thought to tell the tale of a fair young maiden, forced into marriage by her evil stepfather, and rescued by a fair young knight,' said Walter.

'Indeed? And are there parts for all in this pretty tale?' said Hal.

'Why, yes,' replied Walter. 'Carlos could play the stepfather, you the husband, and me the fair young knight . . . '

His voice trailed away when he saw that Hal was trying not to laugh.

'I'm tired of playing wenches in shabby gowns,' he grumbled. ' 'Tis surely my turn to play a handsome knight, now I'm seventeen . . . '

'And I'm to play the ugly old husband, am I?' Hal said, amused. Then, to Walter and Alys's amazement, he went on, 'You're right, it would make a change from Robin Hood and Sir Lancelot! I quite fancy myself as an evil old lecher, lusting after some fair wench! Aha!' he growled, twisting his face into a horrible grimace,

220

so that Alys almost shuddered. Hal was a true actor, and there was something in that expression that reminded her of Sir Henry. If Cecily and I hadn't run away, I could have been married to him by now, she thought. Wed to that awful old man, or starving my days away in the gatehouse tower, with the rats and the spiders!

'But haven't you forgotten something?' Hal enquired. 'If you play the knight, who will play his lady? Juan, with his black beard? Juanita? You and she would not make convincing lovers, Juanita being twenty years older and several stone heavier then you! Matilda can tumble and juggle, but she's no actress, and the same goes for Katrin, though she sings like an angel . . . '

Walter was blushing fiery red again.

'I . . . I thought Alys might play the part,' he suggested.

'Me?' gasped Alys. She had truly never thought of such a thing. In all the plays she had ever seen — not that there were many — the girls' parts had always been played by young boys like Walter. Respectable young women, like Cecily and herself, would not have dreamed of getting up on to a stage in front of rowdy crowds of onlookers, who would pelt them with bad eggs, rotten fruit, or worse, if they didn't care for the performance!

'Oh, I couldn't! I truly couldn't!'

Hal shrugged.

'Without a heroine, I don't see how we can do this play,' he said. 'Though, 'tis an interesting idea . . . '

Walter was looking so crestfallen that Alys felt guilty. After all, she reasoned, there wouldn't be much for her to do, except shout 'Help!' 'Save me!' and the like. No one she knew would see her, or recognize her, in the shabby gown and strawlike wig. And anyway, why was she suddenly worried about being respectable? A young lady who had fled from her home disguised as a boy, faced outlaws on the road, nursed the sick, and travelled across half of England to find the man she loved, could hardly be described as respectable, anyway!

'Wait,' she said slowly. 'Perhaps, if I only had a very few lines to say . . . '

Hal grinned and slapped her on the back.

'We'll make a player of you yet,' he said cheerfully. 'Rehearsals this afternoon, all right? Tell Carlos he's to play a wicked stepfather, and I must go a-hunting for a great padded pillow or cushion so that I look like a fat ugly old husband!'

'And I'm to play a handsome knight at last!' said Walter, tossing his blond curls and preening himself. 'It's all due to you, Alys. How can I ever thank you?'

'Oh, 'twas nothing,' said Alys awkwardly.

Both Katrin and Cecily joined in the preparations with a will. Even though Cecily was shocked at first, she promised that Alys should wear her own gown. It was on the short and tight side, but in better condition than the pink silk that Walter usually wore. Katrin promised that Rough should take part, too, as the heroine's faithful guard-dog.

'He will do exactly as I say, if I stand behind the scenery and give him his commands. The crowds always love to see him,' she explained.

As he'd promised, Hal provided Alys with just a very few lines to say, and those mostly of the 'Ah, woe is me, whatever shall I do?' variety. Most of the action concerned the evil plottings of the stepfather, played by the swarthy Castilian, Carlos, and the husband, played by

Hal. But there was a dramatic climax to the tale when the handsome knight, brandishing a wooden sword and shield, rushed on to the stage, rescued Alys, made short work of both villains who yelled, groaned, and 'died' horribly, and proceeded to take his bow, while Rough bounded around, barking happily!

A fair-sized crowd had gathered by performance time, and Alys, waiting in the waggon while Cecily put a stitch in her dress and Katrin rearranged her wig for about the tenth time, felt thoroughly nervous. How did I get into this? she thought. I shall forget my lines, or faint, or make myself look a complete fool, and the crowd will hate me, and throw things . . .

But it was too late to back out, and Alys found that the performance passed in a blur. One moment, it seemed, Cecily was shoving her out on to the makeshift stage, Rough at her heels, to speak her first line . . . and the next, she was bowing to the audience, Walter's hand in hers, and blushing, as Hal and Carlos got up from where they had fallen and took their bows too, with a great deal of good-natured booing and hissing from the crowd!

'I think we may count this play among

our successes,' said Hal, as he untied the great pillow that had formed his stomach.

'Yes, indeed. The crowd loved me, didn't they? Did you hear them cheer when I rode on with my sword held high, ready to defend my lady?' said Walter.

'They cheered just as loudly when Rough pretended to attack Carlos,' said Katrin sharply. She had little use for Walter, calling him milksop and molly-coddle. 'But you did well, Alys. How did you like your first taste of the player's life?'

'I'm not sure,' said Alys shyly. 'It seemed to pass in a dream, and now I can remember little of what happened.'

'It was like that for me, the first few times,' said Hal. 'But the crowd liked you, Alys, even though I saw some of them looking puzzled as to whether you were a lad or a girl! 'Tis something new, to see a woman in a play. If it became known, no doubt people would flock to see it.'

'Aye, as though I was a dancing bear, or a mermaid from far Cathay, with a tail where my legs should be!' said Alys, laughing. 'I have no wish to be a curiosity, a sideshow for strangers to goggle at. I was pleased to help, but Cecily and I will leave you when we reach York, as we planned.'

'Ah, well,' said Hal, shrugging, and weighing the leather money-bag that Juanita had taken around the crowd. 'This seems well-filled; I'm for the nearest tavern tonight to sample good Lincolnshire ale and perhaps a roast fowl. What do the rest of you say?'

In the end, the men went off with Katrin and Juanita, while Cecily disappeared into the waggon to mend a huge three-cornered tear in Alys's skirt, which she had caught on the point of Walter's wooden sword. Alys herself felt exhausted, and decided she would have a little nap, curled up on the costumes in one of the carts. I wonder what Tom would have said, if he saw me standing up on a stage with a troupe of travelling players? she thought, as she drifted towards sleep. Would he be shocked? No, amused, more likely . . .

She was dreaming, as she often did, of Tom and their secret meetings beneath the Outlaws' Oak when she heard someone call her name. Blinking, she awoke to find it was almost dark and there was no sign of Cecily.

'Who's that? What do you want?' she cried sleepily. Suddenly, two arms went round her, there was a smell of strong ale, and someone was pressing wet kisses on her forehead, her cheeks, her lips.

'Don't do that! How dare you!' she cried, shoving the man away. In the half-light, she saw tangled blond curls, and realized it was Walter.

'What are you doing?' she said in her frostiest tones.

'Ah, Alys, be kind to me,' he babbled, grabbing her hands and covering them with kisses. 'From the first moment I saw you, I . . . oh, Alys, I know you feel the same, you do, you must!'

Alys shook her head, completely bewildered.

'What are you talking about?' she said.

'About you! About us, my dear one, my fair one, my beautiful Alys,' the boy moaned. 'I love you, Alys! I want you to be my wife!'

10

March 1471

'Your wife?' gasped Alys, wide awake at once, trying to push Walter's eager hands away. Not that it was difficult. He wasn't much bigger than she was herself, and was rather flabby, without the muscular strength she was used to in Tom.

'Aye, and why not? Alys, I have loved you from the first. I would not have you think I wish to dishonour you, tumble you in the back of the waggon like some cheap tavern-wench . . . '

'I should think not!' said Alys, pulling her cloak more tightly round her and wishing the others would come back. She peered at Walter. He was flushed with ale, with a pleading expression in his close-set blue eyes and a pouting, sulky look to his mouth. Oh, no, Alys thought, how can he possibly think I'd wed him, with his sulks and his head-tossing and his mincing, girlish ways? How can he believe I love him?

'Say something, Alys!' the boy pleaded, as she wriggled as far away from him as she could.

'Indeed, I . . . I know not what to say,' she said. 'Can't . . . can't we talk about it in the morning, Walter? For sure, you've been sampling that fine ale Hal talked of. You'll maybe feel different after a good night's sleep . . . '

Walter looked uncertain and Alys held her breath.

'Tell me that I may hope! Pray tell me that at least, fair Alys!' he begged, grabbing her hands again. He looked so foolish, crouching at her feet like a pet monkey or lap-dog, that Alys had to bite her lips to keep from giggling.

'I . . . well . . . ' she began.

Then, to her great relief, she heard the others returning. She could hear Hal's deep voice giving orders to big Ludo to make sure the ponies were properly tethered, Ludo's grunts in reply, laughter from Katrin and Cecily, and Carlos the Castilian's voice raised in song. Walter scrambled hastily out of the waggon when he heard them, so Alys was alone when Cecily and Katrin joined her.

'You're awake!' said Cecily, smiling.

Then she frowned as she saw her sister's face. 'Is all well, Alys?'

For a moment, Alys was tempted to tell her what had happened, but she decided not to. 'Twas just the ale talking, she thought hopefully as she settled down for the night. He can't really wish to marry me, nor think that I would ever agree! For sure, it will all be forgotten in the morning. No need to say anything to the others.

There was some groaning and holding of heads when morning came, Lincolnshire ale having proved stronger than some people suspected! Alys made a point of avoiding Walter as far as she could, instead staying in the waggon to help Cecily bundle up the costumes for their journey northward. She was just carrying one of the bundles over to big Ludo when Walter suddenly appeared before her, making her jump.

'Here, let me carry that for you, 'tis too heavy a burden for a maiden's shoulders,' he said gallantly. Not knowing what to say, Alys released the bundle without a word. Katrin, coming around the corner with two heavy pails of water, simply stood and stared.

'In faith, what is Lady Walter about?' she said in amazement. 'Offering to carry a heavy bundle, whatever next? 'Tis normally his way to keep clear of any hard work to be done, lest it spoil his beauty!'

Then she glanced at Alys's scarlet face.

'Oh, ho!' she said teasingly. 'What have we here? Not a real-life romance between our handsome knight and his fair lady?'

'No!' said Alys crossly. 'It's just that . . . well . . . Walter seems to have the idea that he . . . that I . . . ' Her voice trailed off into silence.

Katrin's voice was gentle and sympathetic.

'Take care, Alys,' she said. 'Actors always speak with silver tongues when they want something, but 'tis all play-acting with them. Players and minstrels are passers-by and fly-by-nights, all of 'em, even more than other men. Risk giving your heart to one and 'twill be tossed back to you, smashed into little pieces!'

Alys shook her head, laughing.

'Don't worry,' she said. 'I wouldn't have your 'Lady' Walter, as you call him, handed to me on a silver platter! He . . . he just surprised me, last night, rambling on about his love and how he wished to marry me . . . '

'Marry you?' echoed Cecily, wide-eyed, and Katrin began to laugh.

'He's truly smitten then, poor Walter,' she said, more kindly. 'I never thought I should see the day he found someone he cared for more than himself! What did you tell him, Alys?'

'I . . . well, nothing really. I thought 'twas the ale talking, and he'd think better of it today, but it seems not. What can I do? I don't want to seem unkind . . . '

'But if you are kind, he'll take that for encouragement,' said Katrin briskly. 'Stay away from him if you can, Alys! I'm glad to see you showing such good sense. Those baby-fair curls and blue eyes of his have fooled many a silly wench in towns where we've played.'

'Have they?' said Alys.

'Aye, indeed. You don't find him handsome?' said her friend curiously.

'Handsome? Walter? No, not compared to . . . '

'Compared to . . . ?' probed Katrin.

'Tom Taverner, my true love,' confessed Alys with a sigh. ' 'Tis his home at Broughton Hall in Yorkshire we're heading for.'

'He's kin to you, then? A cousin, perhaps?' Katrin guessed.

'Well, not exactly,' said Alys hesitantly. Perhaps it was time to confide in Katrin, she thought. The older girl surely had secrets of her own, and would be unlikely to betray Alys's.

So the whole story came tumbling out; Tom, and their tender love for each other, their unofficial betrothal and Tom's leaving with the Earl his master to fight for King Edward. Life at the Manor with the gentle Lady Philippa and her boorish husband, the unspeakable Sir Henry Capshaw, Alys's imprisonment in the gatehouse tower, her flight with Cecily, the evil outlaws who stole Beauty and Joliet, the good nuns of St Ursula's, Dame Margery and the Stillington family, Cecily's sickness, Robert Saville and the weasel-faced Frenchman . . .

Katrin listened without interrupting, her eyes wide.

' 'Tis like a romance!' she said. 'You should make a song of it, Alys, when you and Tom are together again, and happily wed!'

'If we ever are,' sighed Alys. 'Sometimes I'm afraid it will never happen, Katrin. I saw Tom in September last, and now 'tis almost April. Who knows what may have happened to him, tossing on the high seas or on foreign soil . . . '

'Foreigners don't all have horns and hoofs, you know,' said Katrin dryly. 'I don't doubt Edward of York and his followers will have been well cared-for in the Low Countries, and that your Tom will be back, one day, to claim his inheritance, and his bride!'

'I hope you're right,' Alys sighed. 'You don't know how I long for him, Katrin.'

Katrin patted her hand.

'There's always sadness at parting, if your love be true,' she said. 'But it means all the more joy, when you meet again! These days will all seem like a bad dream long past, when you are in Tom's arms again.'

There was a wistful note in Katrin's singsong voice and Alys couldn't resist asking, 'Were you ever in love, Katrin?'

'Once,' replied her friend. 'For a short time, then he died of a fever.'

'I'm sorry . . . ' said Alys.

'Don't be,' said the other girl, after a moment. 'For he is always with me, in my heart, in my memory, in the songs I sing.

Till the day I, too, die, he will be with me. True love is never forgotten.'

'Are you girls going to dawdle there all day?' came Hal's impatient voice. 'Come up, come up! We want to be well on the road north before the sun is high in the sky.'

Alys, Katrin and Cecily scurried round collecting their bundles and helping the men to stow the scenery, costumes and props safely. Katrin said no more about Walter, and Alys was able to keep out of his way and ignore the longing looks he gave her. Not so Hal, irritable after spending too long in the alehouse, who soon teased the truth out of Walter, much to Alys's embarrassment.

'Won't you be kind to your love-lorn swain? He pines for a kiss, or even a smile from you!' Hal teased.

'Alys isn't unkind. She doesn't share Walter's feelings, that's all,' said Cecily firmly.

Hal raised his eyebrows.

'Well, 'twill be a new experience for young Walter, to meet a girl who isn't bowled over by his fair face,' he said. 'I can't say that it will do him any harm, either. He can play the part of a spurned lover in our next romance, sighing and groaning and writing verses to his lady-love.'

To everyone's amusement, that seemed to be exactly what Walter had decided to do, once he realized that Alys didn't return his feelings. He began to behave exactly like the tragic lovers in romances, blushing and sighing whenever Alys looked his way, even picking up a ribbon she had dropped, kissing it, and placing it inside his jerkin, next to his heart.

'I don't know whether to laugh or weep, Cecily,' Alys admitted, exasperated, as they rode north. 'Do you think he is really suffering, or is it all play-acting, as Katrin says?'

'I don't know . . . ' Cecily began, as the girls heard the sound of hoofbeats in the distance.

'Who is this that comes so hastily?' said Hal, sounding disturbed. 'A large party, by the sound of them. Ludo, get the carts off the road. Carlos, tend to the ponies. Stand back, you girls, you don't want to be struck down by galloping horses!'

Cecily jumped out of the cart where she had been riding and joined Alys, Katrin and Rough beneath an oak tree at the roadside. The big hound's hackles were up, and Katrin hushed him when he began to growl. Moments later, a troop of fully-armed soldiers galloped by, their horses' hooves gouging great marks out of the half-dried mud in the roadway. Alys, Katrin and Cecily glanced at one another, wondering what this meant. They had seen soldiers heading south before, but never so many nor so urgently as these.

'Where can they be going? And why?' Alys said out loud.

Katrin shrugged.

'I know not. Nor do I care. I keep away from soldiers, if I can,' she said. 'War and fighting, 'tis men's business, and whenever there's fighting, our business is bad, for no one has time or money to spare for travelling players! They've gone now, anyway . . . '

But Alys felt troubled as they struggled back on to the road and headed north again. So many soldiers, she thought, and all riding south!

'Who could they be, do you suppose?' she asked Hal, striding along beside her.

'I'm not familiar with the Northern lords. They bore a blazon on their shields I did not recognize,' he said.

'Perhaps that drunken fellow in the Lincoln tavern spoke truth,' put in Carlos the Castilian.

'Perhaps,' said Hal, without much interest. Alys's spine prickled.

'What drunken fellow?' she wanted to know.

'Oh, a soldier, by his looks,' said Hal carelessly, 'though what he was doing, ale-soaked and stupid and far from his fellows, I couldn't say! He spoke of some rumour from the North, Ravenspur or some such place . . . '

'What rumour?' said Alys.

'Only that Edward of York had landed, with his following . . . '

Alys's heart began to thump so loudly she was afraid the others would hear it.

'Edward of York. The rightful king!' she breathed. 'And . . . and his following! That could mean . . . '

Hal was looking at her curiously.

'Yes?' he said. 'What could it mean?'

'Oh . . . er,' she said, blushing, ' 'tis just that I have, well, a friend I believe to have been in exile with His Grace the King!'

'I see. So if Edward has returned, your 'friend' may be with him?'

'Yes,' said Alys. 'God willing, yes, he may!'

Hal was laughing gently, but sympathetically.

'I wish I could tell you more,' he said, 'but the fellow in the tavern was near to passing out, and could only mumble out his tale. It may just be another rumour, Alys, don't get too excited. We are in Yorkist country now, don't forget. Men may wish for the return of Edward, but he will not have so easy a task, dislodging Daft Henry of Lancaster, with his fierce French wife and the mighty Lord Warwick at his side!'

'King Edward can do it,' said Alys staunchly. 'He's a bonny fighter, or so Tom . . . er, so I'm told, him and the Duke of Gloucester his brother, and their loyal friends and followers. The King will win back his throne one day, I know he will!'

'Aye, well, it may be so,' said Hal. 'England prospers best once there's peace, without all this fighting between York and Lancaster, and when England prospers, then we players prosper too!'

'King Edward will restore peace, when he comes into his own again,' said Alys stubbornly.

'God grant it may be so, and that your friend comes back to you unhurt,' said Hal, his eyes twinkling.

Alys had plenty to think about as the players jogged and ambled along the northern road. Supposing it was true, she thought, supposing King Edward has come back, and Tom with him? Where would they go? What would they do? They would ride south, she supposed, to meet the Lancastrians in battle. God keep you safe, my love, she thought, crossing herself, wherever you are.

As soon as she could, she joined Cecily in the back of one of the carts.

'Cecily, I must talk to you,' she whispered urgently.

'Not more trouble with poor Walter?' her sister teased.

Alys shook her head impatiently.

'No,' she said, ' 'tis something Hal said. There was a drunken soldier in the tavern in Lincoln, spreading rumours that King Edward had landed somewhere in the North!'

Cecily's eyes widened.

'But that means . . . '

'Yes. Tom could be in England again, even now!'

'Oh, Alys!'

'It could be just a rumour, mind you. And even if it were true, we don't know when he landed, or even where exactly. But we've seen all those soldiers, Cecily, I'm afraid the King and his party are heading south to do battle, while you and I are going north to Broughton Hall!'

Cecily thought for a moment.

'But what else can we do, sister? We don't know for sure that King Edward has even landed, or that Tom is still with him. Tom might be at Broughton Hall himself, or he might be anywhere! And even if we could find out where the King's party is, we could hardly follow them. I have no wish to find myself on a battlefield, sister, even if you have! No, we would do better to stick to our plan and make for Broughton Hall. If he has been in the North, Tom will surely have found a way to send word to his mother.'

'I suppose you're right,' sighed Alys. 'Yet . . . yet . . . oh, Cecily, it twists my heart to think that Tom and I might have ridden past one another on the road, all unknowing!'

'Nonsense!' said Cecily the practical. 'You would have recognized the blazon on

241

his shield, or he would have recognized you.'

'Even with my hair cut short like this?' said Alys doubtfully, running her fingers through the rough, straggly mop. She had little time for vanity, but she still sometimes regretted the loss of her long silken braids.

'Of course,' said Cecily. 'What I say is, the sooner we get to Tom's home, the better for us. Then there will be no more guessing and wondering, we shall know what there is to know.'

For the very first time, Alys began to wonder how Tom's family would feel, greeted by a strange young woman claiming to be betrothed to him. I wonder if he has had any chance to tell them of me, she thought. And *what* he has told them . . .

She had caught sight of herself in Katrin's looking-glass one morning and been shocked. The Alys Sherwood she knew, neatly and fashionably dressed as befitted the eldest daughter of the Manor, seemed to have gone for ever. In her place was a grubby hoyden with hacked-off hair and crumpled gowns that looked as if she had slept in them, because she had! I look like a vagabond, she thought ruefully, looking down on her darned hose, scuffed shoes, scratched arms and grimy finger-nails. Tom wouldn't recognize me if he saw me like this, she thought gloomily.

'God's greetings to you, good people!' said a merry-faced friar in the grey habit of a Franciscan, as he passed the players, who had stopped by the side of the road for a meal of bread, cheese and dried fish.

'And to you, Father,' said Juanita, who was always more devout than the others. 'Would you care to share our simple meal?'

Hal and Carlos looked at each other. There was little enough food to go round as it was . . .

'Thank you. I have my own provisions, though,' said the friar, 'thanks to the good sisters at Whitby Abbey, who made up a package for my journey, so I need not take your food.'

He sat down beside them and unwrapped a package of bread and cold mutton.

'Are you travelling far, Sir Friar?' said Alys politely, as he was sitting next to her.

'Only to our nearest house in Derby-shire,' said the friar. 'And you?'

'Our companions are for York,' said Alys, munching, and indicating the rest of the players with a wave of her hand, 'but we were looking for the road to Broughton Hall.'

'Broughton Hall? Not Lady Taverner's place?' cried the friar. 'Why, I passed that way only yesterday. I know it well, and can tell you the road to take.'

Alys's heart began to thump again, and she listened carefully as the friar described the road to Broughton Hall. If we make good time, she thought, we could be there by sundown tomorrow! 'Tis too much to hope that Tom will be there, more likely he'll be away fighting for the King, but no doubt his mother will have news, and the widowed sister he told me of, Elizabeth. Tom's family. I shall meet them at long last!

'You . . . you know the Taverner family, Sir Friar?' she enquired hopefully, and was disappointed when he shook his head.

'I know *of* them,' he said. 'There are few folk in this part of Yorkshire who haven't heard of Lady Taverner. She has managed her estates alone since her husband died, many years ago now, and they say wool from her flocks is the finest in Yorkshire. A formidable lady, by all accounts, who rules her household with a rod of iron.'

Cecily caught Alys's eye and made a face. Tom's mother sounded fierce. What would she do, what would she say, when two young women who looked like vagabonds arrived at her door? Ah, well, Alys thought, biting her lip, 'tis too late to worry about that now!

'You say it's another day's journey to Broughton Hall, Sir Friar?' she asked.

'About that, yes,' said the friar, wiping the crumbs from his lips. 'I wish you Godspeed, ladies and gentlemen, I must be on my way!'

As she and the others trudged northward again, Alys began to feel more and more nervous. Suppose Tom's mother doesn't believe my story, she thought. Suppose she turns us away? Even if the rumours are true, and King Edward has been in Yorkshire, and Tom with him, he might not have had time to go to Broughton Hall. And if he did, he would have had war on his mind, not betrothals! He might not have mentioned me to his family at all. He might have forgotten me, in all these months, taken up with some foreign girl out there in the

Low Countries . . .

The sky had clouded over and soon a thin, miserable drizzle began to fall, seeping through Alys's worn shoes and turning the road into a sea of mud. The wheels of the big waggon soon began to churn helplessly and Hal called to Ludo to stop.

'We may as well rest for the night here,' he said, the wind whipping his words away. 'There's some shelter under the trees and the weather may be clear by the morning.'

It was too wet to light their usual evening fire, so there was nothing but the remains of some rather stale bread and some shrivelled apples for supper. Alys's stomach growled with hunger and she huddled up to Cecily and Katrin for warmth, twisting this way and that beneath her cloak, trying to get comfortable.

'Lie still, Alys! You're wriggling like an eel!' complained Cecily sleepily.

'I'm sorry,' Alys whispered, 'but, oh, Cecily . . . I'm afraid!'

'Afraid? Now, when we're so close to our journey's end?' said Cecily.

'But that's just it. You heard what that

friar said about Lady Taverner. Suppose she turns us away? Suppose . . . oh, Cecily, suppose some harm has come to Tom, in all these long months? Or that he has forgotten me?'

'Forgotten you?' said Cecily. 'Not Tom, sister, he's not the forgetting kind. If you love him, you must trust him; aye, and his family too. All will be well, I promise, once we have found Broughton Hall and explained all to Lady Taverner. She may be strict, indeed, she must be, to run a large estate on her own, but I don't doubt she will be fair, and hear us out!'

'I hope you're right,' Alys sighed.

She still found it hard to sleep that night, and awakening to lowering grey skies and a sullen downpour didn't improve her temper. Thanks to Ludo's great strength, they managed to get the waggon and carts moving, but progress was painfully slow. It was already late afternoon when they reached the fork in the road, just after a tavern and beside a huge oak tree, that the friar had told them led to Broughton Hall. At a word from Hal, the carts stopped.

'Well,' said Hal kindly, 'yonder's your road, Alys and Cecily! We must press on to

York, so 'tis time to say farewell and Godspeed!'

There were tears in Katrin's black eyes as she flung her arms round Alys and Cecily in turn, and Alys felt a lump in her throat. Apart from her sister and her cousin Mary, Katrin was the only friend she had ever had. Now they might never meet again!

'Katrin,' she said, trying not to weep, 'don't forget us, will you? I . . . I know not what lies ahead at Broughton Hall, but if . . . if all goes well, and Tom and I are wed, I . . . I want you to come and sing for us. Yes, and the others too. Promise me you will?'

Katrin was smiling through her tears.

'Aye,' she said, looking at Hal. 'We shall come and play at your wedding feast, if we are still in the North by then! Shan't we, Hal?'

'Why not?' said Hal, smiling. There were hugs and kisses and handshakes from Juanita, Juan, Carlos and the Bohemian tumblers. Even big Ludo patted both girl's hands and smiled in his vague, kindly way. Rough gambolled around, his great paws black with mud and his coat slicked down by the rain. I shall miss these good folk,

Alys thought sadly. I shall miss their warmth and kindness, the way they shared what little they had with two strange girls they barely knew . . .

'Fare well,' sobbed Cecily, trying to shield her face from the rain with her cloak. 'Come, Alys, 'tis time . . . '

Alys was just giving Katrin one last hug when she remembered Walter and looked round, thinking to bid him goodbye. He was nowhere to be seen, so she shrugged and set off beside Cecily. Suddenly, there was a cry behind them, and both girls turned to see Walter stumbling after them, without a cloak, his shirt sodden and clinging to his body.

'I thought I could not bear to say farewell!' he cried dramatically, tossing back his fair curls and clapping a muddy hand to his brow. 'But adieu, my fair Alys! Your cruelty has broken my heart, I might well pine away and die . . . '

Does he really believe that nonsense? thought Alys, trying not to giggle.

'Pine away and die? Not you!' sniffed Cecily unsympathetically, glancing at the beginnings of an ale-belly beneath Walter's shirt.

For answer, Walter tossed his damp

curls again and squelched back to join the others. The carts lumbered forward, Katrin waving and waving until they could see her no more. Warm tears mingling with the cold raindrops on their faces, the two girls struggled on, the wind cutting through cloaks, woollen gowns and linen shifts like a knife.

' 'Tis a foul day to be journeying!' Alys muttered through clenched teeth, thinking longingly of a warm fire, fresh clothes, and a bowl of hot, comforting pottage.

They passed no one on the road, and barely had the energy to notice the countryside they were travelling through, even though Alys had already decided they must be on Taverner land. Darkness was beginning to fall when at last, footsore and weary to the bone, they came to a village that must be Broughton. A few cottages, dimly-lit with rushlights, huddled close to a small, square-towered church. There was a village green, a duck-pond, an alehouse, and an avenue lined with elm trees that must lead up to Broughton Hall itself.

Almost too tired to put one icy foot before another, the two girls struggled towards the gatehouse and Alys rapped on the wooden shutter. After a few moments, it opened, and a wrinkled, toothless face with bright brown eyes, resembling nothing so much as a squirrel, looked out.

'Aye? Who's that comes a-callin' on this wild and wuthering night?'

Exhausted as she was, Alys tried to summon up the remnants of her dignity.

'Is this Broughton Hall?' she asked.

'It might be. Who wants to know?'

Alys drew herself up to her full height.

'I am the Lady Alys Sherwood, of Markstone Manor in Hertfordshire, and this is my sister, Lady Cecily. I am the promised bride of Thomas Taverner. Is he here?' she said.

The brown eyes widened and the squirrel-like face peered harder at the two bedraggled girls.

'Nay,' said the gatekeeper. '*Sir* Thomas is not here, and I know naught of any promised bride!'

Alys's heart sank.

'Please . . . then may we speak to Lady Taverner?'

There was a pause, and then the voice said, 'Wait here. No, under the gateway arch, 'twill shelter you from the worst of the rain. Not that you could get any wetter, from the look of you!'

With a cackle of laughter, he closed the shutter. For what seemed an age, Alys and Cecily stood shivering in the gateway. So Tom's not here, Alys thought. I'm cold, I'm heartsick, but most of all, I'm afraid . . .

At last, they heard voices, saw a lantern-light bobbing across the court-yard, heard hounds barking. The gate swung open, a lantern was held high, and a sharp voice called, 'Come forward, wherever you are! And *who* are you, that claims to be my Tom's promised bride? Step inside, that I may see you!'

A lantern was held high and Alys found herself facing a tall, thin woman, blue-eyed, sharp-featured, and wrapped in a thick woollen cloak.

'What is this nonsense? Speak, girl! Explain yourself!' said Lady Taverner.

Alys tried to say that it wasn't nonsense, but somehow the words would not come.

'I . . . I . . . ' she gasped, then pitched forward in a dead faint at Lady Taverner's feet.

11

April 1471

When she came to, Alys found herself sitting on a wooden bench before a roaring fire in the hall. Cecily was beside her, both girls were wrapped in thick woollen rugs, and Lady Taverner herself was forcing a bitter-tasting hot drink between her lips. Alys gasped and spluttered, but although the drink tasted foul, it was warming. Soon she was able to sit up properly and look around her.

The great hall was lit by flickering torches, and a ring of bewildered and curious faces surrounded her and Cecily. As well as Lady Taverner, Alys could see serving-wenches, kitchenmaids, the little squirrel-faced gatekeeper, and a couple of lads who looked and smelled as though they belonged to the stables. Behind them, most of the household seemed to be staring and whispering.

'Th-thank you, Lady Taverner,' Alys whispered, feeling rather overwhelmed.

Lady Taverner made an impatient noise.

'Don't thank me, young lady,' she said crisply. 'I would not have you die on my doorstep, whoever you are!'

Alys leaned back wearily.

'I told you the truth,' she said. 'I am Alys Sherwood, from Hertfordshire, and this is my sister Cecily. Our mother, Lady Philippa, is sister to the Countess of Aylesbury, in whose service your son Tom was brought up. Before Tom . . . I . . . I mean Sir Thomas . . . left, with his master the Earl, to fight for King Edward, he . . . I . . . well, he said he would ask the Earl to ask my stepfather if we could be betrothed, and I promised that I would wed no other than him.'

'I see. Go on,' said Lady Taverner. Her face was expressionless and Alys had no idea whether she believed her story or not.

'How came you here, then?' went on Tom's mother. 'And why? You had but to wait safely at home until Tom returned, didn't you?'

Alys shook her head.

' 'Twas . . . 'twas not so easy,' she said, feeling close to tears. 'My stepfather Sir Hugh, he was always hot for Lancaster, having served King Henry's queen in the past. He wished me to marry an old crony of his, a Lancastrian knight called Sir Henry Capshaw.'

'And this didn't please you?' said Lady Taverner mildly.

'No!' cried Alys, unable to repress a shudder. 'He was old, and fat, and ugly, and I loathed him! But my ... my stepfather locked me in the gatehouse tower and said I must stay there till I obeyed him. That I would never do, so with Cecily's help I escaped, and fled northward to look for Tom.'

Cecily suddenly nudged her.

'The pendant, Alys,' she whispered. 'Show her the silver rose pendant that Tom gave you!'

Alys felt weak with relief. How could she have forgotten the silver rose, the proof positive of Tom's love for her, and hers for him? She fumbled in the bosom of the shabby, travel-stained gown she was wearing, pulled the pendant out, and unfastened it from her neck.

'Here, Lady Taverner,' she said, handing her the silver rose. 'Here's proof that I have not lied to you! Tom gave me this silver rose pendant when last we met, and I swear I have not taken it off since then!

He said you gave it to him when his father died. He told me to wear it for him until we met again . . . '

Lady Taverner looked down at the silver rose, her lips quivering. She turned it over in her hand once or twice, and swallowed hard. When she looked up at Alys again, her sea-blue eyes were full of tears.

'Welcome, Lady Alys,' she whispered. 'Welcome to Broughton Hall! Welcome home!'

She rose from the big carved chair where she had been sitting and gave first Alys and then Cecily a hearty hug. Her gown and hair smelt of dried lavender and Alys, half-laughing and half-crying, thought what scarecrows she and Cecily must look, soaked to the skin and in their shabby clothes. No wonder Tom's mother didn't know whether to believe my story or not, she thought.

Lady Taverner clearly wasn't the kind of woman to weep and feel sentimental for long. She soon realized that half her household had crept into the hall to have a look at these two strange young women.

'Come, back to your work, all of you!' she said briskly. 'What ever are you all thinking of? Gilbert, back to the gatehouse! Ralph, Harry, the stables, see that the horses are fed and watered for the night. Maud, Mattie, prepare the guest chamber for Sir Thomas's promised bride and her sister!'

Then she turned to Alys and Cecily again and her rather stern face softened into a smile.

'I'm sure you have more to tell me, but tomorrow will do just as well as today,' she said kindly. 'You must be tired, and hungry too. Margaret, bring food for Lady Alys and Lady Cecily! Then it's bed for you both, I think.'

'Please . . . ' said Alys faintly, catching Lady Taverner's hand.

'What is it, child?'

'Is . . . is Tom all right?' Alys breathed, her heart in her mouth. 'We . . . we heard a rumour that King Edward's forces had landed here in Yorkshire, and planned to march south towards London.'

Lady Taverner smiled proudly.

'Yes, 'tis true,' she said. 'Edward of York landed at Ravenspur some two or three weeks past . . . '

'And Tom with him?'

'And Tom with him!' Lady Taverner confirmed. 'At first, Edward claimed it was only his York inheritance he wanted, and not the kingdom, and he and his men entered the city of York with that in mind. 'Twas just after that that Tom got leave to come here, to visit me . . . '

'Tom was here?' Alys cried, not knowing whether to laugh or weep. If we'd been just a few days less on the road, I could have been here to greet him, she thought.

'Yes, Tom was here,' went on his mother. '*Sir* Thomas now, for he's past eighteen, you know, Alys, and King Edward knighted him in Burgundy as a thank-offering for the good and faithful service he has done his king. Ah, Alys, he's a fine young man, though I say it myself, a fine young man and a brave knight! Last time I saw my son, he was but a lad. Now he's a man, and a son any mother would be proud of, brave, honourable, and true!'

'I know it!' said Alys, lifting her chin proudly, though tears were prickling the back of her eyes. So Tom got his dearest wish, she thought. He has proved himself, doing knight's service for his king!

'Did he . . . did he mention me?' she asked wistfully.

'Well, not directly,' said Lady Taverner with a smile. 'His mind was more on soldiering than love-making, Alys, and he couldn't stay long, anyway. But I did say that now he was a knight, and had come in to his inheritance, for all this,' she indicated the Hall and the servants, 'belongs to him now that he is eighteen, I should start to look around for a suitable bride for him!'

'And what did he say?' whispered Alys, her heart thumping.

'He blushed, just a little,' said Lady Taverner mischievously, 'and said that I shouldn't trouble myself about that, for he had hopes!'

'Hopes?' echoed Alys, bewildered.

'Aye, so he said. I assumed he meant there was someone he had his eye on, perhaps some foreign lady he'd met on his travels. I never dreamed of Lady Aylesbury's very own niece!'

'Then . . . then you approve the match?' said Alys, greatly daring.

Lady Taverner tried to look stern . . . and failed.

'It seems I have little choice!' she said. 'My son has chosen his own bride, and she has disobeyed her stepfather and travelled across half of England, having the Lord knows what adventures on the way, to be with him! We shall need time to get to know one another, Mistress Alys Sherwood, but . . . '

'But?' Alys breathed.

'I like what I have seen so far,' nodded Lady Taverner. 'You have courage, my dear, courage, loyalty, and spirit. I like that. I would not see my Tom with some milk-and-water maiden fit for nothing but saying 'Yes, my lord' and 'No, my lord'. Some women, it's true, seek gentle, biddable daughters-in-law they can order about like serving-wenches, but I want to know that my son and his inheritance are in good hands!

'We live in troubled times, Alys. Many's the time I have thanked the Lord for my own good health and strength. Where would I have been, when Tom's father died, if I hadn't had the wit and spirit to run Broughton Hall alone? Married off to some fortune-seeker, no doubt . . . '

'Like my lady mother,' said Alys bitterly. 'She was ready enough to place herself under Sir Hugh Drayton's protection, and she has been cruelly ill-used by him ever since!'

Lady Taverner raised her eyebrows.

'Aye, 'tis a hard world for women,' she

said. 'That's why Tom's father and I sought a good husband for our daughter Elizabeth. Not just a useful alliance for our family, but a kind man who would not ill-treat her . . . but I'm tiring you, and here comes Margaret with your supper! I hope you can relish good Yorkshire mutton, Alys? And you, Cecily?'

'Indeed, yes,' said Cecily faintly, though, like Alys, she felt almost too weary to eat. The long, uncomfortable journey, the heat from the fire, and above all, the relief at being welcomed to Broughton Hall at last, made both girls long for their beds. After a hearty helping of mutton stew, with preserved pears to follow, they could scarcely keep their eyes open.

'Mattie, is the spare chamber ready?' said Lady Taverner.

'Yes'm,' nodded one of the maids, a girl of about Cecily's age with a mischievous, freckled face.

'Then follow me, Alys, Cecily,' Lady Taverner went on, rising from her seat and leading the way to the privy staircase at the back of the hall. Up and up again they went, until Lady Taverner led them into a small, but spotlessly clean bedchamber, with a high wooden bed piled with rugs, a clothes-chest and a couple of stools.

'Mattie will bring you warm water in the morning. She will sleep on a pallet at the foot of your bed, so call her if there is anything you need,' she said.

'You are very kind,' said Alys, remembering her manners.

'Tomorrow, I shall have to find you both clothes befitting your rank and station, I can see,' said Lady Taverner, after a scandalized look at the darned and ragged gowns the girls were wearing. 'Indeed, there's much to be done and much to be told! But first, you must sleep.'

Alys and Cecily needed no second telling. The bed was so soft and comfortable, compared with the cold, hard ground beneath the waggon where they had last slept with Katrin and Rough, that they both tumbled in and were asleep within moments.

Little Mattie, the maid, woke them the next morning with mugs of hot, spiced ale. The sun was shining, and Alys couldn't think where she was when she first saw the maid's freckled face peering shyly at her.

'I . . . I brung your morning ale, milady,' she said, with an awkward little jerk of the knees that Alys realized was meant to be a curtsey.

'No need for that, Mattie,' she said cheerfully. 'I hope we shall be friends, you and I!'

'Yes, milady,' said Mattie obediently, and then her curiosity got the better of her and she said, 'Oh, milady, is it . . . is it true you're to marry Sir Thomas when he comes home from the wars?'

'God willing, Mattie,' said Alys soberly, crossing herself, and touching the silver rose pendant which Lady Taverner had replaced round her neck for luck as well. She had been welcomed to Tom's home, but he was still far away with King Edward, facing who knew what perils and dangers. It might be months still before he and Alys met again.

'He's a handsome knight, Sir Thomas,' said Mattie dreamily. 'He put me in mind of King Arthur himself, or maybe the young Sir Galahad, riding up the avenue with his sword and his shield . . . ooh, 'twas fair romantic, milady!'

'Was it?' said Alys, with a pang of longing. She sipped her ale, and nudged Cecily awake.

'I've brung some fresh clothes for ye,

like the mistress said,' Mattie went on, indicating a heap of garments on top of the wooden chest. 'They're mostly old 'uns of hers, or Mistress Elizabeth's, but they'll serve, the mistress says, until we can get new ones made. And we've a tub we can bring in, if you've a mind to bathe. Maud 'n me can bring hot water from t'kitchen.'

'That would be wonderful,' said Alys, stretching, and trying to remember how long it was since she had soaked her tired, bruised body in warm water. It seemed like the ultimate in luxury. The other maid, Maud, sprinkled dried herbs in the water and was ready with warmed towels when Alys stepped out again, her wet hair dripping around her. I believe my hair is long enough to braid again, Alys thought, as Mattie rubbed it dry beside the fire, and combed it out to remove any tangles.

'I feel like a new person!' Cecily said happily, as they hunted through the clothes Lady Taverner had provided — linen shifts and bed-gowns, warm hose, woollen gowns for every day, sideless surcoats trimmed with fur, even one or two silk and velvet gowns for special occasions. All had clearly been worn, but

264

were so well made and of such good quality that they were still wearable. Cecily whipped out a needle from her travelling bundle, turned up a couple of hems, and tidied up some torn stitching. At last, two neatly-dressed and smart young ladies, with tidily-braided hair, went down the stairs again into the hall; Cecily in a dark-blue gown and Alys in mulberry.

'God's greetings to you both! And what a difference!' marvelled Lady Taverner, when Alys and Cecily appeared.

'Thank you for all this,' said Alys gratefully. 'I fear there's nothing much to be done with the gowns we were wearing, except to burn them. They're so thread-bare, they won't stand laundering!'

'Did you come away with nothing but the clothes you stood up in, then?' enquired Lady Taverner, with interest.

'Indeed, no,' said Alys. 'I have Jack, our stable-boy's Sunday breeches and jerkin in my bundle, and his shirt too! I promised I'd return them to him one day, even though he sold them to me for a silver penny!'

Lady Taverner's eyebrows nearly shot up into her hair at this, and Maud and Mattie just stood, open-mouthed.

'I knew you had more tales to tell!' Lady Taverner exclaimed. 'Buying the stable-boy's Sunday breeches for a penny? Whatever next?'

'You haven't heard half of it,' Cecily teased. 'Alys fought off a dozen outlaws, she was the heroine of a play put on by a troupe of travelling players, she sang songs around a night-time fire, she nursed a whole house-full of children through the scarlet sickness, *and* she saved my life!'

'Hush, Cecily,' hissed Alys. 'Whatever will Lady Taverner think?'

'I think my son has chosen a most remarkable young woman to be his bride,' said Lady Taverner seriously, as she ordered Margaret to bring bread, dried fish, and ale for breakfast. 'No doubt I shall hear more about your travels in due course, but today I must ride out to meet old Dick, the shepherd, and see how his ewes and their lambs are doing. We've a fine flock, Alys . . . '

'I know. We met a friar on our journey who told us that Broughton Hall wool was the finest in Yorkshire,' said Alys.

Lady Taverner seemed pleased.

'Aye,' she said. 'My late husband taught me how to recognize fine healthy sheep;

yes, and cattle and horses too, though our land is best for sheep-rearing. We grow oats and barley, beans and turnips, we have our own fish-ponds and orchards, oh, and beehives, as well as the herb garden I like to tend myself, and the dairy.'

' 'Tis a busy life, no doubt,' said Alys.

'Oh, I don't do it alone, 'twould be impossible,' said Lady Taverner briskly. 'Having the right servants, people you trust, who are loyal and do their jobs properly, that's the secret! Dick's father, and his father before him, were Broughton shepherds too. Everyone here knows what they have to do, and they do it well, or 'tis the worse for them!'

Alys and Cecily exchanged glances, remembering what the friar had told them, that Lady Taverner ruled Broughton Hall with a rod of iron. She caught their looks, and laughed.

'I don't doubt there are those who think me strict and unwomanly,' she said, 'but 'tis not that. I love this place, Alys. I have loved it since I came here as a young bride. I want it to be the finest estate in Yorkshire!'

'I'm sure it is,' said Alys politely.

As she and Lady Taverner rode around

267

the Taverner lands, Alys realized that her new home was, indeed, one of the best-kept estates she had ever seen. The servants were well-dressed, smiling, and obedient. No lecherous bailiffs nor man-crazy kitchenmaids like Moll here! There were fewer horses in the stables than at the Manor, but the sturdy Yorkshire ponies looked sleek and well cared-for, as did the fat cattle and woolly, bleating sheep. Even the fowls, pecking about in the orchard and courtyard, were plump and clean-looking. There were no hunting-hounds, but old Gilbert the gate-ward had a brindled, grey-muzzled dog which looked as old as he was, and there were at least two striped cats, one with a litter of kittens, grooming their whiskers in the spring sunshine.

This was Tom's home until he was eight years old, Alys thought, trying to imagine a sturdy little blond-haired lad riding his pony up the green hills and through the well-kept woodlands. And, God willing, there will be children at Broughton Hall again one day. Our children, mine and Tom's. The thought gave her a strange, fluttery feeling inside.

Suddenly she remembered something.

'Is Mistress Elizabeth not here, then?' she asked. 'Tom's sister? He told me she was widowed, and had returned here with her two young sons.'

Lady Taverner nodded.

'Elizabeth, Robbie and George are away at the moment, visiting her late husband's parents near Warwick,' she said. 'They will be back after Easter, so make the most of the peace and quiet now! They're young devils, my grandsons. Robbie is seven and young George just five years old.'

'Younger than my half-brothers and older than my half-sisters, then,' said Alys with a sigh. The Manor seemed far away, and though Lady Taverner had made her welcome, she still felt a pang of homesickness when she thought of Lady Philippa, Dame Eleanor, and the children. I should try to send word, she thought, aye, and to Cousin Mary Enderby, too. And to Dame Margery in Bedford town, as I promised! And if only, if only I could send word to Tom as well, so that he knows I love him, and that I'm waiting here!

She turned to Lady Taverner.

'What do you think King Edward plans to do next?' she asked eagerly. 'What did Tom say? Are they for London, do you

269

know? Did Tom think there would be fighting?'

'If Edward of York hopes to regain the crown of England, he must go south to London,' said Lady Taverner. 'For sure, there will be fighting, Alys. Even if Daft Harry could be persuaded to give up the throne without a fight, the Earl of Warwick would never allow it. As for that she-wolf Queen Margaret, she's more warlike than the men from what I hear!'

'And Tom?'

Lady Taverner gave a rueful laugh.

'He longs to prove his worth in battle, like most young men,' she said. 'When I told him to take care, he laughed and kissed my hand, and told me not to worry, he was under the protection of King Edward! He hero-worships His Grace the King, Alys, and is sure no harm will come to him while he fights beneath Edward's standard!'

'Aye, that sounds like Tom,' said Alys. 'He told me he had been to London once and seen King Edward. He called him the handsomest knight in England and', she blushed, 'he even said I was fairer than the Lady Elizabeth Woodville, Edward's queen!'

'Did he so?' said Lady Taverner sympathetically. 'There's true love between you and Tom, isn't there, Alys? I can hear it in your voice when you speak his name.'

'Aye,' said Alys. 'I love him truly, Lady Taverner, and with all my heart!'

'And what of you, Cecily?' said Lady Taverner. 'Have you found your true love, also? Did any of the young men in your uncle of Aylesbury's household catch your eye?'

'Not really,' Cecily admitted.

'Thomas and I promised to find her the handsomest knight in Yorkshire for her husband — apart from Tom himself, of course!' laughed Alys.

'Then that's what we shall do,' said Lady Taverner decisively. 'Sir William Mumford of Barlby has three fine sons who must be about the age to look for brides, and there's young Hugh de Winter . . . '

Cecily, who was beginning to look alarmed, changed the subject hastily.

'When do you expect Lady Elizabeth and her sons to return?' she asked.

'Some time after Easter,' said Lady Taverner. 'There may be news of another betrothal to come there, for 'tis three full years since Elizabeth's husband died, God rest his soul!'

'And Elizabeth wishes to remarry?' said Alys curiously.

'Yes, I think she does. She's the kind who wants a man at her side, and she also wants to be mistress in her own home,' said Lady Taverner. 'Besides, those young rascals need a father's firm hand around their backsides, in my opinion! Poor Robert, her late husband, came from a big family. There may be a kinsman in Warwick that she could wed.'

'We look forward to meeting Tom's sister, don't we, Cecily?' Alys murmured.

They didn't have to wait long. Shortly after Easter, which Alys and Cecily had spent quietly at Broughton Hall, 'learning to be ladies again' as Cecily put it, a train of horses and riders came jingling up the avenue towards the gatehouse.

' 'Tis the Lady Elizabeth, and Master Robbie and Master George,' cried Gilbert the gate-ward in excitement. Lady Taverner smiled, rose from her chair, and shook out her violet wool skirts.

'Come, Alys, Cecily,' she commanded. 'Come and meet my daughter, your new sister!'

'Robbie! George! Don't be plaguing the life out of the poor dog the moment you set eyes on him!' snapped an irritated voice as Elizabeth Cooper, once Elizabeth Taverner, dismounted from a fine bay horse. She was fashionably dressed in pale blue silk, an odd choice for a journey, Alys thought. Her fair hair was elaborately arranged beneath her veil, and her eyebrows rose questioningly when she saw Alys and Cecily, one on either side of her mother. She curtseyed formally.

'God's greetings to you, my lady mother,' she said. 'I trust I find you well?'

'Yes, indeed,' said Lady Taverner. 'Elizabeth, I have a surprise for you. This is Lady Alys Sherwood, your brother Tom's betrothed, and this is her sister, Lady Cecily.'

Elizabeth was too well-bred to stare, but she looked astonished.

'Betrothed?' she said. 'But how can that be? He said nothing of this to me . . . '

Alys's heart began to thump.

'You mean . . . oh, Lady Elizabeth, you've seen Tom?' she cried.

'Why, yes,' said Elizabeth, with a rather chilly smile. ' 'Tis quite a tale, and not at

273

all what I expected when I rode down to spend Easter-tide with poor Robert's family. Mother, the whole court was there, the Yorkist court, I mean! King Edward himself had come to make peace with his brother, the Duke of Clarence, so that they might march on London together and take the crown from Lancaster by force. Mother, I was presented to the King himself!'

'To King Edward?' echoed Cecily, round-eyed.

'Who else? Oh, he's a fine figure of a man, Mother. Tall as an oak tree and so handsome, a true king! He smiled, and bade me have a safe journey back to Yorkshire . . . '

She sighed sentimentally.

'I truly thought I'd swoon when he patted my cheek and smiled! To be greeted so, by the King himself, 'tis a great honour.'

Lady Taverner sniffed.

'I'm sure kings are like other men when it comes to a pretty face,' she said sharply. 'Never mind King Edward, daughter, what of our Tom? How did he seem? Was he well?'

'Well, and in good spirits,' nodded

Elizabeth, 'but he didn't mention any betrothal.'

She looked at Alys suspiciously.

'Aye, well, 'tis a long tale,' said Lady Taverner. 'Come inside, Elizabeth, and eat and drink with us. 'Tis well past the boys' bedtime. Alys can tell you her story later, when they are abed and asleep.'

She and Elizabeth turned and went into the Hall arm-in-arm, leaving Alys and Cecily behind in the courtyard, not knowing quite what to do. Ralph the stable-boy had led the horses away, Mattie and Maud had taken Elizabeth's travelling-chest up the privy stairs to her bed-chamber. Suddenly, Alys felt as if she didn't belong.

'What do you think of Tom's sister?' Cecily whispered.

'It would be wrong to judge her when she's journey-tired and faced with two strangers in her own home,' said Alys, trying to be fair. After all, she thought to herself, why should Tom mention me to Elizabeth? He thinks me safe at the Manor, waiting for him, no doubt. He's on his way to do battle for his king, and he has knightly prowess on his mind, not love. He barely knows his sister, he went into the Earl's household when he was but eight years old. Why should he confide in her, when he didn't even tell his own mother who I was?

Yet the tiny seed of doubt persisted and Alys felt heartsick. Tom Taverner, squire of the Earl's household, had loved her. She had the silver rose pendant as proof of that. But what did Sir Thomas Taverner, knight, feel as he rode off to do battle for his king? She had no way of knowing. He could have forgotten her, thinking their love and their sworn promise to each other no more than a childish game.

After all, Alys thought, 'tis six months already since I saw Tom, and who knows how long until I see him again? Will he still feel the same? Or will the love we once shared be no more than a dream that dies with the dawning? Oh, Tom, Tom . . .

Biting back the tears, she followed Cecily, Lady Taverner, and Elizabeth across the crowded courtyard and into the Hall. An icy feeling seemed to have settled round her heart and she felt lonelier than she had ever felt in her life.

12

April 1471

'Why, Alys? What's amiss? Are you not feeling well?' Cecily, coming into their bedroom with a pile of clean linen, was surprised to see her sister sitting gazing out of the window, her chin in her hands. Alys turned round, heaving a deep sigh.

'No, I'm quite well,' she said, trying to smile at Cecily's worried look.

'Then what is it?' Cecily asked, settling down with a shirt of young Robbie's that needed mending, and hunting for a needle and thread.

Alys shook her head.

'I . . . I don't know,' she said. 'Truly, Cecily, I don't know why I feel so sad! Here we are at Broughton Hall at last, after all our journeyings. We're safe, warm and well-fed, and Tom's mother has made us welcome. I know that Tom himself is well, and I'm accepted as his promised bride. Lady Taverner even told me that she approved the match! All I have to do is wait here for Tom's return. I could ask for nothing more, and yet . . . '

'Well?' said Cecily enquiringly.

'I feel dull, and flat, and wretchedly unhappy,' she said. 'More unhappy by far than when we were on the road, cold, hungry and in danger! How can this be? The days just drag by, and I seem no nearer seeing Tom than I was six months ago. 'Tis ungrateful of me, I know . . . '

Cecily patted her hand.

'Remember what Katrin said? That this will all seem like a bad dream, once you and Tom are reunited?' she said comfortingly. 'You faced the dangers of the road bravely, sister. Now you have to face these duller days with the same courage. All will be well when Tom returns, you'll see!'

'But will it?' cried Alys, her lips trembling. 'Sometimes I can't believe that Tom will be the same, will feel the same, after all this time!'

'Don't you trust him?' said Cecily severely.

'Well, I . . . ' floundered Alys.

'Then how can you doubt his love?' demanded her sister. 'If your love is true, then a six-months' parting can only make it stronger. Come, it's not like you to brood. I've two or three more of these shirts to mend. Help me with them, or Robbie and George will be running around as naked as peasants' children! For sure, Madam Elizabeth will not trouble herself with her sons' mending. She prefers to leave such menial tasks to the servants!'

Alys grinned suddenly. After just a few days in her company, she and Cecily had formed exactly the same opinion of Elizabeth Cooper! Tom's sister or not, she was spoiled, empty-headed, lazy, and put on superior airs that made Alys long to slap her!

'Can you believe that a sensible woman like Lady Taverner could have produced such a ninny of a daughter?' she said, for about the tenth time.

Cecily shook her head.

'They had a fearful argument this afternoon,' she said. 'Lady Taverner told Elizabeth that being presented to King Edward might have turned her head, but if she wanted to go on living at Broughton Hall, she was to forget her fancy ways, roll up her silken sleeves, and pitch in and help run the household, like everyone else!'

'What did Elizabeth say?'

'Turned up that pretty nose of hers and said she thought that was what servants were for. From the way she looked at me, I was included!' sniffed Cecily. 'Truly, Alys, I thought Lady Taverner would strike her. She, Lady Taverner I mean, is very tired today. She was up half last night in the stables, with that mare that was foaling. When you think of all the work she does, it's no wonder she has no time for Elizabeth's airs and graces!'

Alys shook her head.

'The quicker Elizabeth accepts an offer of marriage from one of her adoring suitors, the better I'll be pleased,' she said. 'Whether she chooses Lord William with his castle and title, or William Merchant with his chest of gold coins, either one of 'em is welcome to her!'

Cecily gave a shout of laughter. As soon as Elizabeth had unpacked her bags, she had revealed that she carried letters with two offers of marriage, and she had not stopped talking about them, ever since. One was from a rich widower, a merchant of Coventry, with a fine house and grown-up children. The other was from a lord, a follower of King Edward, whose castle and lands had been taken over by the Lancastrians. He had no money, but he did have a title, and that could mean a place at court for his wife when Edward of York became king once again.

'Poor Elizabeth. She really can't make her mind up whom to choose,' giggled Alys. 'She could be a rich, pampered merchant's wife, or she could take a chance on her landless lord, and maybe get pinched on the cheek by King Edward again!'

Alys had once made the mistake of asking Elizabeth which of the two men she loved, and had been greeted by a blank stare.

'Love? Love has naught to do with marriage, Lady Alys,' Elizabeth had said primly. 'I learned to love my late husband, poor Robert, after we wed. We gentlefolk do not marry for love, like peasants! We marry to bring honour and advantage to our families!'

Alys was tempted to retort that the Taverner family had no need of either William Merchant's gold, nor Lord William's title, but she had decided there was no point in arguing with Elizabeth. Instead, she and Cecily avoided her as much as possible. It wasn't difficult, for

Elizabeth seemed to spend most of her time in her room, trying on dresses, experimenting with cosmetic creams and potions, and doing a little light embroidery. Meanwhile, her sons Robbie and George virtually ran wild, for she took little interest in them. Lady Taverner saw to their table-manners at mealtimes, but was too busy to occupy herself with them otherwise. Cecily had found them tormenting some of the Broughton Hall kittens, boxed both their ears, and fled to Alys in tears. Alys then suggested politely to Lady Taverner that they needed to be kept out of mischief.

'Oh, Lord, I know they do,' said their exasperated grandmother. 'They need a firm hand. My daughter is too soft-hearted, and I have no time. What do you suggest, Alys?'

'Could the village priest not come in, in the mornings, to teach them their letters?' said Alys, thinking of her own young half-brothers. 'Then perhaps Harry the stable-lad could teach them to ride? After all, Robbie is seven. Next year he could be placed in another noble household as a page. He'll need some sort of training, or 'twill be the worse for him! Young lads can be cruel if one of their number can't sit on a pony, nor serve wine without spilling!'

Lady Taverner looked at her with respect.

'You're right, Alys. It shall be done,' she said.

After that, Robbie and George were less troublesome, and life at Broughton Hall became easier. But still, Alys felt there was something missing. It wasn't hard to fill her days, riding out with Lady Taverner to see Dick the shepherd and admire the ewes and their lambs, overseeing the work of the kitchens, bakehouse and dairy, planting herbs in the herb garden ready for the new season. Alys had already learned something of herbal lore from Dame Eleanor at the Manor, and she discovered that Lady Taverner was just as skilled. She hadn't forgotten the sickness and death of the Stillington children, or her fears for Cecily. She promised herself that, if anyone in her household was taken ill again, she would know how to heal them.

And there was endless sewing, and music and storytelling around the fire in the evenings, and gossip and laughter with Cecily and Mattie, their young maid. But still, Alys thought, I'm waiting. Waiting, always waiting . . .

Impatiently, she tossed another of the boys' shirts on to Cecily's pile of finished mending. Her sister looked up and smiled.

'Better now?' she said. 'It grows too dark for sewing, Alys, and will soon be supper time. I think . . . '

'Hush!' said Alys suddenly. 'What's that I hear? Hoofbeats?'

Both girls listened for a moment. Above the normal sounds of everyday life, the creak of the well, the shouts of the cook as he lost patience with the slow-witted kitchen boy, the clucking of the fowls as Maud flung them handfuls of grain, there was the distinct sound of a horseman coming up the avenue towards the gatehouse.

'Who can it be?' said Alys. 'Was Lady Taverner expecting visitors?'

'She didn't mention anyone,' said Cecily, putting her sewing aside. 'Let's go down and see who it is!'

The two girls hurried down the privy staircase and across the hall where the servants were laying out trestle tables and benches for supper. Out in the courtyard, Lady Taverner was talking to old Gilbert the gate-ward, and a tall young man in a travel-stained jerkin and muddy boots, who seemed to be swaying on his feet from tiredness. At his side, Ralph from the stables was attending to his horse, which looked as weary as he did. Its flanks were steaming, its mouth foam-flecked, and its head drooping. Ralph spoke softly to it and led it away to the stables.

A wild hope had sprung up in Alys's heart. This young man wasn't Tom, but he might bring news of him. She ran forward, careless of manners, etiquette, or anything else.

'Oh, Lady Taverner,' she cried, 'what has happened, is there news?'

Lady Taverner turned round, her eyes glowing and her face alight with joy.

'Yes!' she cried. 'Alys, Cecily, there is wonderful news! This young man is Tom's squire, and he tells me there was a great battle, at Barnet field, on Easter Sunday. Edward our King was victorious, and the Earl of Warwick slain!'

'And . . . and Tom?' cried Alys.

'Tom fought bravely for his king and came through the battle almost unharmed, apart from an axe-wound on his upper arm, which he says will mend,' said Lady

Taverner. 'And there is more, Alys, and better news still! Tom is on his way home to us! He has been delayed by his horse going lame, and bade his squire, here, ride on ahead to give us the good news!'

Alys found she was weeping, and laughing, and clinging to Cecily and Lady Taverner, hardly able to believe the truth. Tom was safe, and coming home! The stable-lads, the cook, and the kitchen boys all came rushing out to see what was going on. Gilbert the gate-ward, grinning, and looking more like a bright-eyed squirrel than ever, told everyone who would listen that Sir Thomas had proved himself a hero. Robbie and George promptly began a mock battle, with sticks for swords, and Mattie the maid burst into noisy tears.

The young squire stood to one side, silent amid all the rejoicing, until Lady Taverner noticed him again.

'My poor boy, you must be exhausted, and half-starved as well,' she said. 'Forgive us, we have waited so long for good news of Sir Thomas, and the Yorkist cause. And now we're forgetting our manners! This is Lady Alys Sherwood, and her sister Lady Cecily . . . '

The lad looked puzzled for a moment,

but then swept them a courtly bow, and introduced himself as John Barton of Nottingham.

'Welcome, John Barton!' said Alys, feeling as though she would never stop smiling. 'You don't know how welcome you are, how we've longed for news! And such news as this, a Yorkist triumph, and Earl Warwick slain!'

'Not only Earl Warwick, but his brother Lord Montagu, and others besides,' said John Barton. ' 'Twas a bloody battle, and fiercely fought, in a mist some thought sent by God to confuse the Lanca-strians . . . '

'You can tell us all about it later, when you are fed and rested,' interrupted Lady Taverner. 'Indeed, we long to hear tales of brave feats of arms! We live quietly here, and battlefields seem far away.'

'What's happening? What's all the noise about?' came a fretful voice, and Elizabeth Cooper strolled across the courtyard, pausing to pat her hair into place when she caught sight of the strange young man.

'Great news, my daughter!' cried Lady Taverner. 'John Barton, here, has come to tell us that Tom is on his way home! There was a battle fought at Barnet on Easter

Sunday. King Edward and the Yorkists were victorious, Earl Warwick is slain, and our Tom fought bravely, yet sustained no serious injury!'

'Is it so? That is indeed good news,' said Elizabeth, forgetting her dignity in the general excitement, and fluttering her eyelashes at John Barton.

'And what of William, Lord Harefield?' she enquired. 'Did you see aught of him on the battlefield?'

'I'm sorry, my lady. I don't know him,' said the squire politely.

Elizabeth shrugged, and Alys and Cecily glanced at one another, knowing just what she was thinking. If Lord William was in favour with the King, and got his lands back from the Lancastrians, then he would be the man to marry . . .

'Poor old William Merchant. He doesn't stand a chance now, for all his fine houses and chests of gold,' muttered Cecily.

But Alys felt too happy to care about Elizabeth's schemings. Edward of York was king again, and Tom was coming home! She whirled round, meaning to question John Barton further, but found that Lady Taverner's steward had led the young squire off to rest.

'There will be time enough for all our questions later,' Lady Taverner said firmly, at the supper table. 'That poor lad is worn out after his journey. Let him sleep!'

John Barton slept all through the evening, the night, and well into the next morning. Alys, however, was much too excited to sleep. Long after Cecily had closed her eyes, she tossed and turned in bed, imagining Tom riding into battle beneath King Edward's standard, fighting fiercely and bravely, and helping the King to win the day for the Yorkist cause.

Ah, my love, I knew you'd not fail when your courage was put to the test, she thought proudly. No more children's games for Sir Thomas Taverner. He was a battle-hardened warrior now, and Alys's heart swelled with pride when she thought of it. He'll be home soon, she thought to herself, as the night sky paled into dawn. The next horseman I hear riding up the avenue of elm trees could be Tom!

She felt heavy-eyed and her head ached after her bad night, yet far too restless to lie abed after the sun rose. Softly, so as not to disturb her sister, she crept out of bed, dressed, braided her hair and stole down the privy stairs to the hall. It was still dark and silent. Even the maids and the kitchen boys were still in bed.

Alys tiptoed across the hall and out of the door into the courtyard. One of the cats came running up to greet her, winding round her legs with welcoming purrs, and stiffening when two or three of the fowls, eager for breakfast, approached her too.

'Go away! Shoo, you foolish creatures!' Alys murmured in a low voice. 'I have nothing for you, Mattie or Maud will be out shortly. Shoo!'

It was a perfect April morning, dew-drenched and bright with birdsong, as Alys slipped out of the postern gate and made her way round to the main gatehouse. She scanned the avenue anxiously, shading her eyes with her hand, but it was empty. Oh, Tom, she thought longingly, please come today. I've waited so long . . .

Raising her face to the morning sun and closing her eyes, she settled down on a pile of straw.

Only moments later, it seemed, she was jerked from sleep by the whinny of a horse in the distance. She scrambled to her feet, blinking sleepily, and shaking the straw from her gown. For a wild moment, she imagined that the sound she had heard was no more than part of a dream . . . but no. Her heart leapt into her throat as she saw a rider approaching, muddy and weary-looking, mounted on a fine bay warhorse.

The world seemed to spin around Alys. She opened her mouth to speak, but no sound emerged. Then . . .

'Tom?' she managed to croak. '*Tom!*'

The rider paused. Shook his head. Stared, and then spurred his horse into a canter. Alys took a few steps forward as he reined in beside her.

'Tom?' she repeated, uncertainly.

She looked up into a dear, familiar, muddy face and a pair of keen sea-blue eyes. Tom's mouth trembled as he dismounted, took her hand, and knelt at her feet.

'Alys,' he murmured. 'Oh, Alys, my lady, my dearest love, I thought . . . I know not what I thought! How came you here, to Broughton Hall? Alys, is it really you?'

Alys nodded. Slow tears began to roll down her cheeks and she touched his hair gently.

'Tom,' she breathed. 'Oh, Tom, welcome home!'

He rose to his feet. Safe at last, her long ordeal of waiting over, Alys gave a sob of relief and happiness, and fell into his arms. For a timeless moment, they clung to one another, then drew apart. Alys felt suddenly shy. There was so much she longed to say, yet all she could do was look, and look, and look again. He's come home at last, she thought, and we shall never be parted again!

Tom was smiling disbelievingly.

'My love, I had thought you at the Manor, waiting for me in safety!' he began.

Alys shook her head, smiling through her tears.

'I was at the Manor, till just after Christmas-tide,' she told him. 'But safe, no . . . '

She shivered suddenly as she told him about her stepfather's vicious rages, the lecherous Sir Henry Capshaw, the days and nights she had spent alone in the gatehouse tower, with only rats and spiders for company. It seemed a lifetime ago.

Tom slipped his arm around her shoulders.

'If I had known!' he said. 'It seems you have much to tell me, Alys!'

Alys looked up into his eyes, the last of her shyness gone.

'And you have much to tell me!' she said. 'You have crossed the sea to the Low Countries, you have served our king and been knighted, you have fought in a great battle!'

A shadow crossed Tom's face and his arm tightened round her.

'Aye,' he said, 'and, Alys, after all that, you don't know how good it is to be here, and see your fair face, like a spring flower, and breathe fresh Yorkshire air, after the noise and the heat of battle and the bustle of the King's court. My love, you don't know how I've longed for this moment.'

'And I, too,' breathed Alys, feeling as though her heart might melt with love.

Before them, the great gate swung open wide and old Gilbert came rushing out, his old hound at his heels.

'Sir Thomas! Sir Thomas! 'Tis you! Ah, 'tis a fine day for Broughton Hall when its young lord comes home,' he cackled. 'Ralph! Harry! John Steward! Look who's here, 'tis Sir Thomas!'

Alys and Tom sprang apart, the spell broken. Behind Gilbert came Lady Taverner, panting slightly and with her head-dress all askew. She looked from Alys to Tom and back again, her face stern, but her eyes twinkling. Behind her, Cecily was weeping unashamedly and some of the maids crowded round to see what was happening.

'Sir Thomas is home! God save Sir Thomas!' cried Mattie.

Tom knelt at Lady Taverner's feet for her blessing.

'God's greetings to you, my lady mother,' he said formally.

'Get up, you great lummox,' gasped Lady Taverner, half-laughing and half-crying. 'Oh, Tom, Tom! Welcome home, my son!'

Tom towered over his mother when he stood up again. He bent his head so that she could kiss him on both cheeks. Elizabeth came forward for a brotherly hug and, more shyly, Cecily followed her. Everyone began talking at once, and then stopped, silenced.

'Come up, come to the house,' cried Lady Taverner gaily. 'We must have food,

food and good Yorkshire ale to celebrate my son's homecoming! Oh, 'tis good to see you, Tom, you don't know how good.'

Still holding hands, Tom and Alys walked into the Hall together, smiling foolishly at one another, blinking back happy tears, starting to speak and then falling silent. There was so much, too much, to say. The rest of the servants came running in, then Elizabeth's young sons Robbie and George. There were cries and exclamations, shrieks from the boys and loud echoing barks from the old hound who, sensing the excitement, bounded around like a puppy.

'Welcome home, Sir Thomas,' said John the steward formally.

Tom nodded, laughing.

'Thank you,' he said, flushed with pleasure. ' 'Tis good to be home, and to be welcomed by you all, as well as by my lady mother and', he gripped Alys's hand, 'my promised bride!'

There were sentimental sighs from the women servants, and Alys felt herself blushing. Then Lady Taverner took charge again.

'Come, bring food and ale for Sir Thomas. He has ridden long and hard to be here,' she said briskly. Alys saw Tom's broad shoulders droop and realized how tired he must be. He's only a few days from a fiercely-fought battle, she thought, he must be weary to the bone!

'You should rest, my love,' she said gently.

He smiled gratefully at her.

'Aye, I will,' he said. 'I'll eat and drink first, then John Barton can take these clothes I'm wearing and burn them, for they're worn to rags! I must sleep, Alys. I shall tell you of my travels, and Barnet field and Edward our king, and I want to hear how you came here, and what has befallen you these past six months. But first, I must eat, and drink, and sleep!'

Alys smiled, let go of his hand, and sent young Mattie scurrying off to prepare a bedchamber and a tub of hot, herb-scented water.

'Look in the closet in my late Lord's chamber,' Tom's mother added. 'There are clothes there, old-fashioned perhaps, but serviceable. Now that Tom is home and not soldiering any more, he must dress according to his station in life! Let us hope the moths have not been at that closet.'

Bathed, and dressed in a woollen robe

that had belonged to his father, Tom fell on the baked salt beef and new bread that the cook provided as though he hadn't eaten in days. Lovingly, Alys watched every move he made. 'Tis like a dream come true at last, she thought blissfully. Tom is home!

Every so often, Tom would look up from his meal or his mug of ale and smile at her so warmly that her heart skipped a beat. How could I ever have doubted his love, Alys thought remorsefully, her hand going to the silver rose pendant at her breast. 'Tis just as Katrin said it would be. Now that we are together again, the past seems like a foul nightmare, over and done . . .

Tom rose from the table and staggered slightly.

'I . . . I'm weary,' he said, 'or maybe 'tis the strong ale has gone to my head! Good day to you all, my lady mother . . . Alys, Elizabeth, Cecily. If I don't go to bed right now, I shall disgrace myself by falling asleep at the table!'

He yawned, stretched, and headed for the privy staircase.

Alys touched her fingers to her lips and blew him a kiss. Sleep well, my dearest love, she thought.

It was well into the afternoon before Tom surfaced, looking much more like himself. Alys was in the dairy, supervising the churning of butter and the making of the creamy white cheeses for which Broughton Hall was wellknown.

'Household tasks have still to be done, Alys, even though Tom is with us again!' Lady Taverner had said sharply, catching Alys day-dreaming in the sunlit courtyard, her chin in her hands.

'Of course they do. I'm sorry, my lady,' said Alys guiltily. It was hard to keep her mind on butter-churns and cheese-cloths when half of it was with Tom, sleeping peacefully upstairs!

Now he put his tousled head around the door and grinned at her.

'I could fancy breaking my fast with a slice of cheese!' he said cheekily.

Alys ran to the door and gave him a hearty kiss, much to the amusement of the giggling dairymaids.

'I'll bring you some. We're almost finished here,' she told him.

When she went into the hall, he was sitting at the table telling young Robbie and George about his adventures. Lady Taverner passed and stopped to listen, as did Cecily, and Ralph from the stables. Even old John the steward, who had fought for the Yorkists himself once, long ago, was there. Alys crept round to Tom's side, longing to hear more about his other life, the life that had kept them apart for six weary months.

'What was it like, abroad, with them there foreigners?' Ralph wanted to know.

'Well, you know, foreigners are pretty much like English men and women,' said Tom gently. 'We met with great kindness in the Low Countries and in Burgundy. I'd been so wretchedly seasick that I thought I should never have the strength to sit on a horse again! King Edward was ever cheerful, though, when the rest of us were ready to give up hope. He never doubted for a moment that we should come home safely, or that his people would welcome him. And so they did! The city of London opened its gates to him without a fight. The Londoners always loved His Grace well, for he understood their ways, and trade prospered when he was king. 'Twas a wonderful sight, King Edward riding into the city in triumph, the trumpets sounding and his loyal brother, Dickon of Glouces-ter, at his side. I rode in the King's train, and everyone cheered and threw flowers. It was a glorious day for the House of York, in truth. Poor, witless Henry of Lancaster was sent back to the Tower, and King Edward rode on to Westminster, to be reunited with Queen Elizabeth and their little children, in sanctuary there. I rode with him, and John Barton and I were both near to tears, seeing him kiss his lady wife and the bairns, 'twas a sight to touch the heart . . . '

Mattie, the serving-maid, gave a sentimental sniff and Cecily's eyes were full of tears. Alys felt a lump in her throat as she whispered, 'Go on, Tom! What then?'

Tom took a gulp of his ale and wiped his mouth on his sleeve.

'Well, then,' he went on, 'King Edward and his captains learned that Earl Warwick's forces were marching towards London, and the King resolved to engage them in battle before they could join up with Queen Margaret of France and *her* army . . . '

'The she-wolf!' cried Lady Taverner. 'I've heard that she is as doughty a fighter as any man alive, and far more warlike than her poor booby of a husband!'

Tom nodded.

' 'Tis true,' he said. 'Anyway, we received orders to head northward towards Barnet town as quickly as may be, the King hoping to surprise Warwick by attacking in the early morning. The King led the centre, with Lord Hastings on his left flank and the Duke of Gloucester on his right. Just before dawn, in the thick fog, we heard the trumpets sound the alert.'

Alys clasped her hands together, her eyes shining.

'And then?' she breathed.

Tom shook his head.

' 'Twas somewhat confusing, like all battles,' he said, 'especially in the fog! Several times I lost sight of His Grace the King, and feared he was wounded, or even slain. I heard the clash of steel on steel, the whinnying of frightened horses, the groans of wounded men, shouts, rallying-cries . . . and then, as suddenly as it had begun, it was all over, and I was alive to tell the tale! In the thick of the fighting, I never even noticed an axe had sliced into my arm, until I saw the blood, but no matter, it will mend. And the King was smiling, and shaking his brave captains by the hand.'

'And Earl Warwick? Did he die in the battle?' said Lady Taverner.

'No, though his brother Lord Montagu did, and died bravely, God rest his soul,' said Tom soberly. 'Warwick himself was pursued from the field by some of the King's men, and slain. There were other lords too who died, on both sides. They say perhaps a thousand men died in the three hours' fighting.'

'May they rest in peace,' said Lady Taverner, crossing herself. 'And may that be the end of all this fighting, with King Edward safe upon his throne again!'

'I wish that it were so,' said Tom, 'but, alas . . . '

Alys went cold inside. What was this? She had assumed that Tom was home for good, that they could begin to make wedding plans.

'What do you mean?' she gasped.

'On the very day of Barnet, Queen Margaret landed in the West Country with her French army,' said Tom. 'King Edward sent word at once to all his loyal subjects to join him at Windsor, from where he plans to set out westward to destroy her, and with her, the last hopes of the Lancastrian cause. It is to Windsor that

John Barton and I shall return, as soon as we have rested.'

'Return?' echoed Alys. Tom seemed to be avoiding her eyes. She felt Cecily give her arm a sympathetic squeeze, and shook her sister's hand away impatiently.

'You're going away? You're going to fight again?' she cried.

Tom looked at her helplessly, and shrugged.

'Alys . . . ' he stammered, 'I must! His Grace the King has need of me! He needs all his fighting men, I must go to him!'

But I need you, too, Alys's heart cried — but she was silent. Sick with disappointment, she looked at the circle of watching faces, from Tom's mother and sister to the stable-lads, and raised her chin proudly, not wanting them to see her cry. Tom's a soldier, she thought, and I shall be a soldier's wife. If he can face another battle with courage, then so can I!

Tears stung her eyes and her mouth trembled, but she rose to her feet with dignity.

'Then God go with you, Sir Thomas, and bring you back to us safely!' she said formally. She saw Tom's lips curve into a smile, and she knew he understood.

13

April 1471

It seemed to Alys as if the whole of Broughton — the village, as well as the Hall, had turned out to see Sir Thomas Taverner and his squire off to fight for King Edward once more. She looked around her, trying to ignore the ache in her heart and the tears that would keep springing to her eyes, in spite of herself. She could see Father Barnabas, the village priest, Dick the shepherd and all the servants, from old Gilbert the gate-ward to young Mattie, the maid, who was sobbing unashamedly into her apron. Lady Taverner and Elizabeth were there, of course, in their finest gowns. Robbie and George stood wide-eyed and watched as John Barton brought Tom's newly-polished armour, and Ralph the stable-lad held the snorting, stamping warhorse for Tom to mount.

He looks like a true knight, my Tom, Alys thought proudly, not without a pang of longing for the merry-faced boy she knew and loved. They had had little time alone together, Tom had been so busy preparing for the long journey south. He and John Barton carried messages for the family at the Manor and also for Dame Margery in Bedford, for they would need to break their journey more than once before they reached faraway Windsor.

And who knew what tidings awaited them there, thought Alys fearfully. Is King Edward really safe on his throne, or will fierce Queen Margaret and her French army prevail? She shook her thoughts away, remembering Tom's confidence in the King and his captains, not to mention young John Barton's patriotic scorn.

'I've heard these Frenchies turn tail and run when they're faced with strong English archers! Have no fear, ladies,' he had said. 'We shall soon be back with you, and all will be well again.'

God grant it may be so, thought Alys with a sigh.

Now Tom was before her, smiling, the sun glinting on his armour and his bright fair hair.

'God keep you, my lady Alys, until we meet again,' he said formally.

Somehow, seeing the love and pride and courage in his blue eyes, Alys managed to smile.

'And you, my lord,' she said, surprised how strong and clear her voice sounded. I'll be brave, she thought. I will not weep. Not here. Not now . . .

'Farewell!' cried Tom, with a flourish. There was a chorus of farewells from everyone, a 'Godspeed, my son!' from Lady Taverner, a blessing from Father Barnabas, and excited waves from the little boys. Tom and John Barton wheeled their horses round and set off down the avenue at a steady trot, their spurs jingling. Half-way down, Tom turned and waved one last time. Then they turned the corner towards the village, and were gone.

Alys, gazing into the distance with eyes blurred by tears, felt an arm go round her shoulders. To her surprise, it was Tom's mother. She wasn't weeping, but there was a desolate look in her eyes that told Alys that she, also, was feeling the loss of her only son.

'Come, my daughter,' she said kindly. 'He is gone, no use to brood. We have work to do. Believe me, work is the best way to forget your troubles! Besides,' she said determinedly, 'what troubles have we, really? Tom and young John Barton seem very sure that this one, last battle will remove the Lancastrian threat, once and for all! Then, when Tom comes home, we shall have a wedding — the first at Broughton for many a long day, for my daughter Elizabeth was wed from her in-laws' home in Warwick. You must begin thinking, Alys, whom to invite to your wedding feast, and we'll have to begin preparing some of the guest chambers, for they haven't been used since my late Lord's day, God rest his soul . . . '

Still chattering about wedding plans, Lady Taverner led Alys into the hall and sat her down with a mug of mulled ale and a dish of baked eggs. At first, Alys was sure she wouldn't be able to eat a bite, but as Lady Taverner talked on, and Cecily came to join them, her spirits lifted. I must only be patient a little longer, she thought. Just a little longer.

She noticed that Cecily seemed pale and quiet, and that afternoon she came across her sister in their bedroom, sitting by the window sewing, her shoulders shaking with sobs.

'Cecily, whatever's wrong?' she cried.

'N-nothing,' sobbed Cecily, sniffing, and beginning to sew as if her life depended on it.

'No one weeps like that for nothing,' said Alys, sitting down beside her sister and taking her hand. 'Come, can't you tell me? 'Tis not like you to weep, are you ill?'

Cecily's eyes brimmed with tears again.

'N-no, not ill, but', she wept, 'oh, 'tis so foolish, you'll laugh at me, think me lack-wit for even imagining . . . '

Alys hugged her, feeling more bewildered than ever.

'I could never think you lack-wit!' she declared. 'Your good sense has saved my life, saved both our lives, more than once! Cecily, what has happened?'

A blush crept over her sister's pale cheeks and she spoke in a whisper.

' 'Tis . . . 'tis John Barton,' she murmured, 'oh, Alys, did you not guess?'

Alys stared at her, open-mouthed. She had been so preoccupied with Tom, and their rediscovered love for one another, she had hardly given a thought to Cecily, let alone to the quiet, polite lad who was Tom's squire. But, now that she thought about it, Cecily *had* seemed especially cheerful while John was there, with a glow on her cheeks and a light in her eyes. And, once or twice, she had seen them talking together, but had thought little of it.

'But . . . but . . . ' she managed to gasp. 'Oh, Cecily . . . why do you weep? Is it that John has gone away? He will return when Tom does, never fear! And then, well, we could ask Lady Taverner, and Tom . . . I mean, John Barton is of good family, 'twould be a fine match! Indeed, I wonder that I didn't think of it before!'

Cecily wiped her eyes.

'Then . . . you think there's hope? You think he might even, well, like me?'

Alys burst out laughing.

'Why should he not like you, goose?' she scolded. 'You're pretty, good-tempered, of an age to wed, and far better at the housewifely arts than I am! John Barton should be pleased to have you. I'll speak to Lady Taverner about it!'

Cecily seized her arm.

'No, Alys, not yet!' she cried. 'I . . . I would sooner wait until he comes home and I know more of him, and how he feels about me. We have plenty of time, I would not wish to force him . . . '

'No, you're right. For now, it shall be our secret,' said Alys cheerfully. 'Lord, though, Cecily, it makes me feel positively ancient, that I should be matchmaking for my little sister!'

Days passed, and no news came from the south. Gradually, Alys, Cecily and the household at Broughton Hall slipped back into their everyday routine. Tom's visit seemed like a dream, and yet Alys knew it was not, and went about her duties with a light heart. She no longer worried that he might have forgotten her, or their love for one another. Even though he had been knighted, and travelled, and fought in a great battle, he was still Tom.

And when he returns, we'll be wed, she told herself sturdily. I may yet be a June bride . . .

Lady Taverner gave her a length of the finest pale-blue silk for a wedding gown, and she, Cecily, and young Mattie set to work embroidering white Yorkshire roses about the hem and around the close-fitting bodice.

'Oh, milady, you'll be the fairest bride in Yorkshire!' sighed Mattie romantically. 'And you're to wed your true love, too, 'tis like a tale from an old romance . . . '

'Mattie!' protested Alys, blushing.

' 'Tis true!' the maid insisted. 'I saw the

way Sir Thomas looked at you, and you at him. It fair made my heart flutter, milady!'

Alice chuckled, and then sighed. How long would it be before she saw Tom again, and had a chance to wear the sky-blue gown? Almost every morning, she awoke thinking, 'Perhaps it's today! It could be today!' Sometimes, when she could be spared from the household tasks, she would sit beneath one of the elm trees at the top of the avenue, imagining that she heard hoofbeats, saw a tall, journey-tired, dusty figure riding towards her.

The weather grew warmer as the days lengthened into spring. Birds sang, leaves sprang out fresh and green, bluebells danced beneath the trees, and still no news came. Then, one day in early May, Lady Taverner told the girls she was going to York market to arrange the sale of some of her best spring lambs. Elizabeth, who was always complaining that life at Broughton Hall was far too dull and quiet, said she would go too.

'What about you, Alys? Cecily?' asked Lady Taverner. 'You've not been to York, have you? 'Tis a fine, fair city, the fairest in the North!'

'Aye, so Tom said,' smiled Alys,

remembering. 'Yes, my lady, we'd be glad to come.'

In York, Lady Taverner set about her business with the leathery-faced farmers and prosperous wool merchants, some of whom seemed surprised to be dealing with a woman, and a sharp, successful woman at that! Alys, Cecily and Elizabeth wandered among the shops and busy market stalls, exclaiming at the price of cloth, shoes, and the trinkets on sale.

'A silver penny for that trumpery little brooch? 'Tis day-light robbery!' said Elizabeth scornfully.

' 'Twas made by the finest French craftsmen!' said the stallholder indignantly.

'French? That brooch has been no nearer to France than Selby town!' mocked Elizabeth.

The stallholder spluttered angrily, and the girls moved on. Alys's attention was caught by a pedlar selling a selection of brightly-coloured ribbons and laces, and she stopped to look at them.

'The best quality, young lady. Come from Wales and the Welsh Marches, they do,' said the pedlar in a singsong accent.

'Wales? Then you're a long way from

home, Sir Pedlar,' said Alys, smiling.

'Aye. I travelled north with some of the King's men, after the battle,' he said.

Alys stiffened.

'Battle? What battle?' she said.

'Why, the battle at Tewkesbury, where the French Queen was beaten, her son slain, and her captains executed,' said the pedlar. 'I'd 'a thought there would be rejoicing in York, it being the King's own city, but mebbe Yorkshire folk haven't heard the news yet.'

'Indeed . . . indeed we haven't,' said Alys in a shaken voice. Cecily, who had moved on with Elizabeth, turned and saw her sister's white face.

'What is it, Alys?' she cried, hurrying back.

'Another battle, in the West, and King Edward victorious again,' Alys gasped. 'Cecily, we must get back to Broughton Hall at once, in case Tom has sent word!'

Luckily, Lady Taverner had finished her business, and they set off home with as much speed as their ponies allowed.

'Don't be too hopeful, Alys,' Lady Taverner warned. 'That pedlar might have got the story wrong, or Tom might have been wounded, or be weeks on the road!'

They rode through Broughton village, past the church, the village pond and the peasants' cottages, and turned into the avenue which led to the Hall. There, just ahead of them, sitting on a fallen log with his head in his hands, was a dusty, dark-haired figure in stained leather breeches. His horse cropped grass round about.

'Why, 'tis John! John Barton!' exclaimed Cecily, starting forward.

At the sound of their approach, the squire looked up. When she saw the expression on his face, Alys's heart began to thump, slowly and painfully. He looked bone-weary, journey-tired, but there was more than that. She, Cecily, and Lady Taverner dismounted hastily and hurried towards him. He tried to rise and greet them, but swayed on his feet and would have fallen, if Lady Taverner had not supported him.

'God . . . God's greetings, my ladies,' he muttered, seemingly unable, or unwilling, to meet their eyes.

Alys found she could not speak. Something's wrong, her heart told her, before John Barton spoke again. The young squire was filthy and mud-stained, and there was a smear that looked like dried blood on his cheek.

'Tell us, John Barton,' came Lady Taverner's crisp tones. Alys had never admired Tom's mother so much. 'Tell us what news you bring!'

John's knees sagged and he sat down on the hollow log again.

'There was a battle,' he began in a faraway voice. 'We ... we met the Lancastrian and French forces, just outside Tewkesbury town ...'

'And?' Lady Taverner demanded. There was a breathless pause.

'A great victory once more. The Lancastrians routed, Queen Margaret's son and heir slain in the field, her captains captured, King Edward victorious,' went on John, still in the same expressionless voice.

Icy fingers of fear clutched at Alys's heart. If the battle was won, if the Yorkists were victorious, John's return, alone and in such despair, could mean but one thing ...

'Tom?' she whispered, through icy lips.

The young squire raised tormented eyes to her face.

'He's ... he's ...' he began. 'Oh, my

315

poor lady, I saw him struck down, struck from his horse by a huge French knight with a battleaxe. I . . . I tried, my lady, but I could not reach him. After the battle, I spent hours searching the field among the wounded and slain but I . . . I couldn't find him . . . '

He began to cry, great gulping sobs. Cecily, in tears herself, knelt beside him and he laid his dusty head on her shoulder.

'I . . . I have failed my lord, failed you all,' wept the young squire. 'Truly, I would have laid down my life for Sir Thomas, but I . . . I couldn't even find his body, give him good Christian burial . . . '

Lady Taverner laid one trembling hand on the sobbing lad's shoulder.

'You did all you could, John Barton,' she said. 'Come, come up to the Hall, so that we can tend you. You've had a long, weary ride; aye, and naught but grief at the end of it.'

Alys stood a little apart from the others, her mind a merciful blank. Tom's dead, said a small, insistent voice in her head. Tom's dead. She shook her head, wanting to shake the thought away. It's all a mistake, she thought, a bad dream. In a moment I shall wake, and everything will be as it was, and Tom will soon be home, and we shall be married. Indeed, Mattie and I must hasten to complete the embroidery, the white Yorkshire roses on my wedding gown, or 'twill not be ready in time! The White Rose of York has defeated the Red Rose of Lancaster . . . who told me that? John Barton told me! It is good news, so why does he weep?

'Don't cry, John,' she said. 'All will be well, you'll see, when Tom comes home!'

Alys remembered almost nothing of the next hours, the next days. She was dimly aware of Lady Taverner taking her into the hall and up the privy staircase to her bedroom. Then Cecily appeared, a pale Cecily, her face streaked with dust and tears, to peel off her gown and hose, dress her in her linen bed-gown and tuck her into bed, while Lady Taverner forced a foul-tasting potion between her lips. She slept, but her sleep was haunted by strange, terrifying dreams. She woke to the sound of the passing-bell being tolled in the village church. Eighteen slow strokes, one for every year of young Sir Thomas Taverner's life.

I can't bear it, she thought. Why can't I

die, too? Oh, Tom, Tom . . .

When she awoke again, Father Barnabas, the kindly old village priest, sat beside her.

'Peace be with you, my child,' he said, making the sign of the cross.

Suddenly, Alys caught at his hand.

'Father Barnabas,' she cried despairingly, 'why? Why did God take Tom? I . . . I love him so much, we were to wed when he returned. Why did he have to die?'

The old priest shook his head.

' 'Tis not for us to question God's wisdom, Alys,' he said. 'But take comfort from this. A brave knight like Sir Thomas, fighting for his King, why, surely he'll go straight to Paradise, and wait for you there!'

'Oh, go away!' cried Alys. 'I . . . I d-don't want my Tom in P-Paradise, I want him here, with me!'

'Hush, child,' said Father Barnabas helplessly, as Alys tossed and turned, sobbing hysterically. Lady Taverner came into the room carrying a small clay medicine cup. The priest shook his head sadly.

'Poor lass,' he said, 'she's near out of her

318

mind with grief. We must pray she doesn't give way, and die of a broken heart. I've seen it happen.'

'Nay,' said Lady Taverner, 'Alys is made of stronger stuff than that, I know she is. Better for her to live on in Tom's memory, than pine and die!'

Hearing her words, Alys stopped thrashing about and lay still and silent. Lady Taverner is right, she thought. Tom was brave, and so shall I be! I owe him no less!

'I . . . I'm sorry, Father Barnabas,' she said in a small voice. 'I didn't mean . . . '

'I know you didn't. Bless you, my child, and may the good Lord and His Holy Mother comfort you in your sorrow,' said the old priest kindly.

In the following days, the Hall was truly a house of mourning. Even young Robbie and George seemed to have forgotten how to romp and play, Lady Taverner looked white and exhausted, and young Mattie went around with her eyes and nose permanently red and swollen from weeping. Alys felt rather as though she was in a dream. Her only comfort, strangely enough, came from seeing the growing tenderness and love between her sister and John Barton. Cecily would allow no one else to tend the young squire, who still blamed himself, most bitterly, for what had happened. Lady Taverner and Alys herself told him over and over again that they knew he had done all he could, but he felt he had failed his lord. Only Cecily's loving care and often silent sympathy seemed to comfort him. Curiously, seeing their love for each other didn't make Alys feel envious, or sharpen her sense of loss. She knew how highly Tom had thought of his squire, and of his affection for Cecily, and felt that he would have approved. We shall have a wedding at Broughton Hall yet, even thought it isn't Tom's and mine, she thought, half-laughing and half-crying.

So the spring days lengthened into summer, fruit began ripening in the orchards, and Ascension Day approached. Alys had already been told of the traditional fair held in Sowerby, the next village, in which the folk from Broughton usually joined. The day itself dawned bright and clear, but Alys woke up with a raging headache, and elected to stay at home.

'Besides, I . . . I don't much feel like a fair,' she said sadly, as Cecily looked troubled. 'I'll do very well on my own, with just Blackie and her kittens to keep me company!'

Almost everyone from the Hall set off for Sowerby Fair, even Lady Taverner, who was expected to put in an appearance, and Elizabeth Cooper, who grumbled that it would be 'full of rustics smelling of cow-dung, with nothing to amuse the likes of *us!*' The Hall seemed silent after they had gone. Alys took a stool out into the sunny courtyard and sat quietly, watching the two coal-black, one ginger and two striped kittens tumbling and playing among the straw at her feet.

When she heard a commotion outside the gatehouse, she was puzzled, but not alarmed. What did alarm her, seconds later, was seeing old Gilbert the gate-ward fling his door open and positively sprint across the courtyard towards her, like someone half his age.

'Why, Gilbert,' she cried, jumping to her feet, 'whatever is wrong?'

The old man grabbed her arm, breathless and panting, pointing towards the gatehouse with a wrinkled arm.

' 'Tis . . . 'tis . . . ' he wheezed.

'Steady, old man,' said Alys, afraid he might have an apoplexy.

' 'Tis a ghost!' Gilbert declared.

Alys's spine prickled for a moment. A ghost, she thought, and I'm alone here but for old Gilbert! She looked around her. The courtyard, with its clucking fowls and scampering kittens, looked so normal, so un-ghostly, that she was reassured.

'Nay, Gilbert, you were dreaming! 'Twas the hot sunshine!' she smiled.

Then she lifted her head as an unmistakable groan came from the direction of the gatehouse. There's someone there, Alys thought — but why didn't Gilbert's old hound bark? He always barks at strangers! So it can't be a stranger, it must be one of the servants. Perhaps someone has been hurt at Sowerby Fair!

She ran forward, fumbling with the rusted iron catches on the gate. Outside, the avenue of elm trees stood empty. Puzzled, Alys looked to left and right . . . and gave a gasp of disbelief.

There, lying unconscious, face down on a pile of straw, was . . .

'Tom!' Alys breathed. 'Tom . . . or his ghost!'

Hastily, she crossed herself, in case this *was* a spirit, come to taunt her in her grief. Slowly, her heart thumping, and hardly able to believe her eyes, she crossed the path towards him. Touched his shoulder. Rolled him on to his back. This was no ghost! He was real enough — dirty, unconscious, his fair hair matted with sweat, his breathing ragged and uneven, yet still . . .

'Tom!' Alys cried. 'Oh, Tom, wake up . . . oh, Tom, we thought you were dead, please wake up, tell me it's really you, oh, Tom, my dear love . . . '

Gilbert the gate-ward had crept out behind her and was peering suspiciously at Tom.

'I . . . I thought Sir Thomas were dead, and this an evil spirit,' he quavered.

'Well, he's not, as you see,' said Alys, suddenly practical. 'But he is very sick, injured no doubt. We must get him into the Hall, to bed, so that I may tend him. Come, Gilbert, I'll take his shoulders, you take his feet!'

Somehow, they manhandled Tom into the courtyard and then into the Hall, where Alys flew to fetch pillows and a warm cloak to make him comfortable. He tossed and muttered feverishly as she bathed his forehead in cool water and moistened his dry, cracked lips with wine.

There was a huge bruise on his forehead and the skin was broken in places. Alys wiped away the dried blood, applied a soothing ointment from Lady Taverner's medicine chest, and bound the wound as best she could. Then she sat and watched, her thoughts in turmoil. Tom was not dead, he lived, he had come back to her. It was almost too much to take in.

' 'Tis a miracle, my lady,' said old Gilbert solemnly.

Alys could only nod, her heart too full for words.

Suddenly, the door of the Hall swung open and Lady Taverner strode in.

'Alys?' she began. 'Where's Gilbert? I had no stomach for merrymaking, so I have returned, as you see, and . . . Alys?'

She peered at Alys and at the figure who lay propped up with pillows, his head bandaged, gave a gasp, swayed, and almost fell.

'Tom?' she croaked. 'Oh, Tom, my son . . . but how can this be?'

She took two steps forward and hugged Alys as they both dissolved into tears.

'Yes!' Alys wept. 'He lives, Lady Taverner, he has come home to us! On foot, by the look of him, sick, and injured, yet he lives!'

Lady Taverner fell to her knees, kissed her son's bandaged forehead, and clasped her hands together.

'Thanks be to God and His Blessed Mother,' she said devoutly.

The whole of Broughton rejoiced when the news of Tom's return became known. Some of the servants swore that their young lord had actually come back from the dead! No one was happier than John Barton, who, with the help of two of the sturdy stable-lads, carried the still-unconscious Tom up to his own room, where he was cared for night and day by Lady Taverner and Alys. There were anxious moments when his fever rose, he seemed to recognize no one, and fought imaginary battles in his dreams, but after a week of careful nursing, he opened his eyes, saw Alys sitting beside him, and spoke her name for the first time.

'Alys?' he murmured, reaching for her hand.

'Yes, 'tis I. And you are safe, Tom. Safe at home,' she soothed him.

As he grew stronger day by day the whole household gathered round to hear the story of his escape from the field of Tewkesbury.

'Indeed, I . . . I remember little,' he said, laughing. 'I remember the blazon on the French knight's shield, a stag or some such, then my horse was slain under me, and the next thing I knew it was dark, and silent, and I was in some sort of ditch filled with foul water. The battle must have moved on, and I knew neither where I was, nor even who I was, my head hammered so. I managed to stagger to a barn, where a farmer found me. His wife was a true Christian woman and tended my wounds most kindly. They had heard the battle was won, and the King gone to Coventry. I made my way there as best I could — on farm carts mostly — to take my leave of His Grace and ask permission to travel north to Broughton to claim my bride!'

He reached for Alys's hand and held it tight.

'You spoke to the King of me?' Alys gasped. King Edward still seemed like a figure from a fairy-tale to her. She imagined him sitting on a golden throne, with a crown on his head and his beautiful wife by his side. It was hard to believe that he had travelled with Tom, spoken with him, even tried to soothe his seasickness, for all the world like an ordinary man!

'Aye, I did. And do you know what he said?'

Alys shook her head.

'That I should head north with all speed, and claim the lady of my heart,' said Tom. 'King Edward himself made a love-match, don't forget. He could have had a French princess, but instead he chose Dame Woodville. The King knows what true love is, right enough, Alys. He was happy to give me leave to come home, once he knew what, or who, awaited me here!'

'And here you are,' said Lady Taverner. 'Back with us, and the King safe on his throne at last, so there will be no more battles, no more fighting.'

'No, 'tis all over,' said Tom, yawning and stretching, 'and I can't pretend I'm sorry. I have had my fill of soldiering.'

'Tell us about the battle! Did you kill lots of enemies? Hundreds? Thousands?' asked little Robbie.

Tom laughed and ruffled his hair, but there was a shadow across his face as he replied.

'No, not hundreds, you bloodthirsty young wretch. But yes, I did kill. 'Tis a strangely easy thing to do, in battle, when you know 'tis either kill, or be killed yourself. I have had enough killing, young Robbie. 'Tis fearful to see men, living men, crumple, and spit blood, and die, and know that you are responsible for their deaths. Good men fought and died on both sides, at Barnet and Tewkesbury. I saw my lord King Edward weep like a child for his former friend, Earl Warwick. Now, he wants nothing more than to bring peace to England.'

Lady Taverner rose to her feet.

'We have much to be thankful for,' she said seriously, 'and much to do as well, to prepare for your wedding, my son! Alys, I know, has a fancy to be a June bride, so we must send messengers out to her family, and . . . '

A shadow crossed Tom's face and he glanced up at John Barton, standing at the end of his bed, Cecily at his side. The young squire shook his head.

'I have said naught,' he said. 'I could burden these good ladies with no more grief, after I told them you were missing . . . '

'What do you mean, more grief?' said Alys sharply. 'What has happened? Is ... is all not well at the Manor? Did you speak to my lady mother? Dame Eleanor? Tell me, Tom!'

'Alys,' said Tom gently. 'Your stepfather is dead. Sir Hugh Drayton is dead, God rest him. He died of a seizure after a bout of heavy drinking. Your mother, poor lady, is once again a widow.'

Alys felt dazed, unable to take the news in. She turned to her sister.

'Cecily,' she said, 'did you hear that? Sir Hugh, our stepfather, is dead!'

'I heard,' said Cecily.

Then, suddenly, she and Alys were hugging each other, crying, laughing, holding on to one another like little children.

'I can't believe it!' Cecily sobbed. 'Oh, Alys, I know I should not speak ill of the dead, but to know that Sir Hugh is gone, 'tis ... 'tis like a weight lifting from my shoulders! He will never terrorize us again, Alys, nor our lady mother and the children! No more threats, no more beatings! We are free!'

'I know it,' said Alys, her lips trembling. 'I cannot weep for Sir Hugh, Cecily. He made our mother's life a misery. She will not mourn that evil brute, any more than we do!'

'All the same,' Tom went on, 'the Lady Philippa is now alone and unprotected. Alys, His Grace the King promised me a wedding gift. Would you like him to appoint some honest, kindly man to run the Manor in your stepfather's place? It would ease the burden on Lady Philippa, would it not?'

Alys nodded.

'Would the King do that?' she asked.

'Of course. King Edward is a chivalrous knight. How could he refuse a Yorkist household in need of help? I shall see to it, just as soon as I am on my feet again. And we must send word to good Dame Margery of Bedford, too. She told us she relished the idea of a journey to Yorkshire to our wedding!'

Alys laughed, thinking of the bright, birdlike little woman who had been so good to her and Cecily. She shall dance at my wedding, she thought, and my cousin Mary Enderby and her flat-footed husband, though poor Will won't be doing much dancing, if I know him! And . . .

'Tom,' she said, 'there's someone else I'd

like you to invite. You know the travelling players I told you of, that we met in Stamford town and journeyed north with? There was Hal, a fine man though a little too fond of his ale, and Gypsy Katrin, who sang like an angel and had a huge wolfhound called Rough who protected us all. I know they were planning to stay in the North and I'd dearly love to see them at our wedding. Could not John Barton make enquiries for them?'

'Why not?' said Tom, smiling. ' 'Tis years since there was a wedding at Broughton Hall. All will be welcome!'

' 'Tis . . . 'tis all rather like a dream come true . . . ' said Alys.

'God grant you always feel that way, my dearest love,' said Tom.

Epilogue

June 1471

Two days before their wedding, Alys and Tom rode to the top of the hill above the Hall, at twilight, and sat for a moment side by side, while their ponies cropped the clover-scented grass contentedly. Alys's pony, a dark bay with a white blaze on her forehead, was a wedding gift from Tom, a replacement for lost Joliet. Although Alys still missed her gentle chestnut mare, she was delighted with her new mount.

The next day, she and Tom wouldn't meet at all, for it was considered bad luck for the bride and groom to see one another the day before the wedding. Tom, with John Barton, Will Enderby, and the other young men would spend the wedding eve with friends at Sowerby.

' 'Tis hard work, arranging a wedding,' said Alys ruefully, trying to stifle a yawn. 'Even with your mother's help, and good Dame Eleanor, and Dame Margery Salter, I scarce know whether I am on my head or my heels.'

Tom, comfortably removed from the feminine turmoil, grinned at her.

'You know you're enjoying every moment, my little bride,' he said tenderly.

Alys smiled. For a time, she had hardly dared to believe in her own happiness. First Tom had made a full recovery, then messengers brought news from the Manor, from Bedford, from Cousin Mary Enderby in Essex. John Barton had ridden out to make enquiries about a troupe of travelling players, led by a man called Hal and thought to be in the North Country, and had returned that very day, telling Alys and Tom to expect Hal, Katrin and the others on the morrow.

'So everyone we love will be here to see us married, Tom,' Alys said happily.

There had been tears of joy from Lady Philippa and Dame Eleanor, reunited with Alys and Cecily at last, and more tears from Lady Philippa when Tom told her of his plan to beg a wedding boon from King Edward, and find a reliable bailiff for the Manor. When the party from Bedford arrived, Dame Margery was accompanied by little Elizabeth, oldest of the Stillington children, and escorted by none other than

Ned Herring, as loud and jovial and barrel-chested as ever.

'I had business in the North, and I never could resist a wedding,' he roared, kissing Alys noisily on both cheeks and slapping Tom so hard on the back that he made him cough. Cousin Mary and her husband had arrived too; Will Enderby as silent as ever and Mary chattering continuously about her fine new manor-house and the baby she was expecting at Michaelmas.

'So all has turned out for the best, Alys,' she said, 'just as we hoped! And I see young Cecily has found herself a sweet-heart, too!'

It was hard to say whether John Barton or Cecily blushed redder!

Now, in these final few private moments before she and Tom became man and wife, Alys fingered the silver rose pendant at her breast and spoke out loud.

'I would like my sister to be as happy in her choice of husband as I am!' she said.

Tom squeezed her hand.

'And are you, truly, happy, my Alys?' he said huskily.

'You know I am.'

Her eyes met his. In their sea-blue

depths Alys could see all the love-longing she knew was reflected in her own. Tom will be good to me, she thought. Whatever the coming years might bring, the good times and the bad, the joy and the sorrow, the bitter fruit and the sweet, the seed-time and the harvest, we shall face it all in the certainty of a true and lasting love.

'Come,' said Tom gently, ' 'tis time to go home.'

They rose to their feet, their arms around each other, and looked down over the darkening fields to the Hall, where candlelights flickered in the windows and smoke curled up lazily from the chimney.

The air smelled of summer, of honey-suckle. High above the moors, a skylark was singing.

Historical Note

This story of Alys Sherwood and Tom Taverner takes place in the second half of the fifteenth century, during the period known as 'The Wars of the Roses'. These 'wars' weren't actually wars in the modern sense at all. They were a struggle for power and control of the throne of England between two factions, or groups of noblemen — the supporters of the House of Lancaster, whose emblem was the Red Rose, and those of the House of York, whose emblem was the White Rose.

While great noblemen and their followers fought a series of bloody battles, from St Albans in 1455 to Stoke in 1487, the ordinary people of England, peasants in the countryside and butchers, bakers and candlestick-makers in great cities like London and York, simply got on with their everyday lives, probably caring very little who happened to be king!

When the Lancastrian King Henry V

died in 1422, he left as his heir a nine-month-old baby, Henry VI. This kindly, naïve, and deeply religious man was married in 1445 to a fiery French princess, Margaret of Anjou. She bore him a son in 1453. By that time, Henry VI had gone mad, and his rival the Duke of York became Protector. Supporters of the King and the Duke fought several battles in the late 1450s, and the Duke and his second son were both killed at the Battle of Wakefield in December 1460.

After that, the Duke's eldest son, Edward of March, led the Yorkist side. He defeated a Lancastrian army at the Battle of Mortimers Cross in 1461. Shortly afterwards he was proclaimed King of England as Edward IV. With the support of the powerful Earl of Warwick, known as the Kingmaker, he defeated the Lancastrians in several more battles.

In 1464, Edward secretly married a beautiful young widow, Elizabeth Woodville, and members of her large family moved into positions of power. This displeased Warwick, who then decided to support the Lancastrian side and took the King prisoner in 1469. He soon regained power and Warwick fled to France. From there he invaded England and put Henry VI back on the throne. Edward, together with his loyal brother Richard Duke of Gloucester and a handful of followers, fled to Burgundy. He returned to England in March 1471 and defeated Warwick at the Battle of Barnet. Shortly afterwards, on May 4th, Margaret of Anjou and her Lancastrian army were defeated at Tewkesbury. Margaret's son was killed in the battle and Henry VI died in the Tower of London.

Edward IV remained a successful and popular king until his death in 1483.

★ ★ ★

Some aspects of fifteenth-century life may seem strange to us today, and some of the words and expressions used in *Silver Rose* might need an explanation.

For example, fifteenth-century households lived more communally than we do, and privacy was a rare privilege. A lady's *solar* (see p. 19) was a room reserved for her and her immediate family.

Marchpane (see p. 43) was a popular sweet made of almonds, similar to marzipan.

See p. 143. Many medieval travellers couldn't read, so a bundle of twigs was hung outside the door to indicate a tavern or alehouse, rather like a modern inn-sign!

Family Tree of the Houses of York and Lancaster

Edward III

- Black Prince
  - Richard II
- Lionel, Duke of Clarence
  - Anne Mortimer
- John of Gaunt, Duke of Lancaster
  - Henry IV
  - Henry V
  - Henry VI m. Margaret of Anjou
- Edmund, Duke of York
  - Richard, Earl of Cambridge
- Thomas of Woodstock

Anne Mortimer — m. — Richard, Earl of Cambridge

Richard, Duke of York

- Edward IV m. Elizabeth Woodville
- Richard III (Dickon) m. Anne Neville

(Please note: This family tree has been simplified to include characters mentioned in the text)

We do hope that you have enjoyed reading this large print book.

Did you know that all of our titles are available for purchase?

We publish a wide range of high quality large print books including:
Romances, Mysteries, Classics
General Fiction
Non Fiction and Western

Special interest titles available in large print are:
The Little Oxford Dictionary
Music Book, Song Book
Hymn Book, Service Book

Also available from us courtesy of Oxford University Press:
Young Readers' Dictionary
(large print edition)
Young Readers' Thesaurus
(large print edition)

For further information or a free brochure, please contact us at:
Ulverscroft Large Print Books Ltd.,
The Green, Bradgate Road, Anstey,
Leicester, LE7 7FU, England.
Tel: (00 44) **0116 236 4325**
Fax: (00 44) **0116 234 0205**

CIRQUE DU FREAK: BOOK 1

Darren Shan

Darren Shan is just an ordinary schoolboy — until he gets an invitation to visit the Cirque du Freak . . . until he meets Madame Octa . . . until he comes face-to-face with a creature of the night.

Soon, Darren and his friend Steve are caught in a deadly trap. Darren must make a bargain with the one person who can save Steve. But that person is not human and only deals in blood . . .

Point CRIME

AVENGING ANGEL

David Belbin

'The car was almost upon him. Angelo could see the panicked face of the driver. He tried to throw himself out of the way, but he didn't have time . . . '

When Angelo Coppola is tragically killed in a hit-and-run accident, the police are unable to track down the culprit.

But Angelo's sister, Clare, cannot rest till she has discovered the truth. Who was driving the car which killed him? And what is the significance of 'blaze' — the last word that Angelo uttered?

Clare is soon convinced that she has found the killer. But can she prove it? And is she putting her own life in danger?

CRASHING

Chris Wooding

'Slack summer holidays were made to do this sort of thing. And some parties are just asking to be crashed.'

So here it was — the party to mark the beginning of the summer. I guess we'd all brought our own agendas; mine was to get it together with Jo Anderson.

But anyone who's anyone knows stuff like that never goes to plan. Friends were rapidly turning into enemies. The local mob of street-thug wannabes had declared virtual war on me. And looming over it all was the spectre of the Zone, the derelict estate haunted by stoners, psychos and freaks, calling me back one last time. Now I just needed to get my friends on board . . .

THE WILDEST DREAM

Kirsty White

Roscawl, July 1848

My dearest Michael,

I do not know when we can meet again.

My father discovered I stole food to give to the villagers who are starving since the potato famine. Now I am banished to my room, and who knows when I will be set free.

And now they are planning to marry me to a useless fop called Edward Cavendish. But I will not. I will not.

Michael, can you wait for me? Together we WILL find a way. We must . . .

Elizabeth